THREE DEVILS DANCING

BOOKS IN THE
DONALD YOUNGBLOOD MYSTERY SERIES

A DONALD YOUNGBLOOD MYSTERY

THREE DEVILS DANCING

KEITH DONNELLY

HUMMINGBIRD BOOKS
Gatlinburg, Tennessee

Hummingbird Books
A division of Harrison Mountain Press
P.O. Box 1386
Gatlinburg, TN 37738

Designed by Todd Lape / Lape Designs

Library of Congress Cataloging-in-Publication Data

Donnelly, Keith.

Three devils dancing : a Donald Youngblood mystery /
by Keith Donnelly.

p. cm.

ISBN 978-0-89587-398-9 (cloth : alk. paper) 1. Youngblood,
Donald (Fictitious character)—Fiction. 2. Private investigators—
Tennessee—Fiction. 3. Male friendship—Fiction. 4. Cherokee
Indians—Fiction. 5. Serial murderers—Fiction. 6. Drug deal-
ers—Fiction. I. Title. II. Title: 3 devils dancing.

PS3604.O56325T485 2011

813'.6—dc22   2010034184

Printed in the United States of America
by the Maple-Vail Book Manufacturing Group
York, Pennsylvania

To G. Payne Marshall, an inspiration to us all

And to Tessa,
my anchor, my rudder, my sail

Prologue

The little boy wandered the halls of the hospital, as he had often done in the past year. He hated to sit and wait, so he walked and explored. He spent a lot of time in the cafeteria and knew some of the workers there by name, and they knew him. On this day, he carried a grape soda in a cup with a lid and a straw stuck through the top as he headed back to Sammy's room.

Sammy was his best friend, and he was sick, very sick. Sammy was also his brother. Sammy was five years old and wise beyond his years. The little boy was two years older and even wiser.

The little boy didn't understand exactly what was wrong with Sammy. Something about his blood was bad. He kept asking if Sammy was going to be okay but could never get a straight answer from his parents. He didn't like that. It was not a good sign, and he was worried.

As he turned the corner, the little boy saw his parents come out of Sammy's room. Then he saw the minister follow them. His mother was crying. She had cried a lot in the last year, and that worried him, too. His dad, much older than his mother, had a frightened look on his face.

"What's wrong?" the little boy asked meekly, not really wanting to know for fear the news was bad.

His parents were silent. It was as if they couldn't find the strength to speak.

"Why don't you go in and see Sammy?" Brother Dampier said.

Brother Dampier was the Methodist minister at their church. The little boy could never figure out why he was called Brother Dampier. Wouldn't Preacher Dampier make more sense?

The little boy nodded and went into Sammy's room. The frail five-year-old was lying slightly propped up in bed. His brown curly hair was damp. Sammy was hooked up to various monitors that blinked and beeped information the doctors and nurses needed. That's what the little boy had been told. All those things looked so serious that they scared him.

Sammy's eyes moved toward his brother. They were dark and deep-set and tired from fighting the good fight. His head moved slightly, and a tiny smile formed on his lips.

"Hi," Sammy said softly.

"Want a drink of my soda?" the little boy asked. "It's grape."

"Sure," Sammy said.

The little boy brought the grape soda to his brother's bed. Sammy took a long drink through the straw.

"That's good," Sammy said, exhaling the words.

His talking seems to take a lot of energy, the little boy thought.

"Want some more?" he asked hopefully.

"Not now," Sammy said.

"Want to play checkers?" the little boy asked, knowing Sammy loved the game.

"I'm too tired," Sammy sighed.

"Maybe you'll feel like it later," the little boy said.

"I'm going to see Jesus soon," Sammy said to his brother. His voice was soft, every word a struggle.

"You can't leave me," the little boy said, a tear escaping from his eye.

"I have to," Sammy said. "He's taking me, and I'm too tired to fight."

◆   ◆   ◆   ◆

Two days later, the little boy sat at the foot of his twin bed looking out the window and wondering why Sammy had to go to heaven. He had raised the window as he often did and could hear the wind move through the tall oak trees near the house. The trees kept it wonderfully cool during the summertime. Sometimes at night when a storm came, he would raise the window and place his pillow at the foot of the bed and fall asleep listening to the wind in the trees and the rain hitting the roof of the sun porch below. He did not know why, but he loved storms. He marveled at their power and fury. To him, they represented the power of God.

But he was mad at God now. God had taken Sammy to be with Jesus. It wasn't fair. Jesus had many children who died young with him now, so why did he need Sammy? The little boy had only Sammy, and now Sammy was gone, and he was alone. His sadness was slowly being replaced by rage.

His parents had let him go to the funeral home and, the next day, the funeral. Many people were at the funeral home, but he could remember only a few—his mother and father and Brother Dampier and Sammy. He remembered Sammy's clothes laid out neatly on the guest-room bed the day after he died—the same clothes Sammy wore as he lay peacefully in the casket.

He didn't remember much about the funeral, but he did remember the grave—six feet deep with dirt piled next to the tiny coffin. He wanted to scream out not to put Sammy in that deep, dark hole, but his father had told him Sammy really wasn't in the coffin, that he was in heaven. He hoped that was true, so he kept quiet.

He didn't remember much of what Brother Dampier had said. Something about the good dying young and going to be with Jesus. *Well, at least he got that right*, the little boy thought. Sammy was good. Sammy was the best.

The door to his room swung open, and his father walked quietly in. He sat across from the little boy on the other twin bed—Sammy's bed.

"It's windy today," his father said.

The little boy did not respond. He sat and stared out the window.

"Want to try to fly that kite you got last Christmas?" his father asked, desperately trying to distract his older son.

"No," the little boy said. "I don't feel like it."

They sat there a long time staring out the window and listening to the wind in the trees. Finally, the little boy's father broke the silence.

"Sammy's gone, son," he said. "He would want you to get on with your life. Someday, when you're older, you'll understand."

◆   ◆   ◆   ◆

Years later, when the boy was a senior in high school, he attended another funeral. As he stood by the grave, he thought back to the long-ago conversation with his father after Sammy's death. He could come to only one conclusion. His father was wrong. He still didn't understand Sammy's death any more than he understood this one.

Long after everyone left the graveyard, he stood over his mother's grave with his tears falling on the freshly packed earth and knew that he understood only one thing. His last life preserver had been ripped away, and now he felt totally alone, lost forever.

THREE DEVILS DANCING

1

I share my life with two women and one black male standard poodle. Mary, my live-in love, is a six-foot blue-eyed blond police officer. We've been together for almost two years. She is the first in a long line of very fine women I have dated to achieve live-in status. So far, it's working.

Lacy Malone, a teenager who looks like she might be Mary's daughter but isn't, lives with us on a temporary basis. Lacy's temporary residence seemed destined to become permanent. How she arrived in our lives is another story.

My dog's name is Jake. A few years ago, Jake and I lived quite contentedly as two carefree bachelors. My life was a little boring, but it was also uncomplicated. Things have changed. My private investigator business has taken a dangerous turn and I have picked up two females along the way. The females rule the roost and life had become much more complicated. Jake and I are not totally against this, however. Our new life has its benefits. Jake gets a lot of attention—head rubs, ear scratches, and treats. I get all of that and then some.

◆　　◆　　◆　　◆

On a beautiful Sunday in early May, I was on my way out of the Mountain Center Country Club after dropping off Lacy for golf lessons when my cell phone rang. I didn't recognize the number and considered not answering. But not many people had my cell number, and even fewer would call me on a Sunday. I feared bad news.

"Youngblood," I answered.

"Hey, Blood," Jimmy Durham drawled. "Are you busy right now?"

Jimmy Durham was an old friend from my high-school days who had played basketball for a rival school. These days, he was county sheriff. Recently, I had been part of a task force that Jimmy put together to take down a meth lab in the area. I even managed to have a shootout with one of the major players of that little drug ring and lived to tell about it. Ever since then, Jimmy had considered me a consultant to the sheriff's office—unofficially, of course. I knew this couldn't be good.

"Not really," I said. "What's going on, bull?"

"Do you know the picnic area about a mile downriver from Campbell Bridge?"

"Sure," I said. "Campbell Bottoms. What about it?"

"Meet me there as soon as you can," Jimmy said, ignoring my question.

"On my way," I said. "What's this about?"

I didn't get a response. Jimmy had already disconnected.

I took a right out of the club and drove the twenty or so miles toward Campbell Bridge and took another right on a secondary road just before the bridge. The picnic area was a few miles down on the left. The leaves on the trees in the thickly wooded area surrounding Campbell Bottoms had yet to reach full maturity. When they did, the sun would have a hard time penetrating the thick canopy. Sunlight danced off my windshield as I snaked my way down to the Bottoms.

I made a left-hand turn into the Campbell Bottoms parking lot. The Bottoms was a favorite weekend picnic area for Mountain Center residents. I had been here many times with friends as a teenager.

The area was expansive. At least fifty picnic tables with outdoor grills were scattered throughout the Bottoms, with individual parking spots for vehicles. Cinder-block buildings at the north and south ends housed restrooms. Through the trees, I saw two sheriff's cruisers at the far north end of the parking area. As I closed the distance, I saw Jimmy leaning against the front fender of his cruiser, arms folded. I parked a couple of spots down, got out, and walked to meet him. He looked tired.

"You okay?" I asked.

His light blue eyes stared back at me with the resigned look of a county sheriff too long on the job.

"Something I need you to see," he said. "I don't like the look of it."

"Lead the way," I said, dreading what I might find. I had seen enough dead bodies recently to last a lifetime.

I followed Jimmy on a narrow path through the woods to the edge of the lake. Two young sheriff's deputies were waiting for us.

"Wes Lane and Skip Wolpert," Jimmy said, "meet Don Youngblood. Don's a friend and private investigator in Mountain Center."

We shook hands and exchanged greetings.

"You two go back to the parking area and look for any signs of drag marks," Jimmy said. "Keep your walkie-talkies on."

The deputies headed out the path toward the parking area, talking softly as they went.

"What do you make of that?" Jimmy asked, pointing to a picnic table near the edge of the lake.

On display were someone's clothes, complete with socks and running shoes. The clothes were neatly folded. They appeared to be those of an average-sized female. On the picnic table were a pink tank top, a white tank top, faded blue jeans, pink socks, and running shoes, white with dark red trim.

"Billy is on the way to photograph this," Jimmy said. "I called him before I called you. He should be here soon."

I nodded, still staring.

"Who called this in?" I asked.

"Anonymous," Jimmy said. "Called our office, told us where to find the clothes, and hung up. No name, no number, nothing."

"Caller ID?"

"Pay phone," Jimmy said. "We'll track it down and take some prints, but I'm not getting my hopes up."

"Good luck with that," I said. "Hard to guess how many prints you could get."

"What do you think about the anonymous call?" Jimmy asked.

"Makes me think that whoever made it might have something to do with this, and they wanted you to find it right away," I said. "Are you looking for a body yet?"

"Yeah, I have a boat canvassing the shoreline on this side of the lake. It's starting north of us and working south."

The boat would be coming down from our right. We were facing west toward the water.

"Unless this is a hoax, I think you could be looking for a murder victim," I said. "I can't see a young woman laying her clothes out like this and going skinny-dipping."

"Yeah, I was thinking the same thing. The water's too cold right now for swimming," Jimmy said. "I sure as hell hope somebody's just jerking me around."

"Anyone reported missing?"

"Not yet," Jimmy said.

"Find any footprints?"

"No, the ground's pretty hard here," he said. "If someone put a body in the lake or if a girl went and got herself drowned, the body could be anywhere. This lake has all kinds of currents."

I looked at the neatly folded clothes and tried to imagine how they got there. I hoped it was a college prank or something along those lines.

"You should probably have your deputies look north and south for signs of a boat being put to shore. Might find a footprint or something. Whoever laid these clothes here either had to park where we did and walk in or come by boat."

"Next thing on my list," Jimmy said as he reached for his walkie-talkie.

"Skip, Wes, get back here and check the shoreline for signs of a boat coming in," Jimmy said. "Skip, you go north. Wes, you go south."

"Okay, sheriff," they said in unison over their walkie-talkies.

I heard a camera click behind me and turned to see my partner, Billy Two-Feathers. I had not heard him coming. He crept in like a big cat.

"Hey, Blood," he said, glancing up.

"You got here fast, Chief," I said.

"I was in Gatlinburg," Billy said, "shopping for a present for Maggie."

Maggie was Billy's wife. They had recently married. Billy and I had been best friends since college and partners in Cherokee Investigations for over ten years. To supplement his income, Billy did forensic photography for some of the area's sheriffs and for the Mountain Center chief of police, who happened to be my closest high-school friend, Big Bob Wilson. Billy was also a damn fine artist. The shutter continuously clicked as Billy moved around the clothes.

"Get a stick and slowly lift the tank tops off the picnic table," Billy said.

As I did that, Jimmy opened an aluminum case and took out some evidence bags. Underneath the pink and white tank tops was a pink bra. As Jimmy held an evidence bag open, I dropped in the tank tops. After Billy clicked a few more shots, we bagged the bra. I lifted the jeans to find pink bikini panties underneath. Jimmy, who had put on white surgical gloves, carefully folded the jeans and placed them in a separate bag. Then he bagged the panties and the shoes and socks. He put all of it back into the case and snapped it shut.

"Sheriff," the deputy named Wes said over the walkie-talkie. "Better get down here. We have a body."

◆   ◆   ◆   ◆

The body was nude and young—I would guess eighteen to twenty-one, though it was hard to tell these days. She could have been younger. She was face up just below the surface. Her eyes were open and glazed over, and her black shoulder-length hair billowed out, moving ever so slightly with the water. A rope was around her right ankle. It led to a tent stake that had been pounded into the ground at the edge of the lake. I backed away, not wanting to look any longer, embarrassed for the dead girl.

"Fuck me," Jimmy said.

We all stood in silence. The only sound I heard was the clicking of Billy's camera.

"This is not good," I said to Jimmy. "This whole thing was staged. Whoever did this wanted the body to stay right here and be found."

"We are dealing with one sick puppy," Jimmy drawled.

"He's going to do this again, Blood," Billy said softly.

"I think you may be right about that, Chief," I said.

Jimmy was still waiting for the crime-scene tech. Billy stayed to take pictures of the body once it was removed from the lake. But I didn't linger that long. I had seen enough. It wasn't my problem. I went back to the club to pick up Lacy.

◆　　◆　　◆　　◆

That night, Lacy and I sat at the bar playing chess. I had one eye on the TV and the other on the board. Mary was fixing dinner. The six o'clock news was on. The dead girl at the lake was the lead story. Jimmy Durham had evidently kept a lid on it, since all that was reported was an accidental drowning. According to the sheriff's department, the identity of the dead girl was being withheld pending notification of the next of kin.

Lacy and I had often played a game of chess at night after she finished her homework. Now that a boyfriend was in the picture, we played less and less. She had yet to beat me, and I was not about to let her win. But her play was improving, and sooner or later I was going to lose. She made her move and punched the chess clock. Each of us had started with half an hour.

"Never go swimming by yourself," Mary said as she pounded boneless chicken breasts.

I could tell the news upset Mary, and I didn't want to make it worse by telling her I was there. I made a move and punched the clock. Lacy studied the board intently.

"Did your hear me, Lacy?" Mary asked.

"I'm about to lose this game," Lacy said as she made a move.

"Later, Mary," I said.

Eventually, Lacy lost the game because her clock ran out. Then she and Mary had a discussion about not swimming alone. I nodded and kept my mouth shut.

2

The next day, I went to see Wanda Jones. Wanda was the medical examiner for the city and county and also my best female friend. She had looks that almost rivaled Mary's. At one point, I had tried to pursue her, but she could never figure out which side of the street she wanted to walk on. Now, she kissed me lightly on the mouth, as she always did on the rare occasions when I came to her office. The kiss lingered a fraction too long. She loved to tease me.

"You're bad," I said, wondering how Mary would react.

"I admit it," she said. "I just can't help messing with you."

"Good thing I'm taken," I said.

"*Taken* is putting it mildly," she said. "I told Mary one time if I decided to go straight, I was going after you."

"How did she react to that?"

"She said she'd arrest me for trespassing," Wanda laughed.

Wanda and Mary got together for lunch about once a week. I guessed it never hurt to keep an eye on the competition. But I knew Wanda was only kidding. She and Mary had become good friends, and I was pretty sure Wanda preferred women to men. If she had designs on anyone, it was Mary.

"You two wouldn't want to do a threesome, would you?" Wanda asked.

"Wanda," I said, staring hard at her. "Stop it."

She loved to push my buttons.

"Well, hell, Don," she said. "You're probably the best-looking couple in Mountain Center. Can't blame a girl for trying."

"Be serious for a minute," I said. "I need some answers."

"You want to know about the dead body," she said.

"I do," I said. "Do you know how long she was in the water?"

"I'll do the autopsy later today," Wanda said, switching into coroner mode. "But I'm guessing less than twenty-four hours."

"Any other thoughts?"

"Did you see the pictures Billy took of the body?" she asked, ignoring my question.

"No, I left before they removed her from the water."

"Billy emailed them to me this morning, and I printed them," she said, handing me the photos.

I didn't notice anything I hadn't already seen.

"Now, I'll show you one I took," she said. "Billy didn't roll her over, so I'm guessing nobody knows about this except me, you, and the killer."

She handed me another photo. In the small of the dead girl's back was a tattoo—a devil with hands outspread in the air, dancing behind a flame. One leg was raised and bent at the knee, the other partially hidden by the flame. A pitchfork was in the devil's left hand. It was black. Red and yellow flames rose from crisscrossed logs that were shades of brown and black. The tattoo had a lot of detail and vivid colors.

"Has to be a transfer," I said.

"Are you speaking from experience?" Wanda teased.

Actually, I did know from experience. Mary and I had messed around with transfer tattoos at the beach. On Mary, they were pretty damn sexy. On a young, dead female body, not at all.

"I'm a detective," I said. "We just know things."

"You're probably right," Wanda said. "I'll keep you posted. I also found a reddish area on the back left shoulder. I think she was stunned with a Taser. I'll know more after the autopsy."

"Call me," I said as I turned to leave. "And email me a picture of that tattoo."

"I will," she said. "Want to see it on her body?"

"No," I said. "I've seen the body. Once is enough. A picture will do just fine."

"Okay," Wanda said.

"And don't tell anyone you don't have to about the tattoo," I added.

"I understand," she said a little defensively. "You want to keep it a secret."

"Thanks, Wanda," I said.

I reached the entrance to Wanda's office and was almost into the hall when her voice stopped me.

"Don," she called, "are you helping Jimmy with this?"

I turned.

"Maybe," I said.

"You should."

"It's his call," I said.

"She was young and beautiful, and now she's dead," Wanda said, a touch of anger in her voice. "You help Jimmy find this guy and turn his lights out."

"You've been hanging around Mary too long," I said.

Wanda smiled. Her face softened a bit.

"Maybe not enough," she said.

"You're impossible."

I left while I still had the last word.

◆　　◆　　◆　　◆

Late in the afternoon, I was back in the office when the phone rang. I recognized the number as the county sheriff's office.

"Cherokee Investigations," I answered.

"Hey, Blood," Jimmy Durham said.

"What's up, Bull?" I asked.

"We got an ID on the dead girl," Jimmy said. "A missing person report was filed two days ago, and I saw it late yesterday when I got back to the office. I sent a picture this morning to the Washington County Sheriff's

Department. The picture ID was confirmed. The girl was a student at John Sevier."

John Sevier College for Women was a very old, very exclusive, and very expensive school located between Johnson City and Bristol.

"What was her name?" I asked.

"Betty Lou Walker," he said. "Her father owns Walker Trucking."

I had heard of Walker Trucking. It was a pretty big outfit. The Walker family had serious money.

"How old was she?" I asked.

"Nineteen," Jimmy said.

"Damn."

"I want to get this fuckin' guy, Blood," Jimmy said.

I knew Jimmy was pissed because he rarely cussed.

"Anything I can do to help," I said, "you let me know."

"Thanks," Jimmy said. "I will. Got any suggestions?"

"What have you told the press?"

"Only that we have a female drowning victim and that I'll release more details once we have an identification and the next of kin has been notified."

"Good," I said. "Don't tell them this is a murder investigation. Let them think it was an accidental drowning. Don't mention the stake and all of that, and don't let the tattoo information out."

"What tattoo?"

"Wanda found a tattoo on her back," I said. "She has pictures. I think it's a transfer tattoo."

"What are you thinking, Blood?" Jimmy asked.

"I'm thinking that whoever killed the girl put the tattoo on the body like a signature to attract attention. If the local news reports this as an accidental drowning, then that person might contact them to claim responsibility, and we might get a lead. It's just a thought."

"And a pretty damn good one," Jimmy Durham said.

Unfortunately, that lead never came.

3

That night, Mary was in bed reading and Lacy was in her room doing homework. I had my laptop on the bar as I searched out tattoos on the Internet while sipping an after-dinner drink of iced Bailey's Irish Cream. I had not come up with the dancing devil tattoo on the back of the dead girl.

The phone rang. The caller ID read, "The Brewery." The Brewery was a local brewpub where I often went with Mary, Billy, or Roy Husky for the best burgers in town.

"Youngblood," I answered.

"Don, this is Wayne down at The Brewery."

Wayne was a local gym rat I had become friends with working out at Moto's Gym.

"What's up, Wayne?" I asked. I was pretty sure it wasn't good news.

"That older, tough-looking guy you come in here with sometimes is at the bar, and he's had too much. He shouldn't be driving."

"His name is Roy," I said. "Keep him there. I'll be down in ten minutes or less."

"Sure thing," Wayne said.

I ran upstairs to the bedroom and told Mary what was going on.

"You don't have to wait up," I said.

"I'll be up," Mary said. "You be careful. Don't drive like a maniac."

•   •   •   •

I was there in nine minutes. The Brewery was in a shopping center near the center of town. I found a parking place by the front entrance. Stairs led from the edge of the parking lot to the front door. I bounded up them, then slowed and walked casually through the entrance and climbed another set of stairs to the second floor. Roy was at the bar, his head bent like he was about to fall asleep. I nodded to Wayne and sat on the barstool next to Roy. Wayne moved to the other end of the bar.

"Come here often, big fellow?" I asked.

Roy looked up and smiled.

"I think I'm about to be rescued," he said. His speech was slow but not slurred.

"A chauffeur for the chauffeur," I said. "At your service."

In truth, Roy was a lot more than a chauffeur. He was Joseph Fleet's right hand.

"No argument from me," Roy said. "Wouldn't be good for a chauffeur to get a DUI. Want one for the road?"

"It's past my bedtime," I said as I put my hand under his arm and helped him off his stool. "Let's get you back to the mansion."

"I can walk by myself," Roy said. "I'm not that drunk."

Wayne came back toward us. I laid a twenty on the bar in front of Roy.

"You good?" I said to Wayne, nodding at the twenty.

"I'm good," he said.

"Thanks."

"No problem," he said.

◆   ◆   ◆   ◆

Roy was a hard man ten years my senior. We had met on the Fairchild case and become unlikely friends. That friendship grew as Roy helped me with the Malone case. Now, I counted him among my good and close friends. Roy was also friends with Billy and my mentor, T. Elbert Brown. Roy was an ex-con turned jack-of-all-trades for powerful Mountain Center businessman Joseph Fleet. Even though our backgrounds were at opposite ends of the spectrum, Roy and I found common ground in honesty, humor, and a singular goal to see that justice was served.

He followed me down the stairs, using the rail. He got into the passenger side of my Pathfinder, buckled his seatbelt, and fished his car keys out of his jacket pocket.

"Get the gate remote out of the limo," he said. "It's underneath the driver's side visor."

I was impressed—too much to drink but still thinking.

The limo was parked a couple of spots away. I opened the driver's door and retrieved the gate remote.

"That fuckin' Ronnie," Roy mumbled as I slid behind the wheel of the Pathfinder.

The alcohol is catching up with him, I thought.

"Why did he have to take her? Why couldn't he just leave by himself?"

I didn't answer. I wasn't sure the question was meant for me. I rolled the Pathfinder out of the parking lot and headed for the Fleet Addition.

"I loved her, goddamnit," he said thickly.

His head went back, his eyes closed, and he was soon asleep as I headed north. The drive took awhile, and I didn't push it.

The Fleet Addition was an exclusive neighborhood developed by Joseph Fleet on the extreme north side of town. The rumor was that when Fleet purchased the land and built his mansion, he pulled some political strings and had the Fleet Addition annexed so his subsequent children could go to city schools. Fleet was supposedly a devout family man. But for whatever reason, he had only one child, a daughter, Sarah Ann. She was a few years behind me in high school, and I hadn't known her well. Fleet's wife died a few years back, and he hadn't remarried.

Twenty minutes later, I squeezed the button on the remote to open the iron gate, followed the long driveway to the front of the mansion, and parked. I had traveled up this driveway many times in the past couple of years. Roy was snoring. I got out of the SUV and went around and opened the passenger door.

"Wake up, Sleeping Beauty," I said.

Roy was semi-awake as I unlocked the front door and guided him down the hall to his bedroom. Joseph Fleet's room was on the second floor, and I doubted he heard us come in. I helped Roy strip to his shorts and undershirt and got him in bed. His eyes rolled open.

"You're okay, gumshoe," he said sleepily.

"Good night, sweet prince," I said.

His eyes slowly closed, and he rolled onto his right side and was quiet. I turned off the lights except for the one in the bathroom and pulled the door shut so I had just enough light to make my way to a reading chair across the room. I sat there in semi-darkness a few minutes, thinking about Sarah Ann Fleet. Finding her had been my first big case.

When I heard Roy snoring, I flipped on the desk light, found a sticky note, and wrote, "Call me in the morning and I'll pick you up and we'll go get the limo." I went into the bathroom and stuck the note on the mirror. I repositioned the door, turned out the desk light, and silently slipped from the bedroom.

4

We were in my office drinking Dunkin' Donuts coffee and eating bagels with cream cheese. Roy had called early that morning. I had picked him up and driven him back to The Brewery in silence. As I handed him the gate remote and car keys, all he said was, "I'll pick up coffee and bagels. See you at the office."

Roy looked tired. After half a cup of coffee and most of a bagel, he finally spoke.

"Thanks for last night," he said sheepishly. "I owe you one."

"That's bullshit," I said. "You've watched out for me on more than one occasion. And besides, friends don't keep score. If they did, I wouldn't have any."

"You'd have plenty," Roy said. "But thanks anyway."

"Don't mention it."

We ate and drank in silence, as we often did. Roy came to the office once or twice a week when we were both in town and brought coffee and bagels. We would talk women, politics, sports, movies, the weather—anything and everything.

"Trying to drowned your depression will only make it worse," I said.

As a friend I felt I had to say something.

"If I ever do that again I'll do it in the privacy of my own room," Roy said.

I didn't say anything.

"And don't think you can't ask me out for a beer now and then," he scolded. "I'm very controlled around people. Not so much when I start drinking alone."

"Probably shouldn't drink alone," I said.

Youngblood, the master of understatement. Roy pointed a finger at me and smiled. We were silent a while longer. I felt there was something else Roy wanted to say and I was going to give him room to say it.

"I can't stop thinking about Sarah Ann," he said finally.

"Hard not to," I said.

Roy looked down at his shoes and took a deep breath.

"You said one time that I might want to talk to someone about it," Roy said.

"A professional," I said.

"A shrink," Roy said, sarcasm leaking through.

"A therapist," I said.

We were silent as we finished our coffee. Roy stared out my office window with the look of a person sorting something out.

"Know someone?" he asked.

"I do," I said.

"Got a name?"

I took out my portable card file, wrote down the name and number of someone local on a note card, and handed it to Roy. He looked at the card, folded it once, and slipped it into his pocket.

"Maybe too close to home," he said.

"They tend to be pretty hung up on the confidentiality thing," I said.

"I'll think about it."

We were silent awhile longer.

"Know someone a little farther away?" Roy asked.

"I do," I said.

"Have you ever . . . ?" His voice trailed off, as if he wanted to retract the question.

"Yes," I said. "Years ago."

"Did it help?"

"Some," I said. "But some things never go away. You just learn to live with them."

◆   ◆   ◆   ◆

Wanda called later that morning. Typical Wanda. No "Hello, how are you?" Just straight to the point.

"She was stunned with a Taser and then drugged," Wanda said. "Whoever did this put her in the water while she was still alive. She drowned. I found no signs of a struggle. I doubt she knew what was happening."

"Is that all?"

"The tattoo was a transfer," she said.

I was silent, not wanting to ask the next question.

"Wanda." I paused. "Any signs of—"

"No," she answered before I could finish. "No signs of rape or even sex, for that matter. This girl may have been a virgin."

I hoped that didn't have anything to do with her getting killed.

"Anything else?" I asked.

"Not really. She was a healthy young woman with her whole life ahead of her. I'd like to kill the son of a bitch who did this," Wanda said.

"I can't argue with that," I said. "Do me a favor, if you can."

"Anything," Wanda said. "Name it."

"Get rid of it."

"The tattoo?"

"Yes," I said. "Remove it from her body. I don't want anyone else seeing it. We have pictures, so that should be enough."

"It's already gone," Wanda said. "Washed off when I used alcohol prepping the body for autopsy. I'll have to mention it in my report and include a photo, but nobody ever looks at those things."

"Do what you have to," I said. "The less said about the tattoo, the better."

Wanda seemed distant, not quite herself.

"You okay, Wanda?"

"A little bummed out, I guess," she said. "The girl's father came by with Jimmy to identify the body."

"Did he see the tattoo?"

"No, just her face," Wanda said. "By the time he got here, I was finished with the autopsy."

"Did you mention it?"

"Of course not," Wanda said, sounding a little annoyed.

"Sorry," I said. "I should have known better than to ask."

"The father is really pissed, Don," Wanda said.

"Can't blame him," I said.

◆　　◆　　◆　　◆

I had a turkey and baby Swiss sandwich on rye bread, a hundred-calorie bag of Doritos, and a diet ginger ale for lunch, then went online to check the market. It had continued to deteriorate. While doing that, I downloaded and printed the pictures from Wanda of the tattoo on the Walker girl's back. She had sent three, taken from slightly different angles. They were closeup shots with good lighting, showing lots of detail.

Since I closed the file on the Tracy Malone case, nothing much had happened as far as investigating was concerned. I had gone back to managing my clients' investment accounts. I spent hours a day online analyzing potential buys and deciding if and when to sell stocks already on board. The work was satisfying and boring at the same time. My afternoon seemed destined for more of the same—that is, until I heard my outer office door open.

"Hello?" called a big voice, deep and a little gritty.

"In here," I called back.

The middle-aged man was my height or maybe an inch taller, barrel-chested, a few too many pounds protruding over his belt buckle. His blond-gray hair was cut short in either a flattop or a buzz cut, it was hard to tell which. I stood when he entered my office.

"Can I help you?" I asked.

He came forward and extended his hand.

"I'm Troy Walker," he said.

"Donald Youngblood," I said, shaking his hand. "Please have a seat, Mr. Walker."

He sat heavily in one of the oversized chairs facing my desk.

"I understand you were at the lake when they found my daughter," he said, getting straight to the point.

"I was," I said. "I am truly sorry for your loss."

"Thank you," he said, looking down at his hands.

I could tell he was hurting. I couldn't imagine what it would be like to lose a child—no doubt the absolute worst thing that can happen to a parent. Lacy was not even my child, yet if someone killed her I would go crazy until I avenged her death. I waited as Troy Walker gathered his thoughts.

"What do you think the chances are they'll catch the animal that killed my daughter?" he asked.

"Hard to say," I said. "I don't know what kind of evidence the crime-scene tech gathered."

"Sheriff Durham told me they don't have much to go on," he said. "I took that to mean they have nothing to go on."

"I'm sure they'll do everything they can," I said, afraid of where this was heading and of not being able to stop it from going there. "I know Sheriff Durham personally, and I know he wants more than anything to catch whoever did this."

"That may not be good enough," he said, staring hard at me, putting his grief aside.

"Give them time," I said.

"I am not a patient man," he said as he got up and went to stand in front of the window looking down on Main Street. "Did you know Joseph Fleet is a friend of mine?" he asked, turning back to look at me.

"No, I didn't."

"He called me this morning to offer his condolences," Troy said.

I nodded.

"Do you know how many calls I got this morning once the word went out?" he asked.

I didn't think he wanted me to answer, so I waited.

"A lot of calls," he said. "And do you know how many I took?"

I waited some more.

"One," he said. "Joseph Fleet's. Joseph is the only one who called who could possibly have anything to say that might be worth listening to."

I understood that. Joseph Fleet had lost a daughter. She, too, had been murdered.

"Joseph said you found his daughter's killer."

"I was lucky," I said.

"He also told me you know the difference between justice and the law."

I didn't respond to that one.

"I want you to find my daughter's killer," he said. "I don't care how much it costs or how long it takes."

Well, there it was. If I wanted in on the hunt, here was my chance. Boredom was about to take a holiday.

"I'm not sure I can do anything the authorities can't," I said.

He turned and stared out my window and was quiet for a time.

"Do you have children, Mr. Youngblood?" Troy Walker asked.

"No," I said.

"Betty Lou was all we had, my wife and I," he said, turning toward me. "Only my wife and Joseph Fleet know what I'm going through right now."

His pain engulfed the room like a winter chill. His face showed a sorrow I did not wish to visit. I handed him one of my business cards.

"I'll see what I can do," I heard myself say. "But I don't have a lot to go on. You'll have to be patient. I'll call you in a few days."

"Thank you very much," he said. "I won't take up any more of your time."

We shook hands, and then he walked out of my office. Seconds later, I heard the outer door close.

Now what had I gotten myself into?

5

Just when I thought the day couldn't get more complicated, I heard my outer office door open and shut softly.

"Is anyone here?" a female voice called.

"In here," I said.

If this keeps up, I'm going to need a receptionist, I thought.

A young woman came quietly into my office, as if she wasn't sure she wanted to be here.

"Are you Mr. Youngblood?" she asked.

"I am," I said as non-threateningly as I could. "Would you like to sit?"

"Yes," she said. "Thank you."

She sat, and I waited. She stared at the front of my desk, not making eye contact.

"I don't know where to start," she said, finally looking up. "I'm so scared."

"Why don't you tell me your name?" I said.

She smiled, relaxing a bit.

"Of course," she said. "Megan Carter."

"Okay, Megan," I said. "How can I help you?"

"Somebody kidnapped my daughter," she said shakily. "I want you to help me get her back."

She started to cry. I did what any sensitive male would and moved the box of Kleenex on my desk in front of her. In a minute or so, she stopped, pulled a couple of tissues from the box, and dried her eyes.

"Sorry," she said. "I'm just sick and angry over this."

I noticed bruising around her eye where she had rubbed some makeup off on her tissues.

"Tell me about it," I said.

"I got married when I was nineteen," she said.

I listened as she unfolded the story. The father, Ricky Carter, was basically a good-looking bad boy. Now, where had I heard that before? He literally charmed the pants off Megan and got her pregnant. Her words. Ricky was always into something shady. Lately, he had been involved with running drugs in Knoxville. She had threatened to leave him on several occasions if he didn't stop. He had promised he would.

Evidently, Ricky had been given a large sum to make a buy. He skipped with the money instead. Megan had no idea where he was. His employers were not happy. Yesterday, while Megan was at work, two men had snatched three-year-old Cindy Carter from her daytime baby-sitter at gunpoint and threatened Megan with Cindy's life if she called the police. When Megan found out, she called Ricky on his cell phone.

"Ricky said they were bluffing. That they wouldn't hurt Cindy," Megan sniffed. "That he was taking the money and disappearing. He said I would have Cindy back in a few days. He sounded high. Then he hung up on me. I keep calling him, but he won't answer."

Last night, Megan said, one of the kidnappers had called and said the little girl was safe and would be well taken care of. Megan had three days to get the two hundred thousand dollars her husband owed. When she handed over the money, she would get her daughter back. The kidnapper let her say good night to her daughter before hanging up.

"Why would they think you could raise that kind of money?" I asked.

"Have you ever heard of Cox Foods?" she asked.

"Sure," I said.

"That's my family. I was a Cox before I became a Carter."

"So why not go to your father for the money?"

"We haven't spoken since I married Ricky," she said. "My father has kind of disowned me."

"And he isn't interested in his granddaughter?"

"Not yet," she said. "He's very stubborn. I hope he'll come around someday."

"What about you mother?" I asked.

"She sneaks around and sees Cindy," Megan said. "But she's afraid to tell my father."

"Could you get the money from your mother if you had to?"

"Maybe," she said. "But if I do, I want to make sure I get Cindy back. What should I do?"

I needed time to think this through.

"What are you going to do if Ricky shows up?" I asked.

"Ricky and I are through," she said. "I'm going to find a good lawyer and divorce the son of a bitch."

"How often does he hit you?" I asked, catching her off-guard.

"Sometimes when . . ." She stopped. "How did you know?"

"Your makeup is good," I said. "But not quite good enough."

She absently touched her eye and quickly brought her hand back to her lap.

"Sometimes when he gets high," she said. "Ricky thought he had married the golden goose. When my father disowned me, Ricky got mad and stayed mad. He took his anger out on me."

The more we talked, the less shy Megan became. She was beginning to show some spunk.

"Do you know a good divorce lawyer?" she asked. "I've been thinking about it for a long time, but this . . ." Her voice trailed off.

"I do," I said. "Right down the hall. I can introduce you while I think about how to get Cindy back."

"Let's do it," she said with no hesitation. "The sooner I'm rid of Ricky, the better."

I could hear the anger in her voice.

We left my office and walked past the elevators, around the corner, and down the hall, which ended at an office door that read, "Roland G. Ogle, Attorney at Law." I opened the door for Megan and followed her in.

"Well, hello, Don," Estelle Huff said.

"Hello, Estelle," I said. "Is Rollie busy? I have someone here I want him to meet."

◆   ◆   ◆   ◆

An hour later, Megan Carter sat in front of my desk with a whole new demeanor, focused and confident.

"Mr. Ogle sure is something," she said. "I like him."

"He's a very good divorce lawyer," I said. "You can trust him."

"Do you have a plan?" Megan asked.

"I do," I said. "I'm going to try and find the people responsible for taking Cindy. In the meantime, you talk to your mother about the money, should we need it."

"I don't want your plan to get Cindy killed," she said urgently.

"It won't," I said. "I don't think this is a kidnapping for ransom. I think all these people are worried about is getting their money back."

"What if they call me again?"

"Tell them you're working on getting the money and should have it in a couple of days," I said. "Call me if anything happens." I handed her my card and a pad and pen. "Write down your cell-phone number for me, please."

She wrote the number on the pad and handed it back to me as she stood to leave.

"Thank you so much," she said, extending her hand.

"How did you hear about me?" I asked as I walked her to the outer office door.

"Everyone in Mountain Center knows about Donald Youngblood and Billy Two-Feathers," she said, smiling.

I wasn't sure whether I liked that or not.

◆   ◆   ◆   ◆

I could go weeks without anything happening and then get two cases in one day. Sometimes, it just worked that way. Two potential clients visiting me in my office was the equivalent of Grand Central Station at rush hour. It was months since I had a case I could sink my teeth into, and now it appeared I might have two. Most cases I worked on were small and could be resolved in a day or two. Once in a great while, I got in over my head. I wondered if that was about to happen.

After a rather long day, I was ready to leave the office before anyone else opened my door and came in with a problem. I called Lacy on her cell phone.

"What's up?" she answered.

"Mary is working second shift," I said. "What do you want to do for dinner?"

Silence came from the other end.

"Lacy?"

"Yeah, I'm here," she said. "Hannah asked me over for dinner, and then we're going to study, if that's okay with you."

"Where are you now?"

"At Hannah's," Lacy said.

"So what's for dinner?" I asked casually.

"You're so funny," Lacy said, seeing right through my third degree. "Pot roast. Would you like to talk to Hannah's mom? Maybe she'll invite you over."

"No," I said. "Just checking."

"I know," Lacy said.

"I'll pick you up at nine," I said.

"I could walk," Lacy said.

Now she was messing with me. She knew I would never let her walk home after dark.

"Nine o'clock," I said with emphasis.

"Relax, Don," Lacy said. "I was just kidding. See you at nine."

◆　　◆　　◆　　◆

I was trying to decide what to do for dinner when the phone rang and solved my problem.

"Donald," the voice said. "It's Joseph Fleet."

"Mr. Fleet," I said. "I haven't talked to you in a while. How are things?"

"Overall," Fleet said, "I think things are pretty good. But I have something I'd like to talk to you about. When can we get together?"

"How about dinner tonight at the club?" I asked. "That is, if you're free."

"I'm free," Fleet said. "What time?"

"Six o'clock?"

"See you then," Fleet said. "And don't mention this to Roy."

◆   ◆   ◆   ◆

The very private Mountain Center Country Club was not in Mountain Center. It was situated on an unknown number of acres in a vastly under-developed area northeast of the city. Among other things, the club offered golf, tennis, racquetball, and a fitness center with a full-time masseuse. Members could soothe their aching muscles with a variety of saunas, whirlpools, and steam baths. A first-class restaurant with a chef who had graduated from Johnson & Wales University in Providence, Rhode Island, sat atop the third floor of the main building.

Joseph Fleet was seated at an out-of-the-way table for four by a window overlooking the eighteenth green. He had not bothered to wait on me to start drinking. A half-filled glass sat in front of him. I walked over.

"Nice to see you again, Don," he said. He stood, and we shook hands. "Christmas, right?"

"Good to see you, too," I said. "I think Christmas at your place was the last time."

"Sit," Fleet said as a waitress appeared to take my drink order.

"How are you tonight, Mr. Youngblood?" the waitress asked.

"I'm fine, Gloria," I said. "And you?"

"I'm fine, too," she said. "What can I get you?"

"An Amber Bock, please," I said. "Draft."

"And bring me another one, please, Gloria," Fleet said, draining his glass.

Joseph Fleet and I exchanged small talk as we waited for our drinks. When they arrived, we raised our glasses. Gloria appeared again, and we ordered our food. Fleet ordered a beer to be brought with his dinner. Out the window to my right, I watched a few late-day golfers finishing their rounds.

"Did you and Stanley Johns ever get together on your computer security?" I asked.

"Oh, yes," Fleet chuckled. "Stanley is quite a character. He did a great job. I think he was having so much fun being wined and dined that he stretched it out a bit, but his work was first-class. In the end, he billed me for about half of what it should have cost. He added a 'Special Treatment Discount' at the bottom of his invoice."

"I'm still amazed he agreed to do it," I said. "Stanley is such a hermit."

We talked about the weather, the stock market, his business, and the goings-on in Mountain Center. Meanwhile, our food arrived, we ate, and the table was cleared. Fleet didn't mention Troy Walker, nor did I. If that old wound was to be opened, then Joseph Fleet should be the one to do it. We ran out of steam and sat silently with our after-dinner drinks in front of us.

"As much fun as I've had this evening," I said, "I'm sure you have something you want to say."

Fleet smiled.

"Ever the detective," he said, finally getting to the point of our meeting. "I'm worried about Roy. He's drinking way too much. Has been, on and off, ever since Sarah Ann was murdered. It was hard to put that behind me, but I did. Roy hasn't. He needs help."

"Have you talked to him?"

"No," Fleet said. "He doesn't think I know. It would crush his psyche if he realized it. I'd like you to talk to him."

"Why me?"

"He regards you as his best friend—you, Billy, and T. Elbert. I don't think he'd ever tell Billy about his problem because he wouldn't want Billy to think he was weak. He might tell T. Elbert. I know you brought him home last night. I know what kind of shape he was in. I lost Sarah Ann. I don't want to lose Roy. Will you talk to him?"

I was silent for a while. Roy Husky was more than an employee to Joseph Fleet. Under Fleet's guidance, Roy had been educated in the ways of the rich. Roy was more like a son than an employee. I understood Fleet's concern.

"We've already talked a little," I said. "He came by the office this morning. He's thinking about it. Roy has to want help or whatever I say is useless. If the opportunity presents itself, I'll bring it up again."

"Thank you," Joseph Fleet said. He seemed relieved. "That's all I can ask."

"If I can arrange something, will you give him some time off?"

"Absolutely," Fleet said. "As much as necessary. Anything you need, just ask."

I nodded and took a long drink of my Bailey's Irish Cream.

6

Even though I promised Troy Walker to look into his daughter's death before I had taken on the Carter case, the quasi-kidnapping of Cindy Carter was obviously more pressing. *The living before the dead,* I thought as I sat at my desk the next morning.

I called Jimmy Durham.

"Hey, Blood, what's going on?" Jimmy drawled.

"How are you doing with the Betty Lou Walker investigation?" I asked.

"Not very well," Jimmy said. "The crime-scene tech came up with zip. We're talking to all the regulars on the lake to see if they saw anything. So far, nothing."

"Troy Walker asked me to look into it," I said. "Maybe we can work together and save some time. I'll be glad to share what I find."

"I could use the help, Blood," Jimmy said. "God knows you're a better investigator than anything I've got. My guys are eager enough but green as new apples."

"I'm wondering how she got there. Did you find a car unattended?"

"No," Jimmy said. "Her car is missing. We have an all-points out on it now."

"Let me know where you find it."

"Will do."

"I'll meet with Troy Walker in a few days and see if I can get some leads," I said.

"Good," Jimmy said. "Let me know what you find out. We'll stay away from Walker."

"Another thing," I said. "Do you still have Oscar Morales, or have the feds taken him?"

We had captured Oscar in a meth lab bust last year. At the time, I questioned him and suggested he cut a deal with the feds.

"I still have him," Jimmy said. "He must have given the feds some good information. They're paying us to keep him. Looks to me like he's not going to have to do a lot of jail time."

"I need to talk to him today. Can you make arrangements?"

"Sure, what time?"

"A couple of hours," I said.

"What's this about?" Jimmy asked.

"I can't tell you right now," I said. "You'll have to trust me on this one."

"He'll be waiting when you get here," Jimmy said.

◆   ◆   ◆   ◆

"Mr. Youngblood," Oscar Morales said as I came into the interview room. Oscar was wearing the orange uniform of the incarcerated. He had not shaven in a few days and looked as if his uniform was due to be changed. "What brings you here?" he asked.

The last time we talked, we had spoken only Spanish. Oscar had pretended he didn't know English. That was after the meth lab bust. Ballistics had matched a stray bullet that accidentally hit Mary to a gun Oscar had fired. Luckily, Mary was wearing a protective vest. She missed work for a few days with a cracked rib, some bruising, and a lot of pain.

"I'm working a case you might be able to help me with, Oscar," I said.

Oscar looked amused.

"Your English has vastly improved since the last time I saw you," I said.

"The last time, you tricked me with that cultured Spanish of yours," Oscar said. "But that was probably for the best. It looks like I am not going to do much jail time."

"So I've heard," I said.

"My English has been pretty good for a long time. Sometimes, I can learn more by pretending not to speak English. I'll bet you have learned a few things by hiding the fact that you speak Spanish."

"I have," I said.

"How is the lady cop?" Oscar asked.

"Fine," I said.

"That is good," Oscar said. "You can forget, as they say, the small talk. I will help you if I can."

"I want to know who controls the drug traffic in Knoxville and how I can get in touch with whoever does," I said.

Oscar shook his head.

"We never dealt with Knoxville," he said. "We dealt only outside the state. I do not know anybody in Knoxville."

"Know anyone who does?" I asked.

"None of us were very friendly," Oscar said. "I am not getting a lot of visitors."

"I checked," I said. "You're not getting *any* visitors."

"Sad but true," Oscar said. "I am sorry I cannot help you."

I rose to leave.

"What are you going to do when you get out?" I asked.

Oscar shrugged. I took that to mean he was probably going right back into the drug business.

"*Call me if you are interested in a real job,*" I said in Spanish. "*It would be best for you and your family if you left this life behind.*"

He nodded.

"*I might just do that,*" he replied.

7

The following morning, I was cruising down I-81 at a respectable seventy-five miles an hour toward Knoxville with Roy Husky in the passenger seat. I had awakened in the middle of the night with a thought. Now, I was about to follow up on it. Roy and I were drinking coffee and discussing politics. Roy was a bit more liberal than I was. I hadn't brought him along to discuss politics, however. That was his idea. I needed him for backup. I would normally have brought Billy, but he was working on something in Cherokee.

"So you don't think Obama is doing a good job," Roy said.

It was more a statement that a question. I knew he was baiting me.

"I didn't say that," I said. "I think it's too soon to tell."

"I wouldn't have figured you for a democrat," Roy said.

"Actually," I said, "I'm not very political. If you gave me a questionnaire on politics to determine where I stand, I'd probably fall pretty close to the center. I guess I'm an independent."

"So where do you stand on *Roe versus Wade*?" Roy pushed.

"I'd rather row than wade," I said. "Especially in deep water."

"Cute," Roy said.

"If you want to ask someone about *Roe versus Wade*," I said, "try Mary."

"No way," Roy laughed. "Forget it. So who are you going to see?"

"Someone I met while I was looking for Joey Avanti," I said.

◆　　◆　　◆　　◆

I pulled into the driveway of the baby-blue split-level and parked behind a silver BMW coupe. I had been in the neighborhood a few years ago to talk to Amos Smith, alias "Teaberry." Amos was a master forger, supposedly retired. I had not called ahead because I didn't have his telephone number and he wasn't listed in the directory. I should have gotten his number the last time I visited—another mistake by an inexperienced private investigator.

"Wait here," I said to Roy.

I got out of the Pathfinder, went up the walk and a few stairs to the front porch, and rang the doorbell. I heard it chime inside. I waited.

The door opened and there stood Amos Smith much as I remembered him. A lean black man, Amos looked fit and snappy in charcoal-gray slacks, a white shirt with a button-down collar, and a camel's hair sweater vest. Flecks of gray showed in his closely cropped hair. His face was a question.

"Yes," he said. "Can I help you?"

I smiled.

"Hello, Amos," I said. "Or should I call you Teaberry?"

It took a second before my face registered in his memory.

"Ah," he said. "Mr. Youngblood, isn't it? The private investigator."

"Nice to be remembered," I said.

"What I remember is the five bills," he said.

"Want to go for five more?"

"Come in," he said, looking over my shoulder. "Who's in the car?"

"Bodyguard," I said as I stepped into his foyer.

"You going to need one?" he asked.

"Maybe later," I said.

"How about coffee?" he asked. "I was just going to have some."

"Sure," I said.

◆　　◆　　◆　　◆

We sat downstairs in Amos Smith's office. He had two desktop computers, a laptop, and a couple of filing cabinets to go with his crescent-shaped desk. The desk was cluttered. Amos was busy.

"I saw the Beemer," I said. "Things must be pretty good."

"Things are very good," Amos said. "The Internet has unlimited possibilities."

"What are you into?" I asked.

Amos smiled.

"I am a provider of information," he said. "You want the dope on someone, come see Amos. I even have a file on you."

"That must be pretty dull," I said, trying hard to act cool. The thought that someone could prepare a file on me just by using the Internet was rather disconcerting.

"Pretty dull until the last few years," Amos said. "Then it got really interesting."

I nodded. I added cream and sugar and took a sip of my coffee. It was not off-the-shelf.

"Good coffee," I said, changing the subject.

"Special blend."

I took another drink.

"Why are you here?" he asked in that slow, sophisticated voice I remembered. Amos was renegade Ivy League. "I'm sure you weren't just in the neighborhood."

"I need your help," I said.

"I'm listening."

I laid out the story of Cindy Carter's kidnapping. Amos listened without a word, barely moving. Occasionally, he blinked. When I finished, he remained silent.

"Who controls the drugs coming into Knoxville?" I asked.

"What makes you think I know?" Amos asked.

I smiled. I knew he knew. If he didn't, he would have just said, "I don't know," instead of being cute.

"You know," I said. "Or if you don't, you can find out. As you said, you're a provider of information, remember?"

Amos laughed.

"Touché," he said.

"I'll pay," I said.

"I don't need the money," he said.

We sat and drank coffee in silence.

"I'll owe you a favor," I said.

He smiled.

"I can always use favors."

He spun in his office chair, set his cup on a table behind his desk, and spun back around to face me.

"The dude's name is Rasheed Reed, and I doubt very much he had anything to do with a kidnapping. Probably someone who works for Rasheed who panicked."

"Where can I find Rasheed?"

"Forget it," Amos said. "You go looking for Rasheed without being invited, you could end up in a hospital or worse."

I winced at the word *hospital*. I'd had enough of hospitals.

"Can you arrange a meeting?"

"Maybe," he said. "What would compel Rasheed to see you?"

"Just tell him I have information that will avoid a shit storm coming down on him," I said. "That ought to pique his curiosity."

"And if it doesn't?"

"It will," I said. "What has he got to lose by talking with me?"

Amos Smith scratched his chin and drummed a pencil on his desk while considering my request.

"Will you try?" I asked.

"And then you'll owe me a favor," he said.

"I will," I said.

8

Roy and I found a Dunkin' Donuts on Kingston Pike and settled in, waiting on a call from Amos Smith. It came an hour later.

"He'll see you," Amos said.

"Where?"

"McGhee Tyson Airport," Amos said. "You know where people park while waiting on a cell-phone call from an arriving passenger?"

"I do," I said.

"Rasheed will be there at one o'clock," Amos said. "Black limo."

◆　　◆　　◆　　◆

Roy and I were at the airport by twelve forty-five. At precisely one o'clock, a black limousine pulled in behind my Pathfinder. Obviously, Amos Smith had given Rasheed Reed a description of my wheels. A large black man emerged from the driver's side door. He stood and stared at the back of my SUV.

"Showtime," I said to Roy as I got out of the Pathfinder.

The black man motioned me to the limo, and I complied by walking over to face him.

"You carrying?" he asked.

"No," I said.

"You wouldn't want to be lying to me," he said.

"I imagine I wouldn't," I said. "And I'm not lying."

He opened the door, and I climbed in beside a black man I assumed to be Rasheed Reed. He was about my height, a little thicker, with a completely bald head and expensive clothes. I immediately felt underdressed.

"Nice suit," I said.

"Thank you," he said.

He closed the privacy partition and sat back in his seat. I thought he might offer me a drink. He didn't.

"You called this meeting," he said. "Get on with it."

His face showed no emotion. His eyelids drooped a bit, as if he was sleepy, and his jaw was slack. But the eyes didn't miss anything, as they looked me up and down.

"A three-year-old girl was snatched in the Mountain Center area and is being held until the father, whose name is Ricky Carter, returns with two hundred thousand dollars of drug money," I said. "The prevailing thinking is it could be one of your employees and that you might not know about it."

Rasheed took a deep breath and was silent for a minute, staring out the window on his side of the limo.

"Sounds like the father made a serious error in judgment," he said, still turned toward the window.

"The father is an idiot," I said. "But whoever snatched the little girl isn't much smarter. If an Amber Alert goes out, this whole mess could end up on your doorstep."

I was counting on Rasheed's not knowing anything about the kidnapping. If he did, I might be in trouble. He turned and looked at me. His expression never changed, but I knew the wheels were turning behind those dark eyes. He took another deep breath.

"Shit," he snapped, and turned back to the window. "Step out and get some air. I need to make a call."

I closed the door behind me as the driver opened his door, slipped out, and shut it. He leaned against the limo, and I followed suit. I heard another door slam. Roy walked to the back of the Pathfinder and leaned against the tailgate, arms folded and eyes locked on Rasheed's driver.

"Nice day," the limo driver said pleasantly.

"It is," I said.

"Who's your friend?"

"My insurance agent," I said.

Rasheed's driver smiled.

"Personal attention from your insurance company," he said. "I like that."

"Never hurts to have insurance," I said.

"Looks like you have the premium policy," he said.

"And then some," I said.

We waited in silence for maybe a minute. I heard Rasheed's voice, but the words were muffled. Then his voice got louder. Someone was getting an earful.

"Get to Knoxville often?" the limo driver asked.

"Not very," I said.

We were quiet again. Then the window behind me slid down.

"Would you join me again, Mr. Youngblood?" Rasheed asked.

I got back in the limo and made myself comfortable. Rasheed's driver returned to his place behind the steering wheel.

"I assume no Amber Alert has gone out yet," Rasheed said, staring at the privacy partition.

"Your assumption is correct," I said. "I asked the mother to give me a few days to see if I could straighten this out."

"That's good," Rasheed said. "I might be able to help you with that."

"I thought you might," I said.

"There is still the question of the two hundred thousand dollars," he said.

"There is that," I said.

"Any suggestions?"

"The person who made a serious error in judgment is the one who entrusted Ricky Carter with two hundred thousand dollars," I said. "You might have to garnish some wages."

"Might," Rasheed said thoughtfully. He studied his manicure. "But somebody might still like to find Ricky Carter."

We were silent for a while. I guessed he had already made a decision and was just letting me stew. I waited patiently and tried to look relaxed.

"Tell you what," he said. "I'll see the little girl gets back to her mama this afternoon, and you track down Ricky Carter."

"Let's say I spend three four weeks looking for Ricky and don't find him. What then?"

"Then I may have to do the garnish thing," he said. "Or worse."

I didn't want to think about what "Or worse" meant.

"What makes you think I'll actually look for Ricky?" I asked.

"I checked you out after Amos called," Rasheed said. "Your word's good, and I'm a pretty good judge of character. If you say you will, then you will."

I sat silently and let him stew a bit. I even looked out my window. Then I turned back to Rasheed.

"Deal," I said. I felt like I had just made a bargain with the devil. I told myself it was for all the right reasons, as long as the devil kept his word. "How do I get in touch with you?"

He removed a silver Cross ballpoint pen from his shirt pocket, wrote his cell-phone number on the back of a business card, and handed it to me. The card read,

Rasheed Xavier Reed

President, Ace Security

Knoxville, TN 37996

"If you need any help from my end," he said, "let me know."

"I'll do that," I said, sliding out of the limo.

I walked back to the Pathfinder and got in as the limo drove past us and out of the parking area.

"How'd that go?" Roy asked.

"I'll know in a few hours," I said.

I reached for my cell phone to call Megan Carter and explain that her daughter should be back home that same afternoon.

"That sounded a little too easy, gumshoe," Roy said.

"Not that easy," I said. "I promised to try to find Ricky Carter."

"And will you keep that promise?" Roy asked.

"I will."

"Why keep a promise to a drug dealer?" Roy said.

"If I'm going to play private investigator on the dark side," I said, "I need to have the reputation of doing what I say. Otherwise, I'm not going to get very far with guys like Rasheed Reed."

I knew I got lucky with Rasheed. If I hadn't known Teaberry Smith, and if Teaberry hadn't known Rasheed, I'd still be looking for a way in. But I'd rather be lucky than good. And it's not bad being some of both.

We were halfway back to Mountain Center when a joyful and tearful Megan Carter called back. Little Cindy had been returned. That phone call made my day. *Sometimes, Youngblood,* I thought, *this job is worth it.*

◆　　◆　　◆　　◆

Mary and I sat at the kitchen bar and drank red wine and finished the last of our pizza and my infamous Caesar salad. Lacy had received a call from "a boy." Suddenly, eating pizza was far less important than it had been a second before the phone rang.

"So, who is this boy?" I asked.

"His name is Jonah. He's a junior on the basketball team and seems like a nice kid. Taller than you and maybe better looking," Mary said.

"Unlikely," I smiled. "The better-looking part." I drank some wine. "You met him?"

"Sure. Lacy introduced me one day when I was directing traffic after school," Mary said.

I drained my glass and poured more wine.

"Relax," Mary said. "He hasn't proposed yet."

"Lacy is a freshman, and he's a junior," I said. "Why does he want to go out with a freshman?"

"In case you haven't noticed," Mary said, "Lacy doesn't look like your ordinary freshman."

Actually, I had noticed.

"That's what bothers me," I said.

"I made sure he noticed I was wearing a gun," Mary said. "And I'm also sure he knows you are the big, bad private eye who shoots first and asks questions later."

"Brave kid," I said. "But that just proves how much teenage boys are controlled by their hormones."

"And having been one once, you can speak with authority," Mary said.

Laughter came from Lacy's room. Her conversation was animated, but her door was closed, so it was impossible to know what she and the boy were talking about.

"That was a long time ago," I said. "I don't remember much."

"I'll bet," Mary said.

We drank some more wine. This conversation was not going my way, and I saw no reason to pursue it further. I did indeed remember a couple of good-looking and very mature girls a few years younger when I was in high school. I even dated one. Of course, I kept my hands to myself. Her father, an ex-marine, would have killed me if I hadn't.

"What were you doing in Knoxville?" Mary asked.

That was a question I didn't wish to answer because I knew it would lead to a heated discussion on why I hadn't taken the kidnapping straight to the Mountain Center police.

"Confidential," I said, trying to keep it light. It was far easier to avoid the question than to lie about it.

Mary gave me her cop stare.

"Bullshit," she said, taking another drink of wine.

Sometimes when she drank too much, she could get a little mean. Or maybe she just got aggravated with me.

"What?" I said.

"Whatever it was, you know I won't like it, so you're not going to tell me."

Sometimes, smart women can really be irritating.

"Look," I said. "I didn't do anything illegal, and it turned out okay. I don't ask you for every little detail about your day." I could hear myself sounding defensive. I didn't like it. I was on the run.

"I'd tell you anything you wanted to know," Mary said, softening her approach. "Because I love you and trust what we have."

Well, there it was. I was being played by a manipulating female. The cat had cornered the rat. So I did the only thing I could. I told all.

Mary drank wine and listened and didn't interrupt. When I finished, she remained silent for a while. I watched for her face to color like it did sometimes when she was upset with me, but I saw no change.

"You did good," she said finally. "You made a tough call and got it right. Might have saved that little girl's life."

I knew she wanted to say more, and I was sure a lecture was coming, but I was wrong.

Much later, I got something far better than a lecture.

9

I sat in a comfortable chair on the other side of Troy Walker's desk in his third-floor office, which looked out over a vast fleet of eighteen-wheelers with "Walker Trucking" emblazoned on the trailers in red, white, and blue. Adele Walker sat beside her husband. She was an attractive, dark-haired, full-figured woman in her mid-fifties. Billy was in the chair beside me. We had just finished the introductions.

The Walkers looked tired. I couldn't imagine what the last four days had been like for them.

Troy looked at Billy.

"You're a big one," he said.

"So I've been told," Billy said. His bass voice was like a rumble of distant thunder.

"Now I understand Cherokee Investigations," Troy Walker said.

"Billy and I are partners," I said. "He'll be working with me on your case."

Billy and I had predetermined our strategy on the drive up. I wanted the Walkers to know he would be involved.

"Do the police have any leads?" Troy asked.

"None that we know of," Billy said.

"So how will you proceed?"

"We'll start to dig," I said. "Billy and I have more time than the authorities."

"Sounds good," Troy said.

"We'll need a few good pictures of your daughter," Billy said. "I'd like a head shot and a full body shot."

"I'll get those to you right away," Adele Walker said.

Billy handed her his business card.

"Who was her best friend at school?" I asked.

"Sally Thomas," Adele said. "They were as close as sisters. Sally is as devastated by this as we are." Adele pulled a handkerchief from her purse and dabbed her eyes.

"Does Sally also attend John Sevier?" Billy asked.

"No," Adele said. "She goes to East Tennessee State University."

"Have her call me in a day or so," I said. "When she feels like talking."

"I will," Adele said.

"Boyfriend?" Billy asked.

"Not steady," Adele said. "Betty Lou went out mostly with Sally and sometimes in groups, boys and girls. You could ask Sally. She would know more than I do."

"We'd like a list of her professors at school," Billy said.

"And places she frequented," I said.

"And any other friends you think might be able to help us," Billy said.

Adele Walker had removed a pad and pencil from her purse and was making notes.

"Anything else?" she asked.

"Write down Troy's email address, if it's okay for me to have it," I said.

Adele and I simultaneously looked at Troy. He nodded.

"My private one," he said to Adele.

"If I'm not in a position to call, I'll send you an email every few days," I said.

"That would be good," Troy said. "I'm not always easy to reach, and we're in union negotiations right now."

The room got quiet.

"Anything else?" Adele said again.

"Not right now," I said, standing to leave. "This may take awhile. Please be patient."

"We will," Adele said, looking at Troy.

Troy nodded reluctantly.

We shook hands, and Billy and I started for the door. I turned and tossed out the question I was really curious about.

"By the way," I asked, "did Betty Lou have any birthmarks or scars or tattoos?"

"No," Adele said. "None of those. Why would you ask?"

"Sometimes, people remember an identifying mark and not a face," I said. "It could help in determining where she was last seen."

"I see," Adele said. "I'm sorry, but Betty Lou didn't have any of those things."

That you knew of, I thought.

◆   ◆   ◆   ◆

We took Highway 11-E back toward Mountain Center. Billy had left his Grand Cherokee in my parking space behind my office building.

"The tattoo is the key," Billy said.

"I know," I said. "I believe we're going to see it again."

"You think we're dealing with a cult?" Billy asked.

"I have no idea what we're dealing with, Chief," I said.

"How do you want to play it?"

"How available are you in the next few days?"

"I got a few things going," Billy said. "Nothing that can't wait a few days."

"Once I get the list," I said, "I want you to take a run at the professors. I'll talk to Sally Thomas."

"I can do that," Billy said.

Billy had a way of being intimidating and disarming at the same time. The professors would find him a curiosity and would be more likely to open up to him than to me. They also might be a little afraid of him, making them more likely to share information and tell the truth.

"Ask the usual questions. Who did she hang out with? Was she close to any professors? Was she a good student? Like that. And whatever else you can think of. Play it like an accidental drowning. Don't mention the crime scene or the tattoo."

"Aren't people going to get suspicious about us investigating an accidental drowning?" Billy asked.

"Maybe," I said. "Just say you were hired by the father to figure out why Betty Lou was at the lake and if she was with anyone. That sounds plausible."

"Sooner or later, the word will get out that this is really a murder investigation," Billy said.

"Let's do our best to see that it's later, rather than sooner," I said.

10

In mid-afternoon on Monday of the following week, Sally Thomas sat in one of the big chairs on the other side of my desk wearing a black low-cut halter-top. It went well with her blond hair and dark eyes. I guessed Sally wasn't a natural blonde. I'm sure she had on other clothes, but I didn't notice. Sally was obviously proud of her chest. She bent over to tie her tennis shoes, giving me a good view of her braless boobs. I was almost embarrassed for her—almost. I took the opportunity to practice my skills of observation. I saw a rose tattoo high on her left breast. Then Sally straightened back up and gave me a coquettish smile. I resisted the urge to say, "Nice tat," afraid it might come out as "Nice tit." I wondered if her mourning period was over.

"Is everything we say here confidential?" she asked.

And everything we do, I thought but didn't say. She might take the humor seriously. Remaining professional, I took a small black spiral notebook from my center desk drawer and uncapped a pen, ready to make notes.

"It is," I said.

"That's good. What would you like to know?"

Why you aren't wearing a bra, I thought. I controlled myself and moved on.

"Were you Betty Lou's best friend?" I asked.

"Definitely," Sally said. "And she liked to be called Betty. She said Betty Lou was so high school."

I nodded as if I understood. Maybe Betty Lou wanted to reinvent herself. Getting away from your parents and going to college can have that effect.

"Did she share a lot with you?"

"Everything," Sally said.

"Did she have a boyfriend?"

"She wasn't into boys yet."

"Was she into girls?"

"She was into me," Sally said. "We were sort of into each other. I like boys okay, but Betty Lou wasn't ready for boys."

"I see," I said. "So you spent a lot of time together."

"A lot, considering we went to different schools," Sally said.

"I see." I nodded, wrinkling my brow and giving the appearance that I was deep in thought. "Did Betty have a tattoo?"

Sally smiled as if to say, *You saw my rose, didn't you?* I maintained my professionalism, and the smile disappeared.

"No, she didn't," she said. "I tried to talk her into it when I got mine, but she was afraid."

To add to my professionalism, I wrote in my notebook, "No tattoo."

"When was the last time you saw her?" I asked.

"The day before she died," Sally said, her voice quavering.

And then the dam burst and tears came. I grabbed my trusty box of tissues and placed it on the desk in front of her. The sexy coquette was gone. She was crying in earnest, and I could almost feel her pain. Why were women always crying in my office? She removed a few tissues from the box.

"I'm sorry," she sobbed.

"It's okay," I said. "Take your time."

She did. I doodled in my notebook. She had a nice long cry as I sat there praying she'd stop before someone heard her and called the cops. Big Bob would never let me live that down.

Sally finally calmed down and took a deep breath.

"Sorry," she said again. "I've been holding that in all day. That should last me until tomorrow. I'm totally lost without Betty."

"I know it's tough," I said. I spoke from experience. I had still not totally recovered from losing my parents. I guessed I never would. "Did you talk to Betty the day she died?"

"Yes, I did," she said. "She was on her way to Johnson City to go shopping."

"Do you know where?" I asked.

"I know she was going to Barnes & Noble on State of Franklin," Sally said. "I don't know where else. She said she would see me later. When she didn't show up, I knew something was wrong. I kept calling her cell phone and didn't get an answer."

I made another note: "Barnes & Noble."

"What time of day did you talk to her?"

"Late," Sally said. "Just before dark. She said she'd see me in a couple of hours."

"Do you have any idea why Betty would go to the lake?" I asked.

"No," Sally said emphatically. "That makes no sense."

I was running out of questions. Sally stared into space as if trying to figure something out.

"She didn't drown, did she?"

"Yes," I said. "She did. It's on her death certificate. She had water in her lungs."

"There's more to it, isn't there? You wouldn't be involved if there wasn't."

I didn't want to lie, so I stayed silent.

Sally leaned forward toward my desk. She was getting some color in her face.

"Tell me," she said. "Goddamnit, I loved that girl. Tell me what happened."

We had a staring contest. I knew I was going to lose. A determined female wins that one every time.

"You have to keep this quiet," I said against my better judgment.

"I will," Sally said.

"I mean it, Sally," I said with an edge to my voice. "If this gets out, it could really hinder my investigation."

"I promise," she said. "I want you to find who did this. I won't breathe a word."

I told her pretty much everything. I wasn't sure why, but I felt she deserved to know. I didn't mention the tattoo.

She fought back tears and substituted anger.

"You get whoever did this," she said.

"I'll do my best." I didn't know what else to say. "Give me your cell-phone number."

I tore off the top sheet from my note pad and handed it to her. She hurriedly wrote down her cell phone number and handed the pad back to me. I laid it on my desk in front of my computer to remind me to input the information into my Palm Pilot phone file.

"In the meantime, if you think of anything that might help me, give me a call," I said.

I gave her my card as she rose to leave. I walked her to the outer office door and opened it for her.

"Watch yourself," I said. "We don't know what we're dealing with."

"Anyone who messes with me gets a face full of mace," Sally said angrily.

"Be careful anyway," I said. "Having mace and being able to use it are two different things. It's better to feel a little unsafe than too safe."

"That's good advice," she said. "I'll be careful."

Then Sally Thomas turned and walked purposely toward the elevator. I admired her for a few seconds, then shut the door and returned to my desk, wondering what it would be like to be back in college.

◆   ◆   ◆   ◆

I sat and thought about my conversation with Sally. I made a few more notes and then called Jimmy Durham.

"Did Betty Lou Walker's car ever turn up?" I asked.

"No," Jimmy said. "We're still looking."

"According to a friend, Betty Lou went to Barnes & Noble in Johnson City the Saturday afternoon before she was found at the lake," I said. "It's a big mall. Her car may still be in the parking lot, or it could have gotten towed."

"I'll call the Johnson City police," Jimmy said. "Thanks, Don."

11

The following Monday morning, Billy sat in front of my desk drinking hideously strong black coffee and filling me in about his interviews with Betty Lou Walker's professors. Since he had been thoughtful enough to bring me a tall cup of Dunkin' Donuts coffee with cream and sugar and a toasted poppy seed bagel with cream cheese, I kept my usual smart remarks about his brew to myself.

"How many of her professors did you talk to?" I asked, taking a rather large bite of the bagel. I chewed and listened.

"All of them," Billy said. "The headmistress was kind enough to arrange a schedule."

"Headmistress?"

"That's what they call her," Billy said.

"How quaint," I said.

"That sounded like a sexiest remark," Billy said.

"Really?"

"Uh-huh," Billy said. "Probably wouldn't have said that if Mary were here."

"Just because you're afraid of Maggie doesn't mean I'm afraid of Mary," I shot back. I was probing for signs of henpecked-ness from the new husband.

"Relax, Blood, I was kidding," Billy said with a sly smile. "Overreacting a little, aren't you?"

I took another drink of coffee and stared at him. I really *was* over-reacting. Now, why was that? Maybe I felt my days of bachelorhood were numbered.

"And I am not afraid of Maggie," Billy said rather indignantly, though there was obvious humor in his voice.

"Sorry, Chief," I said. "Now, tell me about the interviews."

"All of Betty Lou's professors said the same thing. She was a good student, quiet in class, didn't seem particularly close to any of the other students or professors, and had very good attendance."

"In other words," I said, "a complete dead end."

"Pretty much," Billy said. "Now what?"

"Good question," I said, finishing off the bagel.

We sat and drank coffee and were silent. A basic truth in private detecting was that one interview usually led to another. But in this case, all our interviews seemed to lead nowhere.

When in doubt, return to the scene of the crime. I could go myself, but I knew Billy was much better qualified. He had some kind of built-in genetic code that allowed him to sense things out of place, things not right, especially in remote places like the wooded area where Betty Lou's body was found. He just seemed to know things. I don't think even he could explain it.

"I'd like for you to go back to the crime scene for a second look," I said. "Spend some time there. Meet me at the diner in the morning at seven-thirty. We'll talk then."

Billy nodded and got up to leave.

"I have some things I need to do," he said. "I'll go out later today. I'd like to be there when it gets dark."

After dark? Only Billy Two-Feathers would want to be at a murder scene after dark.

Billy walked out of my office. Seconds later, I heard the outer office door shut.

I called Troy Walker and gave him a quick update on our progress, which was no progress at all. He sounded tired and subdued. I knew he was still hurting. There are some wounds time cannot heal. I knew that from experience. I promised to stay in touch.

Just before I left the office Jimmy Durham called.

"They found Betty Lou Walker's car in the mall parking lot where the Barnes and Nobles store is located," Jimmy said. "Looks like whoever took her took her from there. I'm going to call Troy Walker and let him know."

"You going to canvas the mall to see if anyone recognized Betty Lou?"

"Unless you want to," Jimmy said.

"You go ahead," I said. "I've got something else going on. I may follow-up later. Let me know if anything turns up."

"Will do."

"Before you hang up," I said, "one suggestion. Send your guy in plain clothes and tell him to soft pedal it. We still want to try and keep this thing under wraps."

◆　　◆　　◆　　◆

That night, as we usually did when Mary worked days, we sat at the bar with drinks in hand, discussing events of the past few days. Mary had worked four straight second shifts, so we had found little time to talk. Lacy was in her room doing homework or talking on her cell phone or both. I was nursing an Abita Amber, and Mary was drinking a Blue Moon.

"So tell me more about this Walker case," Mary said. "You're not telling me everything."

I had been purposely vague.

"She did drown, right?" Mary asked.

"Yes," I said.

"Accidental, right?"

"Maybe not," I said.

"So tell me," she said.

"You're better off not knowing," I said.

"I can keep my mouth shut," Mary said. She gave me the familiar cop stare. "Tell me."

I gave in.

"Not a word to anyone about this," I said.

I started with the phone call from Jimmy Durham and went from there. I considered leaving out the part about the tattoo. But in the end, I told her all of it.

"So you take a case to privately look into finding a possible murderer, as if you haven't had enough of being beaten up and shot," Mary said.

"I was set up," I said.

"Unbelievable," Mary said. She sounded annoyed.

On my last case, I had nearly been killed. Twice.

"What does Billy think about this murder?" Mary asked.

I think she trusted Billy's instincts more than she did mine.

"He thinks whoever did this is going to do it again," I said.

"Which would mean we might have a serial killer on the loose," Mary said.

"Well, at least I'm not looking for a missing person," I said. "We know how that turns out."

"You're still looking for Ricky Carter, right?"

"Yeah, I almost forget about Ricky," I said. "Ricky's not missing. He's hiding out. I don't think he'll be too hard to find once I start looking for him."

"Want my advice?" Mary asked.

I took another drink of my Abita and stared at her and remained silent. She knew I didn't want her advice. I knew she was going to give it to me anyway.

"Go look for Ricky and let Jimmy Durham find this murderer," she said.

"I promised the Walkers I'd look into it," I said. "Besides, it could get interesting."

Mary took another drink of Blue Moon and shook her head.

"Men," she said. "You'll never learn."

"One of our most endearing qualities," I said, smiling.

12

The next morning, Billy met me at the diner promptly at seven-thirty, as promised. Doris Black, the owner, was bustling around tending to the early arrivals—taking orders, pouring coffee, and spreading goodwill. She left me alone with a cup of coffee at my usual table in the back because she knew I was waiting on Billy. Once he arrived, Doris swooped in to take our order.

"What'll it be, Mr. Youngblood?" she asked. Attempts to get Doris to call me Don had been pure futility.

"Two scrambled with sausage patties, rye toast, and home fries," I said, mouth watering.

"Billy?"

"Blueberry pancakes with bacon," Billy said.

Doris scurried away.

A short time later, she was back with our food.

"Billy," she said, placing his breakfast in front of him. "Mr. Youngblood. Enjoy, you two."

She was gone in a flash.

"I cannot understand why she calls you Mister and everyone else by their first name," Billy said, shaking his head in mock disbelief. I knew he was teasing me.

"I can't explain it," I said innocently. "I tried for a year to get her to call me Don, and she just can't do it."

"I know why," Billy said cryptically.

"Sure you do."

"I do."

"Okay, wise guy, tell me," I said, forking in a mouthful of home fries.

"It's because you're rich, Blood," Billy said, pouring syrup over his pancakes.

I'm going to have to try those sometime, I thought.

"Because I'm rich?"

"Yes," Billy said.

"Explain."

"Do you call Joseph Fleet by his first name?" Billy asked.

"No," I said.

"Has he asked you to?"

"Yes, but I call him Mr. Fleet out of respect," I said. "He's older."

"And rich," Billy said.

"That has nothing to do with it," I said. But I was starting to wonder.

"You call T. Elbert by his first name," Billy said. "Why don't you call him Mr. Brown?"

"It's different," I said. "I'm a lot closer to T. Elbert. He'd laugh me off his porch if I called him Mr. Brown."

Billy smiled. He really had me going. He did that sometimes. I'd be in waist deep before I knew it.

"Eat your pancakes," I said, feigning annoyance. "And tell me about your trip to the lake."

Billy took his time giving me his impressions of the crime scene. In his opinion, the killer wanted the body found quickly. He was sure the killer had used a boat in the evening—when conditions were dark enough so he would not be easily seen but not so dark that he couldn't see what he was doing.

"Anything else?" I said, finishing my last bite of home fries.

"This guy is crazy," Billy said. "I can feel it."

"You sure it's a guy, Chief?"

"I am," Billy said.

I had learned never to question Billy's instincts. They were never wrong.

13

Early the following day, just after I finished my first cup of coffee, Rasheed Reed paid me a visit. His driver waited in the outer office while Rasheed made himself comfortable in one of my oversized chairs.

"Nice," Rasheed said. "Comfortable."

"Thanks," I said. "My partner suggested them."

"Billy Two-Feathers," Rasheed said. "Cherokee Indian. Big dude."

He wanted to let me know he had checked us out. I tried not to act impressed.

"He is that," I said.

I waited. Rasheed was silent as his eyes moved around my office.

"I was in the neighborhood on business and thought I'd drop in," Rasheed said.

"Lucky me."

Rasheed smiled.

"How are you progressing in your search for Ricky Carter?" he asked.

"I'm working on it," I lied. "I was thinking I had maybe thirty days on this."

"Time's wasting," he said. "I get impatient sometimes. The longer Ricky's out there unsupervised, the more of my money he'll spend. I'm thinking fifteen days should be enough for you."

I remained silent, as if I hadn't heard. Rasheed knew I had but didn't seem bothered by my lack of recognition. He stared out the window.

"How is the little girl?"

Rasheed was reminding me of our deal.

"She's fine," I said.

"That's good," he said.

"I'll see if I can speed up a bit," I said.

Rasheed nodded and then stood.

"Okay," he said. "You let me know as soon as you find Ricky."

I noticed he didn't say *if* I found Ricky.

"Anything you want me to tell him *if* I find him?" I said, using a little emphasis.

"Tell him to send back the money and all is forgiven," Rasheed said.

"Meaning?"

"Meaning I won't kill him."

"Should be a pretty good incentive," I said.

"Should be," Rasheed laughed.

◆   ◆   ◆   ◆

After Rasheed Reed left my office, I brewed my second cup of coffee and called Megan Cox. Megan had started using her maiden name as soon as she filed for divorce. She and Cindy had moved in with her parents. Apparently, all was forgiven now that Ricky Carter was out of the picture.

Once we exchanged pleasantries, I got to the point of my call.

"Part of my deal to get Cindy back," I said, "was to promise to look for Ricky."

"I wondered how you did it so easily," Megan said.

"Any idea where I should look?"

"Not really," Megan said. "He could be anywhere."

"Friends?"

"He hung out with a bunch of losers," Megan said. "I don't know if you could really call any of them friends."

"Any loser in particular?"

She was silent for a moment.

"Well, there was this one guy, Butch Pulaski," Megan said. "He'd hang out some. They'd drink beer and watch football. Butch was okay but going nowhere, if you know what I mean."

"Know where I can find this Butch guy?" I asked.

"There's a redneck bar, the Bloody Duck, on the highway to Johnson City," Megan said. "Ricky got too drunk to drive one night, and I had to go pick him up. I bet you could find Butch there."

"Thanks," I said. "Call me if you think of anything else that might help."

"I will. If you find Ricky, tell him I filed for divorce and that I never want to see his lying face around here again." Her anger came through loud and clear.

When I locate Ricky, maybe I should get Megan after him, I thought.

"Be sure and tell him that," she added.

"I will, Megan," I promised.

"And send your bill to my father. He wants to pay it."

"I'll do that, too," I said.

◆   ◆   ◆   ◆

Later, I called Roy Husky.

"Can I buy you a beer after work?" I asked.

"Sure," Roy said. "What's the occasion?"

"I need a tough guy to protect me while I visit this redneck bar on the Johnson City highway," I said.

"The Bloody Duck?"

"You know it?"

"I know it," Roy laughed. "You will need protection, gumshoe."

"I'll pick you up at the mansion around five-thirty," I said.

"Dress down," Roy said. "And bring a gun."

I couldn't tell if he was kidding about the gun.

14

I wore jeans, boots, a Grateful Dead T-shirt, and a black leather jacket and had a money clip with two hundred dollars in twenties in my left front pocket. I might as well have been in greasy bib overalls. I would have fit in better.

The Bloody Duck was a combination blue-collar and biker bar-and-grill. Some of the patrons looked liked they'd been in the same clothes for a week. Some were just drinking, while others were drinking and shooting pool. I counted six pool tables. The place was quiet. It got even quieter when Roy and I walked in. Every eye was on me, and every face had a "What the fuck are you doing in here?" sneer. I felt like a medium-rare filet mignon hot off the grill in a roomful of hungry carnivores. Bringing a gun wouldn't have been such a bad idea.

No one paid any attention to Roy. I had the feeling he'd been here before. The bartender nodded at Roy, and the barmaid smiled at me. She was attractive in a floozy redneck bar sort of way. After the initial stares, the hum returned to normal. As we walked past the bar, I prepared to get bumped and to be told to watch where I was going, but that didn't happen. Maybe I watched too many movies.

We took a booth in a back corner. Even though it was against the law in restaurants and bars in Tennessee, I was surprised no one was smoking.

The bartender came from behind the bar and made his way to our booth. He was tall and lean, his dark hair slicked back. He wore jeans, black boots, a black T-shirt, and a white apron tied at the waist.

"Roy," he said, nodding.

"How you doing, Rocky?" Roy asked.

"Not bad," Rocky said. "Haven't seen you in a long while."

"Been busy," Roy said.

"Who's this?" Rocky asked, making a head motion toward me.

"Friend of mine," Roy said. "Don, this is Rocky Gibbs."

"Nice to meet you," Rocky said, extending his hand.

It was a normal firm handshake with no macho statement behind it.

"You, too," I said.

"What'll you guys have?" Rocky asked.

"Draft," Roy said. "Bud's okay."

"Same," I said.

Rocky went to fetch our beers.

"I met Rocky in prison," Roy said. "He was young and foolish like me, but he turned it around. He'll help us out if he can."

Rocky returned with our beers and a couple of coasters.

"Want some peanuts?" he asked.

"No," Roy said. "Sit for a minute."

I slid over, and Rocky sat facing Roy. Roy looked at me.

"We're trying to find someone," I said, turning toward Rocky. "Just want to ask him a few questions."

Rocky looked at Roy. Roy nodded. Then Rocky looked at me.

"Who?" he said.

"Guy named Butch Pulaski," I said.

Rocky looked over Roy's shoulder toward the pool tables.

"Butch is shooting pool," he said. "Looks like he's between games."

"Could you ask him to join us for a beer?" Roy said.

"Sure," Rocky said, getting up.

Rocky moved slowly toward the pool tables, taking his time, speaking to patrons as he went. He stopped in front of a scraggly kid wearing a Tennessee Titans baseball cap and dirty coveralls over a long-sleeve T-shirt. He was holding a cue stick. Rocky leaned down, whispered in the kid's ear, and nodded toward us. The kid leaned the cue against the wall and walked our way. He stopped in front of our booth.

"You guys want to buy me a beer?" he asked suspiciously.

"Sure," Roy said, making room. "We know a friend of yours."

Butch sat beside Roy. I smelled a combination of sweat and motor oil. Roy moved a little farther away. Rocky showed up with a draft and set it in front of Butch. Butch raised the glass and took a long pull.

"What friend?" he asked, wiping his mouth on the sleeve of his shirt.

"Ricky Carter," I said.

"Some friend," Butch said. "I haven't seen Ricky in weeks. He owes me money."

"How much?" I asked, taking a drink of my draft.

"A hundred bucks," Butch said.

"I might be able to help you with that," I said.

"How?"

"I'm looking for Ricky," I said.

"What did he do now?"

I looked at Roy, who was finishing his beer. He shrugged. I had the feeling Butch was just a poor working guy trying to make ends meet, so I told him the truth. I was guessing he and Ricky weren't best friends.

"Ricky was always a total dumb-ass," Butch said. "Good-looking wife, rich father-in-law, and all he wanted to do was run drugs and get high."

"Any idea where he'd run to?" I asked.

Butch took another pull on his beer. It was more than half gone. I caught Rocky's eye and put up three fingers. He nodded. Butch leaned in toward me and lowered his voice.

"Some tropical island somewhere," he said, finishing his draft. "He was always talking about scoring big and retiring on some island. Like I said, total dumb-ass."

Rocky showed up and set three more drafts on our table. I handed him two twenties.

"We're good," I said.

"Thanks," Rocky said, and slipped away.

"Any idea what island?" I asked Butch.

"No," he said. "I asked Ricky that once, and even he didn't know. Said he'd just go from island to island until he found one he liked."

I didn't think I'd get much more out of Butch, so I peeled off five twenties from my money clip and handed them to him. He looked like he'd just hit the lottery.

"Thanks, man," Butch said. "You're a lifesaver. I mean it."

"No problem," I said, handing him my card. "If you hear from Ricky, let me know."

"You can count on it," he said, stuffing the card into a coverall pocket.

Butch finished his second beer with a final gulp and slid out of the booth. He smiled at both of us and headed back to the pool tables.

Roy shook his head.

"Sad," he said. "He's never going to be anything but a grease monkey."

"There are worse things," I said.

"Like prison," Roy said, finishing his second beer.

"That's one," I said.

"Let's get out of here," Roy said. "This place is depressing me."

◆   ◆   ◆   ◆

Mary was working second shift, so I dropped Roy, checked in with Lacy, called Stanley Johns, and stopped for a large pepperoni pizza, a cold six-pack of beer, and a couple of sixteen-ounce ginger ales, also cold. Twenty minutes later, I parked in front of Stanley's house on Locust Street. I carried the pizza around to the back door. He had left it open for me.

Stanley Johns—friend and hermit—was in his sprawling basement office doing his best to protect the world from computer viruses. I had long ago nicknamed his office "Oz" because Stanley was a computer wizard. From time to time, with enough coaxing, he did some innocent hacking for me. My persuading him usually took much longer than the hacking. Pizza always helped the cause.

I set the pizza, one bottle of beer, and one bottle of ginger ale on a worktable that Stanley had cleared for the occasion and put the rest of the beverages in the refrigerator. The beer was for me.

"Hi, Don," Stanley said, barely looking up.

He was intently studying one of his many computer screens. It looked like a foreign language to me.

"Take a break, Stanley," I said. "Let's have some pizza."

He tapped his keyboard a few times, and the screen returned to his wallpaper. He pivoted in his chair to face me.

"How are you feeling, Don?" Stanley asked. "How's the arm?"

I had recently taken a bullet in my left arm in a cemetery shootout with a very bad guy.

"The arm is fine, Stanley," I said. "Thanks for asking."

"What kind of favor do you want?" Stanley asked.

I laughed.

"That obvious, huh?"

"You don't bring pizza unless you're after something."

"I need you to see if you can find a record of a Ricky Carter flying anywhere in the last week or so," I said.

"What's this about?" Stanley asked.

I told him the whole story, slowly, as we ate and drank.

"He said he didn't care about his own daughter?" Stanley asked, incredulous.

"That's what the mother told me," I said, starting my second slice of pizza.

"Do you believe her?" Stanley asked, starting on his third.

"I think so," I said.

Although he'd never been married or had children, Stanley couldn't come to terms with a father who would turn his back on his daughter. Stanley led a rather insulated life.

His question, however, did lead me to consider that Megan may have played me by making Ricky sound worse than he was.

"You were brave to go to the drug dealer," Stanley said.

"Or stupid," I said, finishing my first beer. I went to the refrigerator for another.

"Brave," Stanley said. "And lucky."

"Will you do it?" I asked, getting back to the subject at hand.

"Sure," Stanley said. "If you'll smack him hard one time for me."

Stanley hated violence. In his world, a slap upside the head was tantamount to my blowing Ricky's brains out with my Beretta.

"I can do that," I laughed.

"But only if he knew about the kidnapping," Stanley said.

"Agreed," I said, trying hard to keep a straight face.

"Any idea where he might have gone?"

"An island, maybe," I said. "Tropical."

Stanley started singing the Beach Boys' "Kokomo." He couldn't sing a lick.

"Okay," I said quickly. "Don't quit you day job."

Stanley just laughed and kept on singing. I finished my second slice and got up. I was surprised that he seemed to know all the words. Mercifully, I left before the last chorus, taking the rest of my beer with me.

"Call me!" I shouted from his back door.

15

Stanley Johns called after lunch the following day.

"A Richard Carter flew out of Charlotte, North Carolina, to Bermuda four days ago," he said. "No credit card. He paid in cash."

"Thanks, Stanley," I said. "I appreciate your help on this."

No response.

"Stanley?"

The wizard had returned to Oz.

◆   ◆   ◆   ◆

Later that afternoon, I called Roy Husky. I had cut a deal with Joseph Fleet to use one of his jets, if available. It was an indulgence, but what the heck. I would never spend all the money I had anyway.

"What's up, gumshoe?" Roy answered.

"Want to go to Bermuda?"

"Sounds good," Roy said. "What's the occasion?"

"Ricky Carter flew there four days ago," I said. "I want to wrap this thing up."

"I've never been to Bermuda," Roy said.

"Probably be a quick trip."

"Doesn't matter," Roy said. "It'll give me a chance to check it out. How soon do you want to leave?"

"Tomorrow, if possible," I said.

"I'll see if one of the jets is available," Roy said.

◆　　◆　　◆　　◆

"Bermuda!" Mary said.

We were at the kitchen bar. Mary was drinking white wine, and I had an Amber Bock. We were discussing our day. We did that when Mary worked days, which had been a lot lately. I was grateful for that. Lacy was visiting her best friend, Hannah. I was grateful for that, too.

"It's business," I said.

"How long?" Mary asked.

"Not long," I said. "Overnight at the most. It's not that big an island."

"Is Roy going?"

"Yes," I said. "He's picking me up in the morning."

"Have you ever been there?"

"Yes," I said with a hint of sadness. "With my parents. They took me when I was twelve. I fell in love with a sixteen-year-old girl."

"Really," Mary said with an edge. "What was her name?"

Now, what was her name? I thought. A blonde, I remembered. It was her developing body that had intrigued me.

"I have no clue," I said.

"Men," Mary said. "Bet you remember her boobs."

"Unforgettable."

She punched me on the shoulder and smiled and took another drink of wine. We were quiet for a while. I could tell from her look that something was on her mind. If I kept quiet, it would come out. It didn't take long.

"John Williams is retiring," Mary said.

John Williams was a twenty-year fixture on the Mountain Center police force and a detective for the last ten years.

"Why?" I asked. "John's not that old."

"His kids are grown and gone, he just got divorced, and money's not a problem," Mary said. "John wants to move to Florida, buy a boat, and fish."

"Good for him," I said.

Mary took another drink of wine.

"Big Bob offered me John's job," Mary said.

"That's great," I said.

Mary didn't say anything.

"Isn't it?"

"I like it on patrol," Mary said. "But the job would mean working days and an increase in pay."

We both knew the money didn't mean anything. But Mary was an independent woman. She liked to pay her own way, and I didn't argue about that.

"I'm having a hard time making up my mind," Mary said.

We were silent again. I wanted to say it would be nice if we were on the same schedule. I wanted to say it was a safer job. I wanted to say she'd be crazy not to take it. I waited for her to ask me what she should do. She didn't. I kept my mouth shut.

"How long do you have to decide?" I asked.

"Big Bob said to take my time," Mary said. "John isn't leaving for a few months, maybe not until the end of the year."

Mary took another drink of wine and was silent.

"Perhaps you should sleep on it," I said.

"Perhaps," Mary said.

I knew that smile.

"How long is Lacy going to be at Hannah's?" I asked.

"Long enough," Mary said.

Long enough indeed.

16

Jim Doak, our pilot, informed us we'd be in Bermuda in a couple of hours, which would put us on the ground around ten in the morning. Jim was the only Fleet Industries pilot I had ever flown with. Fleet Industries had three pilots—two men and one woman. Jim and the lady pilot were full-time. The other was part-time. The pilots were responsible for everything from maintenance to bottled water. Knowing how meticulous Jim was, I felt perfectly safe.

"Stay out of the Bermuda Triangle," I teased Jim as we boarded. "I'd like to land in the same year we took off in."

Jim laughed.

"Not to worry," he said. "We might be in the tip of it for a few minutes, but we should be okay."

The fall after returning from Bermuda with my parents, I had done a geography paper on the island. I tried to remember what I'd learned. I recalled that Bermuda was nicknamed "Isle of Devils" by early sailors because of all the shipwrecks on its treacherous reefs. And I remembered that the Bermuda Triangle, blamed for many mysterious disappearances, ran from Puerto Rico to Miami to Bermuda. Even as a twelve-year-old, I was fascinated with mysteries.

I talked to Roy about the Walker case and the interview with Sally Thomas. I trusted Roy completely, so I told him about the tattoo and the clothes folded neatly on a nearby picnic table.

"Whoever did it is fuckin' nuts," Roy said.

"Most likely," I said.

I was looking at a list of Bermuda hotels.

"Do you think it'll take long to find Ricky?" Roy asked.

"If he's not hiding, it won't," I said. "And based on how stupid he appears to be, I doubt he's hiding. I'm guessing he'll be at an expensive hotel spreading his newfound wealth around."

By the time we landed at L. F. Wade International Airport on a beautiful Bermuda day, I had compiled a list of expensive hotels and given half the list to Roy. The plan was to hire separate cabs and start searching. We taxied to the north side of the airport, which housed facilities for private jets, and went through customs without a hitch. We both carried small overnight bags. Roy grabbed the first taxi he saw and was gone. I took my time picking out a driver who appeared friendly. I chose a pleasant-looking black man wearing a tag that revealed his name to be Benjamin. He was approximately six feet tall and had a stocky build and a friendly smile. He wore a colorful shirt with black slacks. The shirt was not tucked in.

"What is your destination, sir?" Benjamin asked once I was in his taxi.

"I might have more than one," I said, deciding to go with the truth and hoping Benjamin might be intrigued. "I'm a private investigator from the States, and I'm looking for someone."

I showed him my PI license. I didn't get to do that often and had to admit it felt good.

"It might take a few stops before I find him," I said. "I'll need you to wait."

I handed him two hundred-dollar bills. He looked at them wide-eyed.

"American dollars okay?" I asked, remembering Bermuda had its own currency.

"No problem," he said in his pleasant accent. "I can exchange dollar for dollar."

"I'll have another two of those for you at the end of the day or whenever I find who I'm looking for," I said.

"I am yours for the day," Benjamin smiled. "Will this be dangerous?"

"No, nothing like that," I said. "Just routine."

"Too bad," Benjamin sighed. "I could use a little excitement."

"Let's try The Reefs first," I said as we pulled out of the airport.

"Expensive," Benjamin said.

"That's the idea."

We headed toward an area known as Southampton. It was a good distance from the airport. We went over the Causeway Bridge, which connected St. George's Parish to Hamilton Parish, then turned left on Wilkinson Avenue and left again onto Harrington Sound Road. Motorbikes buzzed around us like flies as the locals sped to and fro. The tourists were slower and a lot more cautious. Everyone drove on the wrong side of the road.

I relaxed and enjoyed the view out the taxi window as we passed Devil's Hole. I remembered the last time I was here. We had stayed at a small cottage community in Sandys Parish, in the direction we were heading. Bermuda is divided into nine parishes, and Sandys is on the southwest end of the island. I recalled the beautiful beaches, the snorkeling, following my father around on a motorbike, and the beautiful blond girl in the one-piece black bathing suit. One day, she was there. A week later, she was gone. I pined over her for the rest of the summer. Then I returned to school, reacquainted myself with the local girls, and completely forgot her. What was her name?

Benjamin sped down South Road at a clip reserved for taxi drivers, occasionally blowing his horn at a slow motor biker or tapping a quick beep at another taxi driver. We passed Lighthouse Road, where I saw Gibbs Hill Lighthouse high on Gibbs Hill to my left. I remembered climbing to the top with my father. It was a bittersweet memory.

Soon afterward, Benjamin made a left turn and pulled up to the front entrance of a very spiffy hotel. I could smell the money.

"I'll wait over there," Benjamin said with a nod of his head.

We had arrived at The Reefs. I got out and walked through the front doors toward the lobby.

A beautiful and expensive hotel on the pink-white sandy beach of Bermuda's south shore, The Reefs was just the kind of place where a high roller would stay. It had three restaurants, two bars, tennis courts, a spa, and a fitness center. I was tempted to book a suite for two weeks and call Mary to come join me. *If Ricky Carter knows about this place, he might be here*, I thought.

I went straight to the desk.

"Has a Richard or Ricky Carter arrived yet?" I asked casually, offering my best smile to the pretty young black woman behind the counter.

"One moment, please," she said in a pleasant English accent. Her hands flew over her computer keyboard. "No, sir. He has not arrived, nor do I see a reservation."

"Thanks," I said. "I must have the wrong hotel. He said something about Southampton."

"Try the Fairmont Southampton, up on the hill," she said.

In case Ricky was smart enough to register under an assumed name, I wandered around visiting the restaurants, the bars, the pool, and other common areas where he might be hanging out. No luck. I went to the edge of the beach and found an attendant. I handed him a ten-dollar bill and a picture of Ricky that Megan had given me.

"Have you seen this guy?" I asked.

The young black man took the ten and the picture, smiled, and looked me over from head to foot.

"Well, you aren't a copper," he said in an island accent. "They don't hand out money."

"Private," I said.

He nodded and took a long time with the picture to let me know he was earning the ten. Then he shook his head slowly.

"Sorry," he said. "Haven't seen him."

"Okay," I said. "Keep this to yourself." I handed him another ten.

"Not a problem," he grinned, showing beautiful white teeth. "You'd be surprised how much I keep quiet about."

"I'll bet," I said as I turned to leave.

◆ ◆ ◆ ◆

Benjamin was parked in the shade. He stood outside his cab, leaning on the front fender and drinking what appeared to be iced tea.

"That looks good," I said.

"Compliments of the hotel," he said. "I know a lot of people who work here. Would you like one?"

"I would."

Benjamin gave a shrill whistle, and a bellhop looked our way. My driver held up his glass and one finger and pointed at me. A quick nod, and the bellhop disappeared inside. Moments later, he came walking toward us with my iced tea. I started to reach for my wallet.

"No, no," Benjamin said. "My treat."

"Thanks," I said.

Benjamin raised his glass.

"Health, happiness, and long life," he said.

"I'll drink to that anytime," I said.

We clinked glasses, and I drank the deliciously cool, sweet elixir. *Friendly place, Bermuda*, I thought.

◆ ◆ ◆ ◆

We proceeded up the hill to the Fairmont Southampton. The last time I was in Bermuda, the hotel was known as the Southampton Princess. Benjamin parked in a shady spot, and I went through the front doors into a spacious lobby. I located the house phone and picked it up.

"Mr. Carter's room, please," I said, fully intending not to give Ricky's first name.

"I have a Charles and a Richard," another pleasant Bermuda voice said.

"Sorry," I said. "That would be Richard."

"One moment, please."

The phone rang seven times, and then I heard a recorded message: "The party you have called is not available at this time. You may record a message after the beep."

I was tempted to leave Ricky a message from Rasheed Reed, but I didn't want him dying of a heart attack before I had a chance to confront him. I hung up and walked back outside.

Benjamin was again leaning against the fender drinking from a tall glass. He smiled as I approached.

"Lemonade," he said.

"I appreciate a man who knows how to enjoy his work," I said. "I'm going to need that overnight bag from your trunk."

Benjamin nodded, walked to the rear of his taxi, opened the trunk, and removed my bag.

"Checking in?" he asked, handing me the bag.

"Maybe," I said.

"Find what you are looking for?"

"Not yet," I said, taking out my wallet and removing two more hundred-dollar bills. "I probably won't need you the rest of the day."

Benjamin shook his head and handed me a card that read,

Benjamin Soto

Bermuda Private Taxi

Tele: 441-844-2662

"Call me when you are ready to leave the island," he said. "We can settle up then, and you can tell me how this turns out."

"Deal," I said.

I turned and walked back inside the Fairmont Southampton.

17

I showed the front desk clerk my passport and paid cash for one night in a poolside room. I told him I'd probably be leaving very early the next day. Then I called Roy on my cell phone.

"What's up, gumshoe?" he answered.

"I'm at the Fairmont Southampton in Southampton Parish," I said. "A Richard Carter is a guest here. I'll bet it's Ricky. Come on over and look for me at the pool."

"On my way," Roy said.

I changed into my bathing suit and put two twenties in the right pocket. I wore sneakers without socks and pulled on a "Life Is Good" T-shirt. I put on my sunglasses and a badly worn UT 1998 National Championship football cap and grabbed my sunscreen. Might as well work on my tan. I went out my door and headed for the pool. I took a towel from the pool-side stack, found a lounge chair in the shade, and spread my towel on it.

I rubbed sunscreen on my face, shoulders, chest, stomach, arms, and legs and then went for a walk around the pool. I found Ricky Carter at the far end on the opposite side drinking something in a tall glass and putting the moves on a curvy young thing in a sparse white bikini. I must admit she had a great tan.

I went back to my lounge chair, gathered my stuff, and moved to where I could keep an eye on Ricky behind the privacy of my sunglasses. He didn't seem like he was in any hurry to move. I wanted to get him alone in his room, but I suspected I'd have a long wait. The sun was hot.

About fifteen minutes later, I positioned a nearby table with an umbrella so I was in the shade. A very attractive pool attendant came by.

"Can I get you anything, sir?" she asked.

"Lemonade would be great," I said, the image of Benjamin Soto's drink fresh in my mind.

"Right away, sir," she said, moving gracefully away.

The attendant was back in a few minutes with a tall, cold glass holding a pale yellow liquid. A tiny colorful umbrella accompanied the lemon slice adorning the rim. I couldn't remember the last time I had lemonade. I removed the umbrella and pushed the lemon slice under the ice. The first sip was a sweet and sour delight. I handed the attendant a twenty, and she returned my change. I gave her a generous tip, and she went away happy. Ricky hadn't moved. I took my time finishing my lemonade. I thought about going in the pool, but I didn't want to have to follow Ricky in a wet bathing suit.

"I can see this detective work is a hard business," a voice said behind me. Roy pulled up a nearby chair and sat at the table.

"I'm just barely surviving," I said.

"And doing a damn fine job of it, too," Roy said.

"Want something to drink?"

"Not right now," Roy said. "If this is going to take awhile, I might go to the bar for a beer or two. What's the plan?"

"Follow him back to his room and find out about the money," I said. "Could be in a few minutes or a few hours."

"Might have to rough him up a bit," Roy said.

"Might," I said.

"Where is he?"

"Over your left shoulder on the other side of the pool," I said. "You can look. Ricky is otherwise occupied."

Roy took a glance, turned back to me, and nodded.

"Trying to get laid," he said.

"Apparently."

"If he's successful, it might complicate things."

"Might," I said.

"Pretty easy finding people when they're stupid," Roy said.

"It is," I said.

"Makes you look good," he said.

"It does."

I outlined a more detailed plan, and then we sat silently for a few minutes as I finished my lemonade.

"I'm going to the bar," Roy said. "Call when he's on the move."

He walked away without ever looking back at Ricky.

◆   ◆   ◆   ◆

An hour later, the white bikini left Ricky and did not return. He stood there looking around, annoyed by the girl's disappearance. A few minutes later, he gathered his things and left the pool area. I followed, flipping my cell phone open as I moved. I speed-dialed Roy. We had both our phones switched to international plans.

"Showtime," I said when he answered. "We're heading for the elevators."

Roy came out of the bar and fell in behind me. I followed Ricky into a waiting elevator. Roy entered a couple of seconds later. Ricky punched the button for the sixth floor and looked at me.

"Six," I said, nodding.

Ricky looked at Roy.

"Me, too," Roy said.

We rode the elevator in silence, ignoring each other. When the doors opened, we waited as Ricky exited left and headed down the hall. He didn't seem to notice us behind him. My timing was perfect. As he opened the door to his room, I pushed through and Roy followed.

"Hey!" Ricky said as Roy shut the door. "What is this?"

"Be cool, Ricky," I said, "and you won't get hurt."

"What do you want?" Ricky was agitated, maybe high on something.

"They took your little girl," I said, looking for a reaction.

"That's just a bluff," Ricky said. "They won't hurt her."

"You knew?" I said, my anger rising. "You knew and you left with the money anyway?"

"She's Megan's kid," Ricky said, eyes darting like a caged animal's. "I'm probably not even the father."

"Bullshit," I said. "You're the father."

Ricky swayed from side to side, trying to figure out what to do.

"Get out of here!" he screamed.

"Shut up," Roy said, sliding a Glock 9mm from his pocket, "or I'll shut you up."

"They'll hear the shots," Ricky said.

"They won't hear shit," Roy said, slipping on a silencer.

Ricky stared wide-eyed.

"Don't kill me, man," he pleaded.

"Where's the money?" I asked, moving close to him and trying to be as intimidating as possible.

"What money?" Ricky said with no conviction.

I slapped him hard with my left hand. He never saw it coming. The sound was like a small firecracker. *That one's for you, Stanley*, I thought.

"The money," I snarled.

"It's not here," he said, gulping for air.

I knew he was lying and didn't want to hunt for the money. I looked at Roy.

"Kill him," I said.

Roy pulled back the slide and pointed the Glock at Ricky.

"Too bad," he said. "Goodbye, Ricky."

"No, wait!" Ricky screamed. "It's in the safe in the closet. The briefcase is under the bed. Please don't kill me." He was almost in tears and near a complete breakdown.

"Open the safe," I said. "Bring the money and put it on the bed."

Ricky did as he was told. When he finished, the bed was littered with bundles of twenties, fifties, and hundreds. Every move Ricky made, Roy followed with his silenced Glock. I neatly stacked the bundles in the briefcase, leaving one bundle of hundreds on the bed.

"Traveling money," I said to Ricky. "You don't deserve it, but I'm giving you a fighting chance. Go somewhere, change your name, and start over. Try not to be such an asshole."

I knew I was probably wasting my breath, but I was big on second chances. He seemed to relax a little.

Looking around the room for something to tie up Ricky, I spotted an extension cord attached to a floor lamp.

"Pick up the desk chair and carry it into the bathroom," I ordered Ricky.

I followed him into the bathroom.

"Sit," I said.

He sat in the chair.

"Hands behind your back," I said.

He complied.

I tied him up tightly with the cord and threaded it through the back of the chair. With some effort, he could probably get loose, but it would take awhile. I turned to Roy, my back to Ricky.

"Take the money and get back to the boat," I said with a wink. "I'll stay here for an hour, then meet you there. Be ready to go when I arrive. Leave the Glock. If Ricky gives me any trouble, I'll shoot him."

"Will do," Roy said.

He backed out of the bathroom. I followed and closed the door behind me. Roy picked up the briefcase as I turned on the television.

"I won't be long," I said softly. "Call Jim and tell him to get ready to move."

"Want the Glock?" Roy asked in a whisper.

"No," I said. "And I'd be very interested in how you got that by customs."

Roy smiled.

"I'll never tell," he said as he opened the door to the hall. "See you soon."

When Ricky heard the door close, he thought we both had left and began to yell for help. I went to the bathroom door and opened it slightly.

"Shut up, Ricky," I said, steel in my voice, "or I'll come in there and put a bullet in you brain. Another outburst and you're dead. Do you understand?"

"Yes."

"I'm leaving in one hour," I said. "If you come out before that, I'll shoot you. If you make any more noise, I'll shoot you."

I closed the bathroom door, turned the volume up on the TV, and slipped quietly from the room, hoping my bluff would work. I took the stairs down to the lobby and called Benjamin on the way to my room.

"I need you at the Fairmont Southampton as soon as you can get here," I said.

"I'll be out front in ten minutes," Benjamin said.

I went to my room, changed, gathered my things, and headed for the lobby. By the time I walked through the front entrance, Benjamin was waiting for me.

"The sooner we get to the airport, the better," I said.

"I understand," Benjamin said.

We drove in silence. I was pretty sure Ricky would stay in the bathroom. Even if he didn't, he would have a hard time explaining why he'd been robbed of so much cash. The only thing he could do was pack up and get out of Bermuda.

I flipped open my cell phone and dialed Roy.

"Yeah?" he answered.

"I'm on my way," I said.

"I'm almost there," Roy said. "See you in a few."

Twenty minutes later, we pulled into the private airport entrance for departing passengers. I handed Benjamin two hundred-dollar bills.

"No time to talk now, Benjamin," I said. "Someday, I'll be back and tell you the whole story."

Benjamin nodded.

"Until then," he said.

"And Benjamin," I said. "I was never here."

"You were never here," he said, smiling.

18

The following Monday morning, I was having my second cup of coffee when the door to my outer office opened. Jake raised his head and gave a low, menacing growl, letting me know it was not a regular visitor. I heard a muffled voice and then Rasheed Reed filled the doorway to my inner sanctum. Jake, none too happy about being awakened from his nap, was on his feet and snarling. He barked once.

"Jake, lie down," I said with authority.

Jake immediately quieted, turned around twice, and plopped down.

One eye on Jake, Rasheed Reed sat in one of the oversized chairs in front of my desk. I had called and asked him to stop in. I hadn't said why, but I guessed he knew.

"I do like this chair," he said.

"I'm so glad."

"That dog bite?" Rasheed asked.

"His name is Jake," I said. "He gets upset when people call him 'that dog.' "

"Good dog, Jake," Rasheed said in a soft voice.

Satisfied, Jake laid his head on his paws, closed his eyes, and resumed his nap.

"So I'm here," Rasheed said.

"Who's in the outer office?"

"My driver," Rasheed said.

"Want him to hear all of this?"

"Ernest," Rasheed called. "Wait in the car."

We heard the outer door open and close. I reached under my desk, lifted the briefcase, and handed it to Rasheed. He took it, placed it on his lap, snapped it open, and stared at the money. A smile grew on his face.

"How much is here?" he asked.

"One-ninety," I said.

Rasheed nodded.

"The rest?"

"Ricky spent most of it," I said. "I took a thousand for expenses."

"Seems fair," Rasheed said. "I really didn't expect to see this again. Where's Ricky?"

"Would you rather know where Ricky is or have the money?"

"You're not going to tell me, are you?" It was more a statement than a question.

"It wouldn't matter," I said. "He's long gone."

"It's a matter of principle," Rasheed said.

I leaned forward and stared at Rasheed.

"Look," I said. "Let it go. Ricky isn't worth the effort. If he shows up again in East Tennessee, you can kill him with my blessing."

Rasheed stared back at me in silence, wheels turning. He got up and walked slowly to the window and looked down at the street, his back to me.

"Nice location," he said.

"It is," I said.

After an awkward silence, he turned to face me.

"Tell me one thing," Rasheed said. "Was Ricky out of the country when you found him?"

"He was," I said.

"Good," he said. "I'd hate to think you found him in my own backyard."

Rasheed picked up the briefcase and walked toward the outer office. He stopped in the doorway and turned to face me.

"You did good, Youngblood," he said. "You're a man of your word. I won't forget. I owe you one if you ever need a favor."

Without waiting for a response, he turned and disappeared into the outer office. I heard the door open and close.

"I wonder why the only people who think they owe me a favor are thugs," I said to Jake.

Jake, ignoring me, continued his nap.

•   •   •   •

Later that day, things got really weird. My friend, college chum, and now special agent in charge of the FBI's Salt Lake City office, Scott Glass, called.

"Hey, Blood, what's going on?" Scott asked.

"Got a few irons in the fire, Professor," I said. "What's up?"

"I found a house I want to buy out here, and I need to run it by my financial advisor," Scott said.

"Always willing to cooperate with the FBI," I said. "Tell me about it."

He did. Scott had found a three-bedroom, three-bath tri-level in a nice neighborhood in Salt Lake City. He was excited about it. Scott had never been a homeowner.

"It has a double garage, gas logs in the fireplace, great kitchen, nice landscaping," Scott said.

"How much?"

"I can probably get it for around two hundred thousand."

"Sounds like a deal," I said.

"I'll need a down payment out of one of my accounts," Scott said.

"No problem," I said. "How much?"

"You tell me," Scott said. "You're the financial advisor."

"Well," I said, "at your age, I'd recommend a fifteen-year fixed-rate mortgage. You should be able to get one for around five percent. The rule of thumb is that your house payment should be around twenty-five percent of your take-home pay. Tell me what you'd like to pay per month, and I'll go from there."

Scott gave me a figure, and I did the math.

"You sure about this?"

"Oh, yeah," Scott said.

"Okay," I said. "I'll UPS a check tomorrow."

"Great," Scott said. "You and the ladies will have to come out again next year to ski. You can stay with me."

"It's a date," I said. "Now, tell me what you're working on."

Scott loved to tease me with his current cases. He wouldn't tell me too much, though he did trust me to keep my mouth shut.

"Okay," Scott said, lowering his voice. "I'll tell you about this case, but you can't mention it to anyone. This one is very sensitive. Last week in Minnesota, a girl was found at Swan Lake, and it was so staged that it was freaky. I can't get into the details. Three days later, a girl was found at Utah Lake south of here with the identical MO. They were listed as accidental drownings by the local authorities, so as not to start a panic and give away details of the crimes. But it was murder, pure and simple."

"Pure, maybe, but not so simple," I said, knowing in my gut that the Betty Lou Walker killing could not be a coincidence.

"Figure of speech," Scott said. "Pure and complicated doesn't have that artistic ring to it."

"Okay, Professor," I said hesitantly. "Tell me more."

He had forgotten about his impending house purchase and was in full FBI mode. The day-to-day business of an SAC can be boring. A juicy case was cause for excitement.

"I can't tell you much," he said. "We feel sure they're serial killings, but we're not sure if it's one or more killers."

"More than one, I think."

"Why do you think that?" Scott said. "Three days is plenty of time to get from Utah to Minnesota."

"True, but let me ask you a question," I said. "Did the locals get an anonymous tip on where to find them?"

"Yes, they did," Scott said hesitantly.

"Were the girls staked out face up?"

A pause followed.

"You're scaring me, Don," Scott said. "Have you hacked into my email or bugged my office?"

"No," I said. "One more question. Were their clothes laid out nice and neat somewhere near the crime scene?"

"Now you're really scaring me. And pissing me off," Scott said. "Damn it, Don, I know you didn't kill them, so how do you know so much?"

"Think about it, Professor," I said, turning the tables. "How could I know?"

It didn't take him long.

"You've got one," Scott said as if a light bulb had gone on inside his head.

I told him about the Betty Lou Walker murder. He listened without interrupting. When I finished, he didn't say a word. I thought the line had gone dead.

"Scott?"

"Son of a bitch," he said.

"What?"

"Does Betty Lou Walker have a tattoo?"

"On her back," I said. "A devil dancing behind a fire."

"God help us," Scott said.

"I've done my best to keep a lid on this one," I said. "Sooner or later, something is going to leak."

"Describe Betty Lou Walker," Scott said.

"I don't know all the vitals," I said. "From what I saw, I'd say about five feet five inches tall, fit, dark shoulder-length hair, dark eyes."

"White?" Scott asked.

"Yes," I said.

"That description fits the others," Scott said.

"Any clues?"

"None," Scott said. "They were hit with a Taser, then drugged—ether, maybe. They were alive when they went in the water."

"They're connected," I said.

"Definitely," Scott said. "The MO and the tattoos connect them."

"But different killers," I said, "each knowing what the others are doing."

"It looks that way," Scott said.

"For a minute, let's assume it's one killer," I said. "He might live near one of the locations. If he did all the killings, it would probably be too far to drive, so he'd have to fly. Check the airlines and see if you can make a connection."

"We're doing that," Scott said. "But I agree with you, I think it's more than one killer."

"So how do they know each other?" I said. "How did they meet? How did they connect?"

"I don't know," Scott said. "There are too many possibilities. The obvious answer is the Internet. But exactly how, I don't know. Call me if you think of something."

"I'll do that," I said.

"You want in on this?" he asked. "Work with us as a consultant?"

"Not officially," I said. "I'll be glad to share information, but only with you."

I didn't want the FBI looking over my shoulder. As a private investigator and a private citizen, I could tread in those gray areas where the FBI couldn't legally go. I didn't want to be restricted.

"Okay, Blood," Scott said. "We'll talk soon. And keep that tattoo a secret. Don't tell anyone who doesn't need to know. If the media gets hold of that, they'll have a field day."

And then some, I thought.

19

The next morning, I was trying to finish my second cup of coffee when Scott called back.

"I've been officially put in charge of a task force investigating these serial killings," he said. "We are calling this the 'Tattoo Killers Case.' "

"Catchy," I said.

"Any thoughts, now that you've had time to sleep on it?" Scott asked.

"Not really," I said. "But I'd like to see pictures of the tattoos on the other dead girls."

"Right now, I'm coordinating with the Minneapolis and Knoxville offices," Scott said. "I'll have Minneapolis email you a photo of their victim, and I'll email the one from ours. Knoxville might want to talk to you, since you were at the East Tennessee crime scene."

"Fine," I said.

"Guess who the SAC of the Knoxville office is." Scott was famous for playing guessing games.

"Phil Fulmer," I said.

"Good guess," Scott laughed. "I heard he might be looking for work. But it's not him."

"Okay, I give up," I said. "Who?"

"David Steele."

"Steely Dave?" I laughed.

"The one and only," Scott said.

"Does he still iron his Jockey shorts?"

"Probably," Scott said. "He is severely toilet trained."

"You think he'll be the one who interviews me?" I asked.

"Probably, since I gave him your name," Scott said.

"Well, that ought to be good for a few laughs."

"He's not a bad guy, but watch yourself," Scott said. "He's never forgiven you for leaving."

◆   ◆   ◆   ◆

That afternoon, I sat at my desk working on the tattoos from the dead girls in Utah and Minnesota. I downloaded and scanned the pictures and adjusted them so they were the same size as those of the tattoo from Betty Lou Walker that Wanda Jones had emailed me earlier. Measurements from the forensic photos told me they were indeed the same size. The colors were identical and the tattoos, at first glance, looked the same. But laying them side-by-side, I could tell they were different. The devil in the tattoo from the Minnesota girl was dancing on the right side of the flame. I could see both his legs. The devil in the tattoo from the Utah girl was dancing on the left side of the flame. I also saw both his legs. The fire and the logs were identical.

I made copies of the pictures of the three tattoos. I took scissors and carefully cut around the outlines. I placed one on top of the other, carefully lining up the flame and the logs. What I saw sent a chill through me. I was looking at three devils dancing. As Scott and I suspected, we were dealing with three different killers, and each had his own signature.

I faxed the separate pictures of the tattoos to Scott, along with one combining the three. Then I picked up the phone and called him.

"You see what I see?" I asked.

"Yes," Scott said. "The tattoos are all different, which leads me to believe there are three killers."

"Probably," I said.

"But you're not completely sold on the idea."

"Not completely," I said. "The timeline is open enough so that it could still be one killer. Maybe he wants it to look like three. Serial killers are smart. Some like to play games."

"So what's your best guess?" Scott asked.

"My best guess is that we're looking at three killers and the leader is here in East Tennessee."

"Because the devil in that tattoo is in the center?"

"You got it, Professor," I said.

"What are you going to do now?" Scott asked.

"I don't know of anything else," I said. "Maybe I'll do some more interviews. I'll let the FBI work on this awhile."

"Let me know if you think of anything," Scott said.

"I will," I said, then quickly changed the subject. "Did you get the money I sent?"

"I did," Scott said. "I made an offer, and I'm waiting to hear something."

"Let me know how that works out, Professor," I said.

"I will, Blood," he said. "And don't go looking for trouble."

Easier said than done, I thought. I didn't have to look for trouble. Trouble had a way of finding me.

20

The next morning, I sat looking down at Main Street and enjoying the silence of my office. Quiet had been in short supply recently. Don't get me wrong. I loved the energy the females in my life brought to my shallow existence, but every now and then I needed solitude.

When the outer office door opened, I knew my brief respite was gone. Jake was on his feet, growling. A few seconds later, an unmistakable figure filled my doorway. Jake barked.

"Youngblood," my visitor said.

"Jake, lie down," I said.

Although the face was older, the voice hadn't changed. I'd never forget that voice—the one that had screamed at me for six months. My visitor boldly walked over and gave Jake a good scratch behind the ears. Jake immediately went from scary watchdog to cream-puff lapdog.

"Agent Steele," I said, standing.

We shook hands.

FBI agent David Steele had been our chief instructor at Quantico when, fresh out of college, Scott and I joined the bureau, a memory I'd shoved into a far corner of my brain. I had known within two weeks that the FBI wasn't going to work for me, but I hung on for Scott's sake until I finally resigned, knowing I wasn't cut out to take orders. I had headed for Wall Street while Scott made the FBI his career.

"You're looking fit, Youngblood," David Steele said. "And a private investigator, no less."

I detected sarcasm in his voice.

"Beats working for the man," I said. "Have a seat."

He took one of the chairs in front of my desk. Jake followed him, looking for more attention.

"And rich, I hear," David Steele said.

I ignored that comment and focused on Jake.

"Jake," I said firmly. "Go lie down."

He looked at me as if to say, *Do I have to?*

"Go," I said, pointing to his bed.

Jake went to the bed, circled twice, and lay down. I turned my attention back to David Steele.

"How can I help you, Agent Steele?" I asked, trying hard to keep an even tone. We had a history, and it was not friendly.

His face reddened a bit.

"Still a hardass," he said.

"You bring out the best in me, Dave," I said.

"You know why I'm here, Youngblood," he said. "So cut to the chase and tell me about the crime scene."

I resisted the temptation to be a wiseass and told it straight, as if I were doing a book report for my college English class. When I finished, David Steele nodded but remained silent. Then he stood and stretched.

"Good report, Youngblood," he said. "Too bad you couldn't cut it. You would have made a good agent."

"Yeah, I regret that every day of my life," I said.

"I'm warning you. Stay out of this," David Steele said. "It's our case now."

He turned and left my office without another word.

Stay out of it? *Not likely,* I thought.

21

The day after David Steele ruined my morning, Roy, T. Elbert, and I sat on T. Elbert's front porch drinking coffee and eating bagels. I had visited T. Elbert less and less in the last few months and felt guilty about it. The early-morning fog had not yet surrendered to the rising sun. I was relating my encounter with David Steele.

"Those fuckin' feds are all a bunch of bitchy little girls," T. Elbert said.

I rarely heard T. Elbert use profanity, so I knew I had hit a hot button.

"Scott's okay," I said casually.

"I guess there are a few exceptions," T. Elbert said reluctantly.

T. Elbert was a retired Tennessee Bureau of Investigation agent who still held some status in the bureau as a special agent. I had always been unclear on exactly what that status was.

Roy was silent. He looked tired, and I suspected he was hung over. He rocked in his chair, sipped his coffee, and stared into the distance.

"What are you going to do next?" T. Elbert asked.

"I think I'll talk to Sally Thomas again," I said.

"A follow-up interview seems appropriate," T. Elbert said. "Especially if you're at a dead end."

We sat, rocked, drank coffee, ate bagels, and watched the sun dissipate the fog.

Roy broke the silence.

"I have a problem," he said.

I looked at T. Elbert. T. Elbert looked at Roy.

"Tell us," T. Elbert said.

He did.

◆　　◆　　◆　　◆

I had met Sister Sarah Agnes Woods at a fundraiser for a drug and alcohol rehab center during my Wall Street days. Silverthorn was being built in the backwoods of Connecticut. It would cater to the very rich and under-thirty addict. The plan was that the very rich would support the center so the less fortunate could get treatment at a reasonable price. Funds were needed. Since I had funds, I was a potential target for a considerable donation. I went to the fundraiser because I liked the idea of supporting Silverthorn. I had seen drugs and alcohol derail more than one life while I was in college.

Sister Sarah Agnes Woods was a tall, rather attractive woman at least ten years my senior. She had short, curly salt-and-pepper hair and intense hazel eyes. Ten minutes after she engaged me in conversation, I knew I had a new friend. Ten minutes later, I was promising a sizable donation. Ten minutes after that, I was in charge of all the donations collected.

I left T. Elbert's front porch and went straight to the office, wanting to strike while the iron was hot. I knew Sarah Agnes would be up early. I was way overdue to check in with her. We usually talked ever month or so, but it was a long time since we'd last spoken. I reminded myself that the phone worked in both directions.

I called her private number. She answered on the second ring.

"It's Don," I said.

"Well," she said. "Long time, no talk. How are you?"

"I'm fine," I said. "Haven't been beaten up or shot in months."

"Good to hear," she chuckled. "Are you still living with two women?"

"And one dog," I said.

"And how it that going?"

"Surprisingly well," I said. "Sometimes, it gets a bit hectic."

"Good thing you have an office to run away to," she said.

"A real good thing," I laughed.

As much as I loved Mary like a wife and Lacy like a daughter, I was easily smothered. The door to my office was my escape hatch.

"Sounds like you're growing up," Sarah Agnes said.

"Good of you to say so," I said.

A few seconds of silence followed.

"What else?" Sarah Agnes said. "You're stalling. You have something else."

"Roy Husky needs some help dealing with the death of Sarah Ann Fleet," I said. "He's trying to drown the memory with alcohol. Needless to say, it's not working."

"I have a top-floor corner suite available. When can he come?"

"Tomorrow," I said. "I'll bring him myself."

"I'll see you then," Sister Sarah Agnes said.

♦   ♦   ♦   ♦

That afternoon, I got another surprise. I heard the outer office door open and close and then a voice with a Spanish accent.

"Is anyone here?"

"In here," I said.

Seconds later, a familiar figure wearing tennis shoes, faded jeans, and a T-shirt entered, grinning widely. He looked better than the last time I saw him. The few days' growth of beard was gone from his face, and the eyes were bright and mischievous. I stood, my surprise evident.

"Oscar," I said. "Did you break out of jail?"

He laughed.

"No, no, nothing like that. They let me go," Oscar said. "May I sit down, please? I'll tell you the whole story."

The short version was that Oscar had made a deal. Apparently, he had enough good information for a Get Out of Jail Free card and some cash. He handed me a check. The amount was surprising.

"I'm impressed, Oscar," I said, handing it back. "You're a better negotiator than a meth lab manager."

"My heart was never in that," he said, waving off the check. "I did it for my family. I would like to open a checking account with a modest sum and have you invest the rest for me, if you would be so kind."

"I can do that," I said. "Are you in this country legally?"

"I am," Oscar said. "I was born in Miami. Being a citizen was a requirement of my former employer."

"Are you in danger from that former employer?" I asked.

"Probably not," Oscar said. "The things I told the *federales*, he would not know that I know. Besides, I had no choice. I could not go to jail and leave my family."

I nodded and stood. Oscar seemed like a good guy caught up in a bad business. Until he proved me wrong, I was willing to help him.

"Let's go downstairs and take care of your banking needs," I said.

Half an hour later, we were back in my office.

"What's next for you, Oscar?" I asked.

"The last time I saw you," he said, "you told me to call if I wanted a real job. I do. Can you help me?"

"Maybe," I said, a light going on in the back of my mind. "Give me your cell-phone number and let me make a few calls."

◆　　◆　　◆　　◆

I dialed his private number at his office. He answered on the second ring.

"This is Fleet," Joseph Fleet said.

"Mr. Fleet," I said. "Don Youngblood."

"Don, I'm glad you called," Joseph Fleet said. "I just talked to Roy a few minutes ago. He told me he's going to be away for a while. We both know why, but it was not actually discussed."

"A definite step in the right direction," I said guardedly. "I feel pretty positive about Roy's decision. I really shouldn't say anything else."

"I understand," Joseph Fleet said. "As long as the outcome is successful, that's the main thing."

"You'll need a driver for a while," I said.

"You have someone in mind, I take it," Joseph Fleet said.

"I do."

"Tell me about this person," he said.

I told him.

"You trust this Oscar?"

"I do," I said.

"Why?" Fleet asked.

"Gut instinct," I said. "Like I knew I could trust Roy. You'll like this guy. He tells it like it is, and he's fluent in English and Spanish."

"Good enough for me," Fleet said. "The Spanish might come in handy. Have him call me on this number at eight o'clock tomorrow."

22

Silverthorn wasn't easy to find. I guess that was intentional. I had printed the directions stored on my laptop. Roy was acting as navigator. If he was nervous about rehab, he didn't show it.

"Take a right at this stop sign," he said.

I turned right. The road meandered through the lush green foliage of the Connecticut backwoods. Without a compass, I had no idea in what direction we were traveling, but I knew we were getting close. The drive took an hour from Bradley International Airport north of Hartford, where Fleet's private jet had dropped us that afternoon.

"Did you get to meet Oscar?" I asked Roy.

"I did," Roy said.

"What did you think?"

"I think he'll do fine," Roy said. "And I think you have some kind of compelling need to help people like Billy and Oscar and me."

"A guy has to have a hobby," I said.

"Better than coin collecting," Roy laughed. It was a nervous laugh. "Take the next left."

We were silent for a while.

"You sure this Sister Sarah Agnes is the right person?" Roy asked, as if looking for an excuse to back out.

"Absolutely," I said. "I often seek her counsel. She's one of the smartest and most no-nonsense women I know. I value her opinion highly."

"Relax, gumshoe," Roy said. "I'm not backing out. Just looking for a little reinforcement."

"Consider yourself reinforced," I said.

It was late in the day when we turned into the entrance. Built in the European style, Silverthorn reminded me of an old hotel. Five stories tall in the center, it was flanked with three-story wings on both sides. Following its completion, Silverthorn had developed a reputation as the *in* place to rehab on the East Coast.

Sarah Agnes tolerated the rich and famous by charging them outrageous amounts of money that went directly to the general fund for operating expenses. The funds that remained were invested. I knew this because I handled the investments, which were thriving.

Sister Sarah Agnes was a tough nut. I had paid a price of honesty, openness, and directness to gain her friendship, but the return was invaluable.

I parked at the entrance and went to retrieve Roy's luggage from the trunk of the rental car as he stood and looked at the place where he would spend at least the next few weeks. I didn't try to reassure him. Roy was tough, and his mind was made up. I felt certain that with Sarah Agnes's help, he would exorcise the demons that possessed him.

I watched as Sarah Agnes came through the double doors of the main entrance and walked purposely toward Roy. She stopped in front of him, smiled, offered her hand, and said, "I'm Sister Sarah Agnes Woods. Welcome to Silverthorn."

"Roy Husky," he said, shaking her hand and returning her smile.

"Come inside and I'll get you situated," Sarah Agnes said to Roy. "Don, wait in the study. I'll see you later."

I parked the car and obediently made my way to Sarah Agnes's study, carrying my backpack with my laptop inside. I knew she'd be awhile, and I was curious to see if the market would continue to tumble. I had a bad feeling. Like a high-strung thoroughbred, the market was easily spooked.

◆　　◆　　◆　　◆

We sat in the study drinking a predinner glass of wine, a very good vintage of red zinfandel I had brought with me for the occasion. The sun had disappeared behind the lush growth of trees surrounding Silverthorn, and night was set to make an appearance. I knew from experience the evening would be cool. The low flames from the gas logs glowing in the fireplace were for more than just ambiance.

"Got anybody famous on the grounds?" I said.

"One rock star and one starlet," Sarah Agnes said. "Of course, I cannot tell you who. You've probably never heard of them anyway. Both are likely a waste of my time, but they're paying top dollar."

"Well, there's that," I laughed.

Sarah Agnes ignored me and took another sip of wine.

"So, tell me," she said. "What's new?"

"Something interesting and sinister," I said.

"Tell me all," she said.

I did. I told her about the murder of Betty Lou Walker, the clothes folded neatly, the tattoo, and the other two murders with the same MO in other areas of the country.

"Mercy," she said at one point, shaking her head.

Then I told her about Ricky Carter and Rasheed Reed.

"That's about it," I said. "Other than that, everything is fine."

"You are a master of understatement," she said. "I'm out of breath just listening to you."

"What do you think about these tattoo murders?" I asked. "Any insight?"

"I don't know what to think," Sarah Agnes said. "The tattoos and the clothes laid neatly out don't seem to fit. I'll have to think about it."

We fell silent. Sarah Agnes looked tired. Running a rehab center and listening to patients' problems all day long must have been exhausting.

"What do you think about Roy?" I asked.

"I like him," she said. "He seems to want help. I'll have to convince him that's okay for a tough guy. He looks up to you, and the fact that you approve of his being here helps me. We'll just have to wait and see."

I knew she wouldn't make any promises, but I could tell she was optimistic. We watched the flames dance as we finished our wine. I felt as tired as Sarah Agnes looked.

"What can I do?" I asked.

"Nothing," she said. "And I mean nothing. No phone calls, no emails, nothing."

"Okay," I said. "For how long?"

"At least two weeks," she said. "Maybe, more. We'll see."

"What if he calls me?"

"You have caller ID," Sarah Agnes said. "Don't answer. And tell his boss the same."

"Will do," I said. I wanted this to work and trusted Sarah Agnes to make it so.

I shared out the last of the red zin.

"Why do you think I've been a confirmed bachelor all my life?" I asked.

Sister Sarah Agnes raised an eyebrow.

"Are you seeking counsel from me on a professional level?" she asked.

"No," I said. "I'm having a casual conversation with a friend over a glass of wine. I'm just interested in your take. I don't need to be on your couch, so to speak. A drugstore, over-the-counter, off-the-top-of-your-head opinion is fine."

She laughed.

"What do *you* think?" she asked.

"I think I should have known better than to ask," I said. "You shrinks are all alike. When you don't have a good answer, you ask another question."

"That's Shrink 101," Sarah Agnes laughed. "So often, the patient knows much more than we do. Are things about to change for you?"

"Sooner or later, I think."

We finished our wine and set the glasses on the coffee table beside the empty bottle, which was changing color as it caught the reflections of the flickering flames.

"Let's get some dinner while we can still walk a straight line," Sarah Agnes said. "The cafeteria closes soon."

23

The next morning, I spied Roy tucked in a far corner of the cafeteria reading, of all things, the *Wall Street Journal*. I purchased a cup of coffee and a cheese Danish. I added half-and-half and sugar to my coffee and took a sip. Not Dunkin' Donuts, but not bad. I took my coffee and Danish to his table and sat. He looked up from his paper and smiled.

"The *Wall Street Journal*?" I said.

He folded the *Journal* and put it in his briefcase.

"What can I say?" Roy said. "You're a bad influence."

"How did you sleep?" I asked.

"Like a baby. Good mattress. I have a suite. You have anything to do with that?"

I shrugged.

Roy smiled.

"Jim will be at the airport around noon," he said.

"I'll be there."

I was getting spoiled flying around the country on Joseph Fleet's private jet.

"And tell Mr. Fleet that I won't be in touch for a couple of weeks," Roy said.

"Okay," I said. "I'm sure that won't be a problem."

We were silent for a while. I got up and went to get another cup of coffee.

"What do you think of Sarah Agnes?" I asked when I returned.

"I like her," Roy said. "If she wasn't a nun . . ." He raised his eyebrows.

"Behave yourself," I said.

"I'm teasing," Roy said. "I know why I'm here. Still . . ."

As if on cue, Sister Sarah Agnes arrived at our table.

"Good morning, gentlemen," she said in a formal tone. "Time for you to go, Mr. Youngblood."

"Yes, ma'am," I said, and stood quickly. I knew she was establishing her authority, and I had no problem with that.

I was about to say, "Call me if you need anything," but I caught myself. I nodded at Roy and Sarah Agnes, turned abruptly, and walked out of the cafeteria.

◆   ◆   ◆   ◆

"Ready?" Jim Doak asked as I hurriedly crossed the tarmac to the sleek little Lear jet.

"Ready," I said as we climbed the stairs.

In a crystal blue, cloudless sky, we cruised five miles above the earth, heading back to Tri-Cities Airport. If Jim Doak was curious about why Roy wasn't making the return trip, he didn't show it. Maybe Roy had given him a heads-up.

"We've got smooth air, Don," Jim said over the intercom. "If you want to move around, you can."

I unfastened my seatbelt, walked back to the bar, and fixed a diet ginger ale with ice. I returned to my seat and refastened my belt, adjusting it loosely for some wiggle room. I took a sip of my drink, sat back, and thought about the murder of Betty Lou Walker.

I had no leads. Billy's interviews with Betty Lou's professors had turned up nothing. No evidence at the crime scene pointed us toward anything. The tattoo had to be the key, but I couldn't find the right door to unlock. Thinking about the tattoo gave me an idea. Then I replayed my conversation with Sally Thomas in my head, and Barnes & Noble popped up and gave me another idea.

Finally, I had something to work with.

24

I had just ordered. I tried to have breakfast at the Mountain Center Diner at least once or twice a week when I was in town. I relished the peace and quiet of the place early in the morning. Doris had just opened, and the hustle and bustle that would mount as the morning rolled on had yet to materialize. I was reading the sports section of the *Mountain Center Press*, absorbed in the baseball box scores. I didn't follow baseball much anymore and was surprised at how few players I recognized.

I felt his presence before I looked up. Big Bob Wilson changed the dynamic of any room he entered. The quietness of the diner got even quieter. I thought I detected a slight smile as he moved toward my table. Maybe it was a smirk. He sat without asking—no big surprise.

"You're up early," he said.

"Seeking respite from the females," I said.

"How's that going?" Big Bob asked.

"It's going fine," I said. "I just need some space every now and then."

"Puts a dent in your bachelorhood, doesn't it?" Big Bob said as he picked up a menu.

"Why look at the menu?" I asked, ignoring the barb. "You know it by heart."

"Want to be sure Doris isn't price gouging," he said.

Doris Black hurried over to get the big man's order.

"Pancakes and sausage," Big Bob said. "And give me a side order of hash browns."

"You got it," Doris said.

"Hold my order until his is ready," I said to Doris.

"Sure thing," she said, hurrying away.

"Heard the FBI was in town," Big Bob said.

"Really?" I said.

"Heard they were at your office."

"Nothing gets by you," I said.

"Damn it, Blood," Big Bob said. "Tell me what's going on."

"They questioned me about the drowning at the lake," I said.

"Why is the FBI interested in a drowning?"

"Because it wasn't a drowning," I said. "It was murder."

I told him the rest of it while we waited for the food to arrive. We were silent as we dove into our breakfast. I had my favorite, a feta cheese omelet with home fries and rye toast.

"Why didn't you tell me this sooner?" Big Bob asked as he drowned his pancakes in maple syrup.

"I haven't seen you to tell you," I said. "Besides, it's Jimmy Durham's case."

"Jimmy's a good sheriff," Big Bob said softly, "but he's in way over his head if this is a serial killer."

"Keep that serial killer stuff to yourself," I said.

"Don't worry about that," he said. "You'd be surprised what I keep to myself."

"Probably not," I said. "You always could keep a secret."

"I've certainly kept a few about you," he said, grinning.

Well, that was the truth.

We finished up breakfast talking football, even though it was months from the season. Then the big man stood, tossed some bills on the table, and leaned toward me.

"If you need any help on this, let me know," he said. "And watch your ass. You draw trouble like shit draws flies."

And with that unpleasant simile, he was gone.

◆ ◆ ◆ ◆

I walked to my office building, went into the bank lobby, took the elevator to the second floor, and went down the back steps to my Pathfinder. That was the shortest route to my SUV, since a rear exit wasn't available on the first floor. Couldn't make robbing the bank too easy.

I drove out of town and took the old highway to Johnson City. I wasn't happy that it had taken me almost two weeks to follow up on the Barnes & Noble lead. I'd been sidetracked by Rasheed Reed. At this point, it was unlikely anyone would remember anything. On the way up I called Jimmy Durham.

"Did your guy find out anything useful at the shopping mall?" I asked Jimmy when I got him on the phone.

"Nothing," he said. "You know how big that shopping mall is. Finding someone who saw her and remembered would have been like hitting the lottery."

"I'm on my way up there now," I said. "It's probably a dead end but it's a lead and I need to follow it."

"Well," Jimmy said, "Good luck."

The old highway connected to a four-lane, and I took that straight to State of Franklin Road. I turned left at a major intersection, drove a few miles, and spotted the Barnes & Noble on the left. I made a left turn, and then a right, drove past a Cheddar's, and parked in the rear lot. I went through the front entrance—or maybe it was the back entrance—and found the help desk. The store wasn't very busy, and the young man—a college student, maybe—seemed eager to help.

"May I assist you?" he asked.

"I need to see the store manager," I said casually. "I forget her name."

"Missy," he said. "I think she's in the back. Let me call her."

He picked up a phone and punched in a number.

"Is Missy back there?" he asked. A few seconds later, he said, "Tell her someone at the help desk wants to see her." Then he turned back to me. "She'll be right out."

"Thank you," I said, the friendly detective.

About a minute later, a tall, slender, attractive auburn-haired woman approached me.

"How can I help you?" she said, smiling.

For a second, I lost my train of thought. She was stunning. *Regroup, Youngblood*, I thought.

I made a motion with my head and steered her away from the desk. Once out of earshot, I handed her my ID. She studied it for a few seconds and didn't seem overly impressed or alarmed.

"Is there somewhere we can talk privately?" I asked.

"Sure," she said, smiling again and handing my ID back. "How about I buy you a cup of coffee?"

"Lead the way," I said.

She turned and headed toward the Starbucks at the back of the store. Or was it the front? I followed, practicing my observation skills on her very attractive backside.

"Have a seat and I'll get coffee," Missy said. "What's your pleasure?"

"The mildest they have," I said. "Small."

I always found Starbucks coffee a little too strong for my taste.

"Black?"

"Yes," I said. A tough PI couldn't be seen drinking coffee with cream and sugar. Well, at least not in a Barnes & Noble in front of the attractive store manager.

Missy returned quickly with two small black coffees and set them on the table. I waited until she sat. Chivalry was not dead in East Tennessee.

"Be careful," Missy said. "It's very hot." She blew on her coffee, and then took a sip. She was sexy without trying to be. "How can I help you?"

"I'm curious," I said. "You didn't seem too surprised when you saw my PI license."

"My father was a cop," she said. "I've seen badges and IDs before, and I've known a few PIs. I just figured something must be going on in the shopping center. So, how can I help?"

I slid the picture of Betty Lou Walker across the table.

"Have you ever seen this girl?"

Missy studied the photo and then slowly shook her head.

"Pretty girl," she said. "She looks like the same girl the sheriff's deputy was asking about. The girl who drowned."

"Yes," I said. "Her father hired me to supplement the police investigation. I am trying to find out if she was with anyone the day she drowned." I didn't want to get into a long, involved explanation so I pushed on. "She was in here on the first Saturday of this month. Did you work that day?"

"Yes," she said. "I was here. I work most Saturdays. I'm not always out front. I can keep the photo and ask around. The deputy might have missed some of my employees."

"I'd appreciate that," I said, handing her my card. I took a sip of coffee. It was less than desirable. "I won't take any more of your time. Thanks for talking to me." I stood to leave and picked up my almost-full cup. "I'll take this for the road," I said, not wanting to seem ungrateful by leaving it.

Missy walked with me as I headed to the door.

"Do you have far to go?" she asked.

"Mountain Center," I said.

We reached the exit.

"You married, Don?" Missy asked. She must have taken a close look at my license. I hadn't introduced myself.

"Almost," I said.

"Too bad."

"In another life," I said cryptically.

"Yes," she said, as if she understood my meaning. She handed me her business card. Missy Stone, it read. "Call me if you need anything," she said, smiling.

I had the feeling her offer had nothing whatsoever to do with books. I nodded, smiled and went through the door. To cover all the bases

I visited the stores that were close to Barnes and Noble with no success. Big surprise, nobody saw or remembered anything.

◆   ◆   ◆   ◆

That afternoon, I called Sally Thomas on her cell phone. She didn't answer. I left a message and went to work on my investment accounts. The stock market continued to fall. I had sold a bunch of stocks when the market went under ten thousand, and I was itching to buy them back. They were now bargains, but I wasn't convinced the market had bottomed out. I was playing cat and mouse with the Street, and for once I felt like the cat. I put a few more stocks in my tracking folder and signed off as the phone rang.

"Cherokee Investigations," I answered.

"Mr. Youngblood, this is Sally Thomas."

All business. No sign of the flirty girl in my office. I guessed she was over me.

"Thanks for calling me back, Sally," I said. "I have a couple more questions."

"Okay," she said flatly.

"Even though Betty wasn't interested in boys," I said, "were they interested in her?"

"Probably," Sally said. "She was pretty hot."

"Can you think of anyone in particular?" I asked.

"Well, she went to an all-girls school, so that's ruled out, unless a professor was interested in her," Sally said. "If there was, she never mentioned it."

"Her mother said you went out in groups," I said. "Any of those boys interested?"

Sally laughed, but I heard no joy in it.

"That's what she told her mother. Betty didn't want her to know she hadn't quite figured out the whole sex thing."

"Can you think of any guys hitting on her when you two were out?" I asked.

"Well," Sally said, "I remember this one guy at the gym where we worked out. He worked there. Lawrence, I think his name was. Nice guy. He tried to get Sally to go out once or twice, but she turned him down."

"Did he seem upset?"

"No, not really," Sally said. "Betty told him she already had a boyfriend."

"Which gym?"

"Hard Bodies, near the ETSU campus. There wasn't a good gym near John Sevier College, so Betty worked out there with me."

"Okay," I said. "Thanks. If you think of anything else, let me know."

"I assume your investigation isn't going so well," Sally said.

"You assume right," I said.

◆   ◆   ◆   ◆

That night, Mary and I were in bed reading. The sex had settled down to every second or third day, and tonight was a reading night. After all, we were both past forty. I was working on James Lee Burke's latest novel, while Mary was browsing catalogs. At the moment, she was absorbed in a Chico's catalog. Well, I thought she was.

"I saw a Barnes & Noble card on the kitchen counter," she said casually.

Oops. I thought I had put that away. I was about to be interrogated.

"Uh-huh," I mumbled, pretending to be absorbed in my book.

"Missy Stone?"

"Uh-huh."

"So?" Mary said, her voice rising a little.

"I was interviewing her in conjunction with the Betty Lou Walker case," I said, looking over.

"Was she any help?"

"Not much," I said.

"But you ended up with her card anyway," Mary said.

"Un-huh," I said, pretending to return to my book.

"Good looking, I'll bet," Mary said.

"Very," I said, looking over at her again. "But not as good looking as you. And *she* doesn't carry a gun."

Mary smiled.

"And don't you forget it, buster."

"Yes, ma'am," I said.

Mary loved to tease me by feigning jealousy. Actually, I felt she was more secure in our relationship than I was. I had dated and bedded some good-looking women without really caring if the relationships lasted or not. This time, I did. That scared me a little. I shook it off and returned to my book. Dave Robicheaux was in a mess down in Bayou country.

A few minutes later, Mary clicked off the light on her nightstand.

"Good night, my love," she said.

I had heard those words every night for a while now, yet they always sent a surge through me.

"Good night," I said.

I finished the chapter and turned out my light. I drifted off with a feeling that everything was right in my world.

The outside world was a different story.

25

The next day, I drove back to Johnson City. I stopped at a Bojangles' off I-40 and bought a sausage and egg biscuit, then went to a nearby Dunkin' Donuts for a medium coffee with cream and sugar. I found a secluded spot in a mall parking lot and enjoyed my quasi-breakfast and read *USA Today*.

Forty-five minutes later, I pulled into the Hard Bodies gym parking lot near the campus of East Tennessee State University. The best time to visit a gym if you want peace and quiet is late morning or early afternoon. The working class mainly exercises in the early morning before work or the early evening right afterward. A few work out at lunchtime. But with college students, I wasn't so sure. I hoped to interview Lawrence with as few people as possible around.

The gym was empty except for an attractive coed on one of the treadmills and a dark-haired young man in the rear office who was clearly visible through the mostly glass wall. He rose and came out toward me, no doubt anticipating a potential new member.

"I'm Lawrence," he said. "May I help you?"

Lawrence was about my height and slender. He spoke softly with a bit of an accent that was hard to place. I had the feeling he was older than he looked.

"I hope so," I said. "I'm a private investigator, and I'd like to ask you a few questions about one of your members. Can we go in your office?"

I handed him my ID. He studied it and handed it back.

"Mr. Youngblood," he said as if trying to make a connection. "I think I read about you in the paper last year. You were involved in a shooting or something."

"Yeah, that was me," I said. "But you can relax. I'm not armed."

"Well, that's a relief," he said, smiling. "Come on back."

I followed him to his office. He went behind a desk and sat.

"I really can't talk about our clients," he said.

"Even a dead one?"

His face showed surprise. Then it registered.

"Betty Lou Walker," he said.

"Yes," I said. "Betty Lou Walker."

"I couldn't believe it when I heard she drowned," Lawrence said. "She was in here that day working out."

"You're sure?"

"Yes, real sure," Lawrence said. "She was in here that morning. Some of the regulars were talking about it."

"Did she work out alone that day?"

"Yes," he said.

Something in the way he said it indicated more.

"Did she usually work out alone?"

"Not that much," he said. "Until recently."

"Mostly with Sally Thomas," I said.

"Yes," he said flatly.

The tone was still there.

"You know more," I said. "Tell me."

He hesitated, looking through the window toward the front of the gym. I knew he was trying to decide how much to tell me. He nodded and turned back to me.

"Betty Lou usually worked out with Sally," Lawrence said. "But when Sally was around, no one could get close to Betty Lou. Betty Lou started coming in by herself once or twice a week the last few months but told me not to tell Sally."

"I heard she wanted to be called Betty," I said.

"That's Sally talking," Lawrence said. "Betty Lou was fine with Betty Lou."

"I heard you asked her out a couple of times."

"I did," Lawrence said sadly. "And I think she wanted to say yes, but Sally quashed that idea. Sally was very possessive of Betty Lou."

"Have you seen Sally lately?" I asked.

"Not since Betty Lou drowned," Lawrence said.

"Got any idea what time Betty Lou left that day?" I asked.

"Definitely before lunch," he said. "I'm not really sure what time. It's pretty busy on Saturday mornings."

"Do you think Sally and Betty Lou were an item?" I asked.

"You mean, as in a lesbian relationship?" Lawrence seemed surprised by the question.

I nodded.

"I'm not sure," Lawrence said. "I can see Sally being that way, but I'm not sure about Betty Lou."

"Okay," I said. "Thanks for your help."

"Why all the questions?" Lawrence asked.

"The family wants to know what she did on her last day and why she decided to go to the lake," I said. "You know, closure."

He nodded. I'm not sure he bought it, but I turned and walked out before he could ask another question.

◆　　◆　　◆　　◆

I drove back to Mountain Center thinking about what I'd learned. Sally's version of the truth didn't quite mesh with what Lawrence said. The truth was probably somewhere in the middle. I didn't think Sally had anything to do with Betty Lou Walker's death, but it did open up the possibility that Betty Lou was seeing a guy without Sally's knowledge.

I went to the office, sat at my desk, and stared out the window down at Main Street. The day was overcast, perfectly matching my mood. I had lost my way on this case. Unless something happened, I was out of options.

And then something happened. The phone rang. The call did nothing to improve my mood.

"Mr. Youngblood, it's Bayne Roberts," the voice said.

"Hey, Bayne. How are things?"

When I met Bayne, he was a ranger at the Great Smoky Mountains National Park. I had done some work for him awhile back when he thought his wife was cheating on him. I put Billy on the case. It turned out the wife just wanted a night out with the girls. Then I recommended counseling. They went to counseling and saved their marriage. Right or wrong, I got the credit. Now, Bayne called me occasionally for advice.

"Things are not good, Mr. Youngblood," Bayne said hurriedly. "We just discovered a dead body in the Sugarlands Valley Nature Trail area. It's a murder. To make matters worse, a bad thunderstorm is heading toward us and is going to wash the crime scene clean away. I was wondering if you could get that Indian partner of yours to photograph the scene before it's too late. I hear he's real good at that. I need him fast."

"I'll call Billy now," I said.

"Will you come, too?" Bayne asked.

"Sure, Bayne," I said. "I'm on my way."

"Thanks," Bayne said. "I really appreciate it."

"By the way, Bayne," I said. "Congratulations on your promotion."

Bayne had recently been made head ranger. He was responsible for over fifty park rangers.

"Thanks," he said. "On a day like this, I wish I was just a plain ole ranger."

I dialed Billy's cell.

"Chief," I said, "I need you to get over the mountain to the Sugarlands Valley Nature Trail, and bring your camera. They have a dead body and a storm closing. I'll see you there."

"Leaving now," Billy said, knowing the urgency.

I wondered if the FBI would get called in on this. I had no doubt David Steele and his junior G-men would love to take over the investigation, but I was unsure about the protocol.

I picked up the phone and called T. Elbert.

"Brown," he answered tersely.

"Want to have some fun?" I asked without introduction.

"What's going on, Donald?"

"A dead body in the Smokies. I'm told it's a murder," I said. "The Feds could show up. Fire up the Black Beauty and pick me up out front of my office as soon as you can."

"You bet," T. Elbert said. "I'll be there in ten minutes."

He made it in nine.

26

O n the way, I called Bayne back and told him Billy would be there soon. I told him to let the other rangers know I would be in a black Hummer, so they'd let us into the parking area.

T. Elbert drove with due haste. I could tell he was excited. The traffic was light, and we made good time. I saw dark clouds hanging on the mountaintops. We drove past the Great Smoky Mountains National Park sign at the entrance forty-five minutes after we left Mountain Center, slowed only by the downtown traffic in Gatlinburg. The Sugarlands Valley trailhead was about a mile from the entrance. As we neared the trailhead, T. Elbert turned on his flashers. A ranger directed us into a parking space. I saw Billy's Grand Cherokee.

As I got out of the Hummer, a young ranger approached.

"Mr. Youngblood?" he asked.

"Yes," I said.

"The head ranger is waiting for you up the trail about halfway in," he said. "Go left where the trail splits."

T. Elbert came around the back of the Hummer in his motorized wheelchair. I was always surprised at how fast he could get out of his vehicle and into that chair.

"He's with me," I said to the young ranger. "He's a special agent with the Tennessee Bureau of Investigation."

I went down the trail with T. Elbert following. We crossed a foot-bridge and turned left. The trail was a concrete half-mile loop. The hard surface allowed T. Elbert to navigate easily. About a quarter-mile from the split, I saw Bayne standing with two other rangers, one a white male and the other a black female. He said something to them, and they moved past us with a nod and went back toward the trailhead. Bayne walked to meet us.

"Thanks for coming," he said as we shook hands.

"Glad to help," I said.

"I'm not sure why, but I wanted you to see this," he said in a low voice. "The FBI is on the way."

"Who called them?" I asked.

"Can't say," he said. "There's a lot of politics going on. I'll fill you in later."

I introduced Bayne to T. Elbert, and we followed the head ranger up the trail. Bayne introduced me to two National Park Service special agents who investigated crime only inside the Great Smoky Mountains National Park. We shook hands. They seemed none too happy to see me. I could understand. I was intruding on their territory.

I introduced T. Elbert to the two special agents and was immediately distracted by the clicking of Billy's camera. I turned and in the distance saw the body of a nude female hanging from a tree limb, her arms tied behind her back. Then up the trail on a park bench, I saw neatly folded clothes. At that moment, I had no doubt one of our serial killers had been here. Thunder rumbled in the distance.

"I suppose no one saw anything," I said.

"You're right about that," Bayne said. "We don't patrol the park from two to six in the morning. Very few cars are on Route 441 during those hours. That would have been a perfect time to do this thing."

"I'm going to take a look," I said to Bayne. "In ten minutes or so, it's going to open up."

Bayne nodded.

I went toward the girl, watching every step I took, looking for signs of anything that seemed out of place. I saw nothing. I reached Billy. He looked at me sadly and shook his head.

"I'm done," he said, and headed out the way T. Elbert and I had entered.

The victim hung there in a grotesque display. She was a dark-haired, dark-skinned girl probably of Spanish descent, a little over five feet tall, weighing maybe 110 pounds. I was embarrassed for her—and for myself for having to look at her. I hoped we could take her down soon and cover her up. The anger rising in me made me physically hot. I felt my face flush. The freshening breeze spun her slowly around to reveal her back. I noticed what could have been a mark made by a stun gun behind her left shoulder.

I knelt to look for signs that this was the killing place. I saw none. Her feet dangled a yard above my head, and I almost missed it as I stood up. The sight sent a chill through me that reached my very core. On the sole of her left foot was the tattoo of the dancing devil—the one directly behind the fire. It was a smaller version of the one on Betty Lou Walker. The same son of a bitch had done it again.

"Youngblood!" an unmistakable voice yelled. "Get the hell out of there."

I knew before I turned that it was the SAC of the Knoxville FBI office, David Steele. I walked slowly out exactly the way I had come in.

"What the hell do you think you're doing?" a red-faced David Steele barked.

"Taking a look at the crime scene on your behalf before it gets washed away," I said calmly, with a hint of sarcasm.

Before he could respond, lightning cracked in the distance, as if supporting my impertinence. A few raindrops backed up the lightning.

"Get a body bag in here on the double," David Steele called to one of the agents. "Photograph the crime scene," he said to the other.

"No need," I said. "We have that covered."

"Christ, Youngblood," David Steele said. "Why didn't you just stay in the bureau? You seem to be doing all our work for us."

"Just trying to be a cooperative citizen," I said.

"I knew there was something you weren't telling me," T. Elbert said.

"Who the hell is this?" David Steele said. "Ironside?"

I felt the anger rise in me again. I was seconds away from punching the smirk off Agent Steele's face when T. Elbert rescued me.

"I'm Special Agent T. Elbert Brown of the Tennessee Bureau of Investigation," he said.

"Like hell you are," David Steele said. But there was little conviction in his comeback. He seemed to wish he hadn't said it.

"Like hell I am," T. Elbert answered, and whipped out his ID.

David Steele took the ID, studied it, and handed it back. Then he said something that gained a degree of respect from me.

"Sorry, Agent Brown, no disrespect intended," he said. "I'm just surprised to see the TBI here."

"No offense taken," T. Elbert said. "I'm here as a friend of Donald's, to observe. I'm semi-retired."

The wind picked up.

"Now, if you'll excuse me, I must leave posthaste," T. Elbert said. "Water does little good for my chair."

He did an about-face in his wheelchair and headed back down the trail toward the Hummer as the rain intensified. In the woods, two agents were bagging the body.

"Let's get out of here!" David Steele shouted to his agents. "Youngblood," he said to me, "come sit in my car for a few minutes."

I'm sure I looked surprised by the invitation. A smart remark formed on my lips, but I swallowed it and remained silent.

"Please," he added.

I nodded, said my goodbyes to Bayne and the agents, and followed SAC David Steele to his car. The park rangers and special park agents were close behind, also seeking shelter in their vehicles. The other FBI agents carried the body to an SUV close by.

We reached the nondescript Taurus just as the heavens opened up. Sheets of rain blew across U.S. 441. The few cars that passed did so at a crawl.

◆　　◆　　◆　　◆

Inside the Taurus, David Steele was silent. He gripped the steering wheel with both hands and stared straight ahead, looking like a man with a big decision to make.

"Sorry about all that back there," he said. "We Feds get too possessive sometimes. I used to tell trainees to watch that, and now I'm not following my own advice."

"Not a problem," I said, knowing the scene we had just witnessed could unnerve anyone.

Tiny hailstones bounced off the hood of the Taurus.

"Scott Glass told me I could trust you," David Steele said.

"You can," I said.

"Tell me what you saw."

"Billy's pictures will tell you more than I can," I said.

"I'm interested in your gut reaction," he said. "So walk me through it as if I wasn't there."

"Okay," I said. "When I walked in, I didn't see any signs of a struggle or anything disturbed. He must have come in from the opposite direction. Billy will know. I didn't see any signs that the girl died there from the hanging. I'm sure she was killed somewhere else and brought here. Her hands were tied behind her back. That was unnecessary. The killer wanted us to know it wasn't a suicide. He knew we would figure that out, but he wanted to announce it. The clothes were the calling card—neatly folded like those at the lake, and placed just so on the bench. I don't know what, but that means something to the killer."

"Good observations," David Steele said.

"Dave, one more thing," I said. "I saw a tattoo on the sole of her left foot—a devil dancing behind a fire, a smaller version of the one on Betty Lou Walker's back."

He stared at me like a man who had been given really bad news.

"Well, fuck me," David Steele said. "We have a serial nut job on the loose. The clothes and the tattoo pretty much seal the deal."

"Serial nut jobs," I said. "I'm pretty sure there are two more."

"God help us," he said.

"Want me to call Scott, or do you want to?"

"You can," he said. "You saw more that I did."

The hail ceased, replaced by heavy rain. It beat down as if we were inside a car wash. The wind continued to blow. Leaves and other debris skittered across the highway.

"Where will they take the body?" I asked.

"Knox County," David Steele said.

"Will you let me know how the autopsy goes?" I asked. "I'd like to know the official cause of death."

"You working with us on this?" he asked.

"Unofficially."

"Probably better that way," he said, "knowing how you like to bend the rules."

"Sometimes that helps," I said.

"Sometimes it does," David Steele said. "I don't have that luxury."

"But I do."

"Yes, you do," he said. "So take advantage of it."

I couldn't believe what I was hearing, not from this buttoned-down, closed-up, severely toilet-trained FBI agent. But I certainly understood. I felt a little desperate myself.

"I never thought I'd hear that come out of your mouth," I said.

He turned to face me, more relaxed now but with a tired and beaten-down look.

"That girl hanging there," he said. "That's really fucked up. I have a daughter, you know."

"No, I didn't."

"If that was my daughter, I'd go fucking crazy. You know what I mean?"

I thought about Lacy—not my daughter but beginning to feel like it.

"I do know what you mean," I said.

"So," David Steele said, "we're going to pull out all the stops on this one. If you have to bend some rules, bend them. I'll back you up as best I can."

We sat in silence and listened to the rain pound down on the Taurus.

T. Elbert was in his Hummer waiting for me a couple of cars down. I called his cell phone. He answered on the first ring.

"When the rain slackens a little, I'll make a run for it," I said without preamble.

"No hurry," T. Elbert said. "Are you and the fed making nice?"

"That's an affirmative," I said. "I'll tell you about it later."

"Good," T. Elbert said. "Never hurts to have those paranoid little bastards on your side."

"I'll see you in a few minutes," I said, then flipped my phone closed and slipped it back into my jacket pocket.

"I don't think he likes me much," David Steele said.

"You didn't exactly come across all warm and fuzzy, Dave," I said. "He'll get over it."

"Let's keep a lid on this murder as long as we can," he said. "I'll take care of my end if you can take care of yours."

"T. Elbert is as closed as an oyster before shucking time," I said. "And I never was a big talker."

"Thanks," David Steele said. "I'll keep you posted."

I nodded, opened the car door, and made a run for the Hummer. The rain had slackened some, but I still got good and wet. T. Elbert drove away in silence.

When we got out of the park, I called Scott Glass and filled him in on the events of the day. He was as angry and upset as the rest of us.

"I have a feeling that a couple more bodies are going to turn up real soon hanging in trees," I said to Scott.

"You may be right," he said.

"If you could stake out national parks in the areas of those other murders, you might get lucky," I said.

"I don't have the manpower," Scott said. "All I can do is alert the park rangers."

"It's something," I said.

"I'll do it first thing tomorrow morning," Scott said.

"One other thing, Professor," I said, dreading the next words out of my mouth.

"I'm listening," he said as if he knew it wasn't going to be good news.

"Better have the rangers look around," I said. "As far as I know, the locals didn't get a phone call about this one. Dead bodies might already be out there somewhere."

"That's what I'm afraid off," Scott said with resignation. "I just didn't want to say it out loud."

The rain continued falling hard. The windshield wipers on the Hummer were working furiously to keep up.

"David Steele said he'll share the autopsy report with me," I said.

"You two big buddies now?" Scott asked.

"We're getting there," I said. "This dead girl hanging nude in the woods really got to him."

"Doesn't sound like Steely Dave," Scott said.

"Did you know he has a daughter?" I asked.

"No, I didn't. He's never shared his personal life."

"For him, I think it hit too close to home," I said. "You had to be there, Professor. It would have really pissed you off. You'll understand when I send you the pictures."

"Okay," Scott said. "Send them as soon as you can. I'll talk to you tomorrow."

After I was off the phone, T. Elbert finally broke his silence.

"Hell of a thing," he said. "Never could understand the kind of person who would do that."

"Insane," I said. "Loose wiring in the brain. No sense of right and wrong."

"You're right about that," T. Elbert said. "So tell me about you and the FBI."

I told him all of it.

"I can see why it didn't work for you," T. Elbert said. "You're creative, and you like to be in control. Bad combination for an entry-level agent."

"Yeah," I said. "I'm not easily toilet trained."

"So what were you going to tell me about Agent Steele?" T. Elbert asked.

"Turns out Agent David Steele is a stand-up guy," I said. "He wants this asshole as bad as the rest of us."

◆   ◆   ◆   ◆

That night when I came to bed, Mary was still awake and reading the latest book by James Lee Burke, the one I had just finished. She had never read James Lee before. I slid in beside her with a copy of *Rocky Top News* featuring Tennessee's new top-ten football signing class.

We read for a while, and then Mary closed her book and placed it on her nightstand.

"This guy is pretty good," she said.

"He is that," I said.

"You're pretty good, too," she teased, rolling toward me as she ran her hand underneath my T-shirt.

"Not tonight," I heard my voice say, surprising both Mary and myself. I had never turned down an opportunity to make love to her.

She removed her hand and sat up and gave me a long, concerned look. I had told her about the latest tattoo killing but hadn't gone into detail.

"The murder of this girl in the park is really bothering you, isn't it?" Mary said.

"Yes," I said. "I can't get the image of her hanging there out of my mind. I keep thinking it could have been Lacy. I'm having flashbacks of looking up and seeing that tattoo. It sends a chill through me like an ice cube going down my spine. Seeing Betty Lou Walker in the lake didn't disturb me as much as this girl. Betty Lou made me mad. This new murder not only makes me mad but disturbs me on a level I cannot describe." I felt off balance and had a sense of dread. I knew more bad news was yet to come. "And the tattoo didn't bother me the first time I saw it. It was more of a curiosity."

"You never saw it on the body," Mary said. "You looked at a picture. Believe me, that's a big difference."

"It may take awhile to get that image out of my mind."

Mary got out of bed and went into our bathroom and came back with one hand closed and the other carrying a cup of water. The closed hand opened to reveal a little white pill.

"Take this," she ordered.

"What is it?"

"A very effective sleep med," Mary said.

"You take these often?" I asked. I was finding out more about Mary every day.

"Only once since moving to Mountain Center," she said. "Last year when I took that bullet in my vest that cracked a rib. A few times in Knoxville when I saw something so disturbing I couldn't sleep. You'd be surprised how many cops need something to get to sleep."

"Not after today, I wouldn't," I said.

I took the pill, popped it in my mouth, and drained the cup of water. I reached over and turned out the light on my nightstand.

Mary slipped back into bed, turned out her light, and moved close to me.

"I want to get this guy," I said.

"I haven't known you that long, Don," Mary said. "But you're one of the smartest people I've ever met, and you have the natural instincts of a good cop. If anyone can get this guy, you can. Now, close your eyes and relax."

I had a smart, self-effacing retort, but it didn't seem to want to come out. My mind was shutting down. Somewhere in the distance, I heard that familiar voice whisper, "Good night, my love."

27

The next morning, I arrived at the office much later than usual. Whatever that little white pill was, it had knocked me out for over nine hours. By the time I showered and shaved, Mary and Lacy were long gone. I parked in my usual spot and walked around the building and across the street to Dunkin' Donuts. I picked up a medium coffee with cream and sugar and a poppy seed bagel with cream cheese.

I settled into my leather chair, booted up my computer, and took that first glorious drink of coffee. I had a bite of bagel and checked caller ID. No calls, just the way I wanted it. I could relax for a while.

I went online and peeked at the Dow Jones. It was falling like a lead weight in deep water, below nine thousand with no bottom in sight. I had nothing to do but wait. Investing in the stock market or real estate held one universal truth—sooner or later, the value would return. Youngblood's rule in a tough economy: Don't panic, be patient.

I next went to the CBS Sports website. I finished my bagel and coffee looking at baseball box scores, stats, and the standings in both leagues. I played a game of Spider Solitaire on the most difficult level and won. I was trying to decide what to do next when the phone rang. Caller ID was blocked.

"Cherokee Investigations," I answered in my radio announcer's voice.

"Mr. Youngblood?"

I knew that deep, gritty voice.

"Yes."

"Troy Walker. Anything new on my daughter's death?"

I paused and considered whether or not I could trust Troy Walker to keep his mouth shut. I knew he needed closure and was looking for me to give it to him. Any positive news would help.

"Yes," I said hesitantly, "there is."

"Tell me," he said.

"Mr. Walker," I said, "if I tell you this, it has to stay between you and me. Nobody else. Not your wife, not your best friend, not even your priest in the confessional. Understand? If any of this leaks, it could hinder the investigation."

"You have my word," he growled. "And I am not Catholic."

"There are other dead girls," I said. "Their deaths were similar to Betty Lou's, and I know they're connected, but I cannot say how. Sooner or later, we're going to get this guy."

I heard a sigh. His silence conveyed a sense of hope. He was grasping at any news that might give him peace.

"You said *we*," Troy Walker said. "Who are *we*?"

"Besides me, the FBI is involved, and another federal agency. A lot of manpower is on this case."

"You'll stay on it?" he asked.

"I will," I said. "To the end."

"Thank you," Troy Walker said. "It keeps me grounded, knowing someone is giving this personal attention. Do you know what I mean, Mr. Youngblood?"

"I think I do," I said.

"Stay in touch, please."

"I will, Mr. Walker," I said. "I will."

◆　　◆　　◆　　◆

I sat around the rest of the morning waiting for the phone to ring. I was hoping David Steele would call and tell me something about the dead girl in the Great Smoky Mountains National Park. He didn't. I was also hoping Scott Glass would *not* call and tell me about a dead girl somewhere else. Thankfully, Scott didn't call either. No calls came in—well, except for two telemarketers saved from my impending brush-off by caller ID.

I spent a boring morning updating investment portfolios and periodically checking the market. *I might have to hire a financial assistant,* I thought. Finally, I sent an email to T. Elbert to let him know I hadn't heard anything from David Steele. Then I changed into my running gear and drove to the parking lot where I could access the Mountain Center Nature Trail. I did a five-and-a-half-mile loop in just under forty minutes. I was exhausted by the time I got back to the office. I showered, then snacked on cheese and nuts and drank a diet ginger ale.

I put my feet up on my desk, leaned back in my black leather chair, and thought about dead girls and tattoos. The tattoos were good temporary transfers that had no doubt been placed by the killers. But why two different locations on the bodies, and why two different sizes? I had no idea. I picked up the phone and called Scott.

"Glass," he answered.

"That voice," I said. "Like a seasoned veteran."

"Practice," Scott said. "What's up, Blood?"

"Any luck tracking down those tattoos?" I asked.

"None," Scott said. "Most transfer tattoos are made outside the U.S., some in countries that aren't talking to us."

"Not talking to the Federal Bureau of Investigation?" I said. "Imagine that."

"Hard to believe, isn't it?"

"Shocking," I said. "Any other leads?"

"None," Scott said. "And thankfully, no dead girls hanging from trees."

"Well, Professor," I said, "let's hope it stays that way."

◆　　◆　　◆　　◆

An hour later, my phone rang. Caller ID told me it was Mary on her personal cell phone.

"Whatever it is," I said without preamble, "I didn't do it."

She laughed.

"But you're about to," Mary said.

"I am?"

"I got off early, and Lacy won't be home for two hours," Mary said. "Any thoughts about that?"

"Well, I've thought about going to the gym and fine-tuning my body." I thought it best not to mention my five-and-a-half-mile lunchtime run.

"You hurry your butt home and I'll give you a workout you can't get at the gym," Mary said.

"Ten minutes," I said.

I placed the phone on its charger, closed the office, and rushed to the parking lot.

Ten minutes later, Mary and I were helping each other off with our clothes like two horny newlyweds.

28

Friday morning, David Steele phoned. I had promised myself I wouldn't call him. I wasn't eager to get bad news and was trying to purge the image of the latest dead girl from my thoughts, with little success.

"Youngblood," I answered, guessing it might be him, based on the "No data" readout on my caller ID.

"Youngblood, it's David Steele."

"What's going on, Agent Steele?" I asked.

"Cut the crap, Youngblood. Call me Dave," he said. "The M.E. finished the autopsy. The girl was killed late the night before we found her. The killer used a stun gun, then ether. Then she was suffocated."

David Steele sounded tired. I bet he hadn't been sleeping well. I couldn't imagine having his job. If I wanted to, I could walk away from this. He couldn't.

"Who was she?" I asked.

"We don't know," he said. "No ID was on the body, and no one has claimed her or filed a missing person report. We think she might be an illegal. She may have been from the Sevier County area, but no one wants to talk to us."

"You printed her, I assume."

"We did, and no hits," David Steele said. "Think you can help us with this? The locals might talk to someone who isn't law enforcement."

"I'll see what I can do," I said, "though I'm not sure a private investigator will make illegals feel any more secure."

"I know you speak fluent Spanish," he said. "That should help."

"Can't hurt," I said. "I'll give it a shot. Send me a picture of the girl. Have one of your guys Photoshop some life into it. I don't want it looking like a corpse. And send me a picture of the tattoo on her foot. I want to add it to my file."

137

"Will do," David Steele said. "And thanks. I'll keep in touch. You do the same." He gave me his private cell-phone number. "Day or night," he said. "Even if it's just kicking around an idea."

"You sleeping okay, Dave?" I asked. "You sound beat."

"I am beat," he said. "And no, I'm not sleeping well. I keep seeing that dead girl hanging there."

Well, I can relate to that, I thought.

◆   ◆   ◆   ◆

Helping the FBI was not tops on my list, but identifying the dead girl might get her a proper burial and her family some closure. It was worth a try. The question was how. I thought about that for a few minutes and came up with an idea. I dialed Joseph Fleet's private number at Fleet Industries.

"Who's calling please?" a professional female voice asked.

"Donald Youngblood for Joseph Fleet," I said.

"One moment, please."

I don't know exactly how fast a moment is, but it's quick.

"Donald," Fleet said. "Is everything okay?"

I found it interesting that Joseph Fleet sometimes called me Donald and sometime Don. Someday, I'd have to ask him about that.

"Everything is fine," I said. "I haven't heard from Roy and don't expect to for a while."

"Of course," Fleet said. "What can I do for you?"

"How is Oscar Morales working out?" I asked.

"Fine," Fleet said. "You were right. I like him. He knows when to talk and when to be quiet."

"I need his help on something. I may need to borrow him on Monday, if you can spare him," I said.

"Sure," Fleet said. "Does this have to do with Betty Lou Walker?"

"In a way, yes," I said.

"Troy told me about his daughter's murder," Fleet said. "Whatever you need from me to catch the son of a bitch, you got it."

"I appreciate that," I said. "Have Oscar drop by sometime today, if possible."

"He's picking up a client at the airport in half an hour," Joseph Fleet said. "I'll have him come by your place after lunch."

"Thanks," I said. "And don't worry about Roy. He's in good hands."

◆   ◆   ◆   ◆

As promised, Oscar was in my office after lunch. He sat clean-shaven in one of my oversized chairs, decked out in a dark blue pinstriped suit complete with white shirt and fashionable tie. His black lace-up shoes sparkled. I was impressed. Oscar cleaned up nice.

"You look prosperous," I said. I couldn't help smiling.

"I feel prosperous," Oscar said, grinning. "I am in your debt for this job."

"Since you brought it up," I said, "I could use your help."

"Anything," Oscar said.

I told him about the unidentified murdered girl in the park. I left out the part about serial killers and tattoos. When I finished, Oscar slowly shook his head.

"*Bad business,*" he said in Spanish.

"*Very bad,*" I replied.

"What would you like me to do?" Oscar asked.

"Take a trip with me to Sevier County to visit some of the Spanish-speaking communities and see what we can find," I said. "Law enforcement is coming up empty."

"I am not surprised," Oscar said. "I know a few people in Sevierville I can talk to. They should be able to point me in the right direction. I'll make some calls this weekend."

"Tell whoever you talk to, green card or not, that we're not looking to jam anyone up," I said. "All we want to do is get this girl to her family for a proper burial. If anyone asks, the state is paying for it."

"The state?" Oscar said.

"Whatever it takes, Oscar. I'll make sure it happens."

"Ah," Oscar smiled. "I understand."

"Meet me here Monday morning after you drop Mr. Fleet at his office," I said. "I'll drive."

"Good idea," Oscar said. "The limo would stick out like a red-hot chili pepper."

29

We stayed the weekend at the lake house. Mary and Lacy spent a lot of time on the water. I spent some time on the lake with them and the rest taking care of some long overdue maintenance. I had a list that seemed to grow longer. For every item I crossed off, two appeared. I could have afforded to hire the work done, but I wanted it done my way.

Early Sunday night, we sat at the dining-room table celebrating with Lacy that school was out for the summer. We went over the events of the year. Jake lay peacefully on his bed a few feet away.

Although I was mostly a forward-looking person, sometimes it was good to turn around and see where we'd been and look at the progress that got us where we were. Lacy had been with us for about a year. Her mother had tried to come to grips with a deep, dark secret from her past and in doing so lost her life. Mary had moved in with me, and then Lacy followed. My life was complicated, but I was okay with that.

"I may not work at the diner much this summer," Lacy said. "Maybe just Saturdays."

"Really?" I said, looking at Mary, who showed no sign of being surprised.

"Stanley wants to teach me to write computer code," Lacy said.

"Really?" I repeated, waiting for the trap to spring.

"Yes," Lacy said. "It's complicated. He wants me to work thirty hours a week until school starts."

"Sounds fine," I said. "Did you talk to Doris about this?"

"I did," Lacy said. "She thinks it's a good idea."

"So," I said, "there must be something else."

Lacy smiled and looked at Mary. Mary smiled back.

"What do you need?" I asked.

"A laptop," Lacy said. "Stanley said it would be good to have my own to carry back and forth."

"Sounds reasonable," I said.

"I don't have enough money saved to get the one I want," Lacy said. "So what I need is a loan."

"What you need," I said, "is a congratulations-for-making-it-through-freshman-year gift. Pick out the laptop you want. I'll consider it an investment in your future."

"Yes!" Lacy said. "I have to call Jonah. And then I'll go online and do some more research."

She left the table faster than Superman looking for a phone booth. I looked at Mary.

"Why didn't you just tell me she needed a laptop?" I said. "It's no big deal."

"Lacy thinks it's a big deal," Mary said. "And she hates to ask you for stuff, even though she knows you can afford it."

All I could do was shake my head and look confused.

"Besides," Mary said, "it's more fun this way."

◆   ◆   ◆   ◆

After I helped Mary clean up, we went out the back door and down to the lower deck to watch the sunset. What was left of the day was cooling fast. Mary drank another glass of white wine while I sipped a Bailey's Irish Cream. I stretched out in a lounge chair. Mary sat beside me in a folding chair.

"What should I do about the detective job?" Mary asked.

The question caught me off-guard. I hadn't heard anything since we discussed it a few weeks ago. The decision was obviously still bothering her.

"Your call," I said.

"I'm asking *you*," she said, sounding a little annoyed.

Something in her tone sent up a red flag.

"If it feels right, do it," I said. "If not, don't."

"Oh, you're a big frigging help."

"What's wrong?" I asked, surprised at her reaction.

She didn't answer. I wasn't sure she heard me. She stared out at the lake. Then she got up, walked to the deck railing, and poured the rest of her wine over the edge.

"Sorry," she said, turning toward me. "I've had a bit too much wine. And when I have too much, I sometimes get bitchy, a product of the old days. It's not your fault. I'll tell you about it sometime."

She came over, worked her way in beside me on the lounge, kissed me gently on my cheek, and laid her head on my shoulder. I listened to the cicada serenade as night descended on the lake.

"I love you," Mary said sometime later.

"I know," I said.

"And I know you love me," she said. "So you don't have to say it just because I did."

"I do love you," I said. "And I don't mind saying it."

"I should have met you sooner," she said.

"Later is better than not at all," I said.

"Yes," Mary sighed. "It sure is."

We stayed like that for a long time.

Much later, we made our way inside to the master bedroom for a very close encounter. Luckily, our bedroom was on the opposite end of the house from Lacy's.

30

At midmorning the next day, I drove the back roads into Sevier County. Oscar Morales rode shotgun. We were going to pick up a friend of Oscar's who lived in a small Spanish community in Sevierville. We exchanged small talk in Spanish. Thanks to Raul Rivera, a longtime college friend, my Spanish was good. But as with any foreign language, practice was necessary.

Once we reached Sevierville, Oscar gave me directions to a small white house in a modest neighborhood. When I pulled up in front, Oscar got out.

"Wait here," he said, returning to English. "And do not let Luis know you speak Spanish, so he might more freely give information."

Oscar knocked on the front door. It opened slightly, then all the way. Oscar disappeared inside. A few minutes later, he returned with a short, dark-skinned man. Oscar took his place in the front passenger seat, and the man slid into the backseat behind him.

"Mr. Youngblood," Oscar said, "this is my friend Luis."

I reached into the backseat and shook hands with Luis. He seemed surprised.

"Nice to meet you, Luis," I said.

Luis nodded. I guessed his age to be around thirty. He had big, dark eyes and short black hair.

"*Where are we going?*" Oscar asked in Spanish.

"*Gatlinburg,*" Luis said. "*To a small Spanish community there. They call it Little Honduras. It's just off Airport Road. I know a few people who live there. A guy I know said something is going on, but he did not know what it was. I think it is a good place to start.*"

"You know the way to Airport Road in Gatlinburg?" Oscar said to me in English.

"I do," I said.

We drove in silence through Pigeon Forge on U.S. 441 South. We entered the Great Smoky Mountains National Park for a few miles on a section the locals called "the Spur," then exited the park into Gatlinburg. I headed down the main drag toward the center of town.

"*How long have you known this guy?*" Luis asked Oscar.

I kept silent.

"*Long enough,*" Oscar said. "*He has helped me out from time to time.*"

"*Do you trust him?*"

"*With my life,*" Oscar said. "*He is a very honorable man.*"

I tried not to laugh. I was sure the "honorable" part was for my benefit.

"*That is good,*" Luis said. "*Even so, when we get there, he should stay in the car.*"

"*Whatever you say, Luis,*" Oscar said.

I took a left onto Airport Road, which did not lead to an airport. I guessed at some time an airport must have been located around here somewhere. Or maybe they landed small planes on the road back in the day.

Following Oscar's instructions, I went up Airport Road, took a left, and stopped in front of an apartment building on the right. A few people were milling about. Luis got out of the car. Oscar looked at me. I handed him the picture of the dead girl that someone had slid underneath my office door over the weekend. It looked presentable.

"This is the girl," I said. "I had them doctor it so she doesn't look so bad."

Her eyes were open, and she was smiling. Amazing what could be done on a computer these days.

"That was thoughtful of you," Oscar said, looking at the picture. "It is best if you wait in the car unless I signal for you."

"Will do," I said.

Oscar got out. I watched as Luis introduced him to a man who had just come outside. They talked a few minutes. Then a woman came out who looked upset. A few more men and women followed. A group was starting to form. Oscar handed the picture to the first woman. She took one look at it and collapsed screaming hysterically into the arms of the man standing next to her. The man helped her inside. The rest of the women followed.

Oscar motioned to me. I got out and walked over to where he stood with the remaining men. He introduced me to an older man.

"This is Miguel. Miguel speaks English. He is the unofficial leader of this community," Oscar said to me. Then he turned to Miguel. "This is Mr. Youngblood. He can arrange for the girl's body to be given to the family. No questions will be asked."

"Thank you," Miguel said to me.

"You're welcome," I said. "I know this is difficult, but I need to find out the last time anyone saw the girl."

"Maria," Miguel said. "Her name was Maria Cruz. The woman Oscar showed the picture to was her sister."

"I'm sorry for her loss," I said. "What can you tell me about Maria's disappearance?"

"She went to clean chalets on the mountain on Monday," Miguel said. "That was the last time anyone saw her or heard from her."

"Do you know which chalet company she worked for?" I asked.

"I do not," Miguel said. "If I find out, I will let Luis know."

"Did anyone call the police?" I asked.

"No police," Miguel said, looking at the ground. He didn't bother to explain further.

"What can you tell me about her death?" he asked.

I looked at Oscar. He nodded and remained silent.

"She was suffocated," I said. "It looks like the killer used a stun gun and then drugged her. She was unconscious when he suffocated her. She didn't suffer."

Of course, I had no idea if that was the case. But it was the best spin I could put on a bad situation.

"Who would do such a thing?" Miguel asked, his pain evident.

"A very sick person," I said. "And I promise you, Miguel, we are going to catch him."

◆   ◆   ◆   ◆

On the way back to Sevierville, we were quiet. Delivering bad news was a sobering experience. I considered what others had lost and gave thanks for what I had.

I parked in front of Luis's house and turned to him before he had a chance to get out.

"It was nice meeting you, Luis," I said, offering my hand. "I wish the circumstances could have been different. Thanks for your help."

We shook hands. Luis looked at Oscar. Oscar translated.

"*I think I like your friend very much,*" Luis said to Oscar. "*Goodbye, Oscar.*"

We watched as Luis disappeared inside his house.

"One of these days, I'll tell him you speak Spanish," Oscar said. "I cannot wait to see his face."

"*Want to drive?*" I asked Oscar in Spanish. "*I want some time to think about all of this.*"

"*I would be honored,*" Oscar said.

While Oscar drove, I sat in silence. I wondered if he was as unsettled as I was about the events of the day—a dead girl far from home, a grieving sister also far from home, and a psycho killer with a tattoo fetish who probably had accomplices in two other parts of the country. We had to find the three devils before their dance of death continued.

"They may want the girl's body returned to Honduras," Oscar said, concern in his voice.

"I know people who can handle that," I said.

"Could be expensive."

"I'll pay for it," I said.

"Why?" Oscar asked.

"Because I can and because I want to," I said.

"That is good," Oscar said. "I would like to help with that."

"No need," I said. "I can cover it."

"I am sure you can," Oscar said. "But you do not understand. In a way, these are my people. You must allow me to help with the expense."

"Sorry," I said. "I do understand. You most certainly can help."

Oscar went silent again, so I called David Steele's private cell phone.

"This is Steele."

"The girl's name is Maria Cruz," I said without introduction.

"That was fast work, Youngblood," he said.

"I had some help, and we were lucky," I said. "She lived in Gatlinburg. She cleaned chalets on the mountain. The last time anyone heard from her was the previous Monday."

"Do you know which chalet company?" David Steele asked.

"No, I don't," I said. "You have her picture. Your guys should be able to track that down."

"We'll try. But what do you want to bet no one has ever seen this girl?" he said.

"No bet," I said. "But you have to make the effort."

"We will, Youngblood," he said wearily. "What about the body?"

"I'll have someone be in touch with you," I said.

"Good work, Youngblood," David Steele said. "You've got a knack for this kind of work."

I wasn't sure whether that was a compliment or not.

"Yeah," I said. "Lucky me."

"Anything breaks, I'll let you know," he said.

◆   ◆   ◆   ◆

Later, I called Thaddeus Miller, the owner and operator of a local funeral home that had handled my parents' burial. I asked him if he could provide for Maria Cruz. He said he could. He had been a friend of my father's and was very caring toward me during the whole ordeal.

I flipped my cell phone closed, wondering how I had stumbled into this mess. Too many young girls were dying. I didn't want to hear about any more deaths. I felt as if I were trapped in my own sadistic version of the movie *Groundhog Day*.

31

I was in the office early the following Monday morning. The rest of my week had been quiet. I had updated Troy Walker and told him I was out of ideas for the moment and that I was hoping the FBI came up with something. He wasn't happy about it but seemed to understand. Mary, Lacy, and I then spent an uneventful weekend at the lake house. I was ready for something to happen.

I had made a fresh pot of coffee and settled into a game of Risk on my computer when I got the call I didn't want.

"We found another body," the voice said.

"Where?" I asked, closing down the game.

"Superior National Forest," Scott Glass said. "Way up in northern Minnesota, almost to Canada. And a hell of a long way from Swan Lake."

"Same MO as ours?"

"Yes, identical," Scott said. "We haven't been able to identify the body yet. She was of Latin heritage and looked a lot like the girl in the Smokies."

"Maria Cruz," I said.

"Yes, I know," he said. "Steely Dave told me. Good work on that, Blood."

"Tattoo on the sole of her foot?"

"Yes," Scott said.

"Any tips leading you to the body?"

"No," he said.

"Any leads?"

"None so far," Scott said. "She was there a day or two. I'll know more once the autopsy comes in. TOD is going to be hard to pin down. It's still very cold at night up there. We're going over the crime scene now, but at first glance I'm told it looked very clean."

"There's going to be another one near you," I said. "I can feel it."

"I believe you, Blood," Scott said. "We've got to catch these bastards."

*   *   *   *

An hour later, I heard footfalls in the hallway growing louder as they came toward my outer office door. A big man with leather-heeled boots walking on a marble floor can make that sound. The door opened and closed. I heard a cup of coffee being poured. The big man came through my door and made himself comfortable in one of my oversized chairs. He took a long drink and nodded approval.

"Good as always," he said.

"Is this a social call?" I said.

"I'm afraid not," Big Bob said. "But as long as I'm here, I might as well get a good cup of coffee."

"Mary okay?" I asked, slightly panicked. Now, why was that?

"Hell, Blood," Big Bob said. "You think I'm going to walk in here and pour myself a cup of coffee if Mary's not okay?"

"Sorry," I said. "That was stupid."

"Man, she's got you by the balls."

"Okay, cut the crap," I said, annoyed by the jab. "Why *are* you here?"

"Megan Cox," Big Bob said.

"What about her?"

"Somebody beat the hell out of her last night in the Mountain Mall parking lot," he said. "She's in a coma. Might make it, might not. Her father is sure it was Ricky Carter. He said to talk to you and you would explain why."

"It's a long story," I said.

"I've got time," Big Bob said, taking another drink of coffee.

"You're not going to like some of it," I said.

"I was guessing I wouldn't," the big man said.

I told him about Cindy Carter and Rasheed Reed. I told him about going to Bermuda with Roy to retrieve Rasheed's money. He drank coffee and shook his head and frowned. I expected an explosion when I finished. I didn't get it.

"You were lucky," he said. "Damn lucky."

"I know," I said.

"Might have saved that little girl's life," Big Bob said.

"That's what Mary said."

"Mary knew?" he asked, his voice getting louder.

"After it was over," I said. "The little girl was already back home with her mother."

Big Bob drained his cup.

"So you think Ricky came back just to beat up his wife?" he asked.

"Soon to be his ex-wife," I said. "I wouldn't have thought he had the balls. I know he knocked Megan around sometimes when he got high. And I know he wanted a piece of Daddy's money, and that it wasn't forthcoming."

"So it was probably Ricky," Big Bob said.

"Unless you've got a better choice," I said.

"I don't," he said. "We'll be on the lookout for Ricky. I know you're going to stick your nose in this. So if you find him first, let me know."

"Might be hard to prosecute him if Megan doesn't wake up," I said.

"You wanting to take the law into your own hands again?" Big Bob asked. "Like you did with Victor Vargas?"

"That was self-defense," I said.

"Sure it was," the big man said.

◆   ◆   ◆   ◆

After Big Bob left, I sat in my black leather chair thinking about the last time I saw Megan Cox Carter and getting angrier by the minute. Big Bob was right. I was going to stick my nose in this. Maybe it was my fault Megan was in the hospital. Maybe if Roy and I had leaned harder on Ricky, he wouldn't have come back. Maybe Ricky didn't do it. Maybe the sun wouldn't come up in the morning.

But I knew the sun would be up, and I was just as sure Ricky had assaulted Megan. *I'd really like to find Ricky before Big Bob does*, I thought. Let the FBI worry about the three devils for a while. I had things to do closer to home.

32

The Mountain Center Medical Center was a state-of-the-art hospital and looked the part. The modern architecture gleamed in the late-morning sun. The center had been built a little more than a year ago. I had already been an overnight guest, thanks to a bullet from Vegas bad boy Victor Vargas.

The ICU was on the fourth floor. I went to the nurses' station.

"How is Megan Carter doing?" I asked the nurse on duty.

Her nametag said she was Brenda Knox. Brenda was an attractive brunette around five and a half feet tall with a slender frame and good figure. Her short, dark hair showed flecks of gray—whether from the job or genetics, it was hard to tell.

"You mean Megan Cox?" she asked.

"Yes, Cox," I said.

"Are you family?" she asked, acting like she knew I wasn't.

"No, I'm not," I said, showing her my private investigator's ID. "I'm looking into the assault."

She looked at my ID and warmed a bit.

"Donald Youngblood," she said. "I've read about you in the local paper, and I remember when you were here after being shot. It was the talk of the hospital."

"It's nice to be remembered," I said. "Now, about Megan?"

"Still in a coma," she said.

"What's her prognosis?"

"I can't comment on that," Nurse Brenda said. "You'll have to ask her doctor."

"Can I see Megan?" I asked.

"That's her over there," Nurse Brenda said.

I turned and looked across the hall through a window into a room where Megan Cox lay hooked up to various monitors. She was on a respirator. I barely recognized her. An older woman sat on the other side of her bed. She was holding Megan's hand and talking to her.

I turned back to Nurse Brenda.

"Her mother?"

"Yes," she said. "Her father was in there a few minutes ago, but he went down to the courtyard to use his cell phone."

"Thanks, Brenda," I said. "I may see you again."

"Anytime," she said.

◆   ◆   ◆   ◆

I took the elevator to the first floor and found the courtyard. A lone man on a cell phone sat on one of the benches near the fountain that was the focal point. The water made the soft sounds of a mountain stream, and the air was pre-summer warm. The courtyard was a peaceful place to escape for a few minutes from the stress of waiting and the fear of death. The man looked up when I entered. I kept my eyes on him, and he picked up my signal as I moved closer.

"I have to go," I heard him say. "You handle it. I'll talk to you later." He snapped his phone shut and stood.

"Mr. Cox?" I asked.

"Yes," he said.

I thought I detected fear in his voice. I hoped he didn't think I was bearing bad news.

"I'm Don Youngblood," I said. "I heard about Megan. I'm very sorry."

"Howard Cox," the man said, extending his hand and seeming relieved. "It's nice to meet you, Mr. Youngblood. I wish the circumstances were different, but I do thank you for taking care of my granddaughter."

"I'm glad I could help," I said. "Any news on Megan?"

"Well, she's in a coma," he said. "She has strong brain-wave activity, so we're hopeful. She has a concussion and a skull fracture."

I knew all about concussions and skull fractures, having recently had my brains scrambled by a goon squad in Las Vegas. The memory was not pleasant. It had taken me awhile to recover. My head hurt at the mention of the words.

"It may take her a few days to wake up," I said. "I know it's hard, but hang in there."

"A few days is what the doctor told us," Howard Cox said, looking away. "If anything happens to Megan, I don't know what I'll do. I haven't treated her very well since she married that jerk Ricky Carter."

There was nothing I could say to that, so I didn't say anything. Howard Cox sat back down. His tiredness showed. I let him regroup.

"The best thing you can do right now is get some rest," I said. "Is there anything I can do?"

"You can find Ricky Carter and kill the son of a bitch," he said, recovering some energy.

"I intend to look for Ricky," I said. "And I can't blame you for wanting him dead. But right now, we have no evidence it was Ricky."

"That's what the police said," Howard Cox said. "Until Megan wakes up, we can't know for sure. But I know it was Ricky." He put his head in his hands and stared at the tile floor of the courtyard as I sat and waited. Finally, he stood. "I have to get back up to Megan's room. Consider yourself on retainer. Any expenses you incur tracking down Ricky, bill to me."

I handed him my card.

"Call me if anything develops with Megan," I said. "If Ricky's around, I'll find him."

Howard Cox nodded, pocketed my card, turned, and walked out of the courtyard in the direction of the elevators.

Heading for the parking lot, I thought how I had seen far too much of hospitals and cemeteries the last few years. Maybe they just went with the territory.

◆   ◆   ◆   ◆

If Ricky was still in the area, I didn't think he'd be hard to find. The obvious place to start was the Bloody Duck. I was brave enough to go alone but not foolish enough. It could turn dangerous. And in a dangerous situation, even cops asked for backup. My theory: If you have it, you won't need it.

Since Roy was out of circulation, I decided to press the newlywed into service. I had intentionally left Billy alone, and I think he was getting a little annoyed by it.

"I need some backup this afternoon if you're available, Chief," I said when he answered his cell phone.

"About time, Blood," Billy said. "Tell me about it."

I told him.

"What time do you want me at the office?" Billy asked.

"Around five," I said.

"See you then," Billy said.

33

We went through the front door of the Bloody Duck at five-thirty. The place was hopping. Most of the crowd was at the bar and around the pool tables. Rocky saw us and did a head nod toward the back booth where Roy and I had sat. I nodded back to him.

We sat and waited. In a few minutes, Rocky was at our table.

"Hey, Billy," Rocky said. "Long time, no see."

I didn't expect that. I hoped the surprise didn't show on my face. I was always finding out things about Billy that surprised me. He wasn't one to share what he felt was trivial information.

"It has been awhile," Billy said.

"Haven't seen Roy either," Rocky said. "I'd say it's been at least two weeks."

Then I got another surprise.

"Roy is out of town," Billy said. "He may not be back for a while."

So Billy knew Roy was gone. I wondered if he knew the reason. I wasn't about to ask.

"What can I get you?" Rocky asked, looking at me.

"Fat Tire," I said.

Fat Tire was a Colorado brew I had been introduced to during a long-ago ski trip. I noticed it on one of the draft taps as I walked past the bar. Observation is all.

"The usual?" Rocky asked, looking at Billy.

Billy nodded.

I was curious to see what "the usual" was, since Billy didn't drink alcohol.

A few minutes later, Rocky returned with my Fat Tire and a large club soda with lime.

"Got a minute?" I asked Rocky.

He slid in beside Billy.

"I didn't think this was a social call," he said.

"Seen Ricky Carter around?"

"Not in a very long while," Rocky said.

"How about Butch Pulaski?"

"Butch? Sure, Butch is in here two or three times a week."

"Think he'll be in tonight?" I said.

"I don't know," Rocky said.

"Can you get in touch with him?"

Rocky stared at me with the look of a man who didn't want to answer any more questions.

"What's this about?" he growled.

I looked at Billy.

He nodded.

I told Rocky about Megan.

"I'm pretty sure Ricky did it," I said. "I just can't prove it right now."

"The little cocksucker," Rocky said. "If he shows up in my place again, I'll kick the shit out of him."

"Call Butch for us," Billy said. "Tell him we have some money for him if he can help us."

Rocky slid from the booth and headed back to the bar. I took a long drink of Fat Tire and did some people-watching.

A few minutes later, Rocky was back.

"He's on his way," Rocky said.

◆　　◆　　◆　　◆

Butch Pulaski sat beside Billy looking about the same as the time I met him. He didn't appear any more prosperous. We exchanged some small talk as we waited for the beer I had ordered for him.

"So what's this about?" Butch asked, taking a long first drink from his draft.

"Ricky Carter," I said.

"What'd he do now?" Butch asked.

"Have you seen him?"

"No," Butch said. "Not since before the last time I saw you."

"We think he beat up his wife," I said. "She in a coma, so we're not sure."

"Beat up Megan? What an asshole."

I took a hundred-dollar bill out of my pocket and slid it across the table to Butch.

"Think about where he might be if he's hiding out," I said.

Butch stared at the hundred and slid it back across.

"If that son of a bitch beat up Megan, I'll help any way I can," he said. "You don't have to pay me."

My regard for Butch Pulaski rose a notch or two.

"Fair enough," I said. "Any thoughts?"

Butch paused for a few seconds.

"Two," he said. "Ricky's parents have a fairly good-sized farm down in Byrd County. It wasn't much the last time I saw it—house, broken-down barn, chicken coop. I was there once a long time ago. He might be there."

He finished his beer. I signaled Rocky for another. Butch was enjoying his newfound importance.

"You said two," I said.

"The first place I'd look would be Lola's trailer," Butch said. "She a no-good little tramp Ricky was banging even after he married Megan. I think he planned to take Megan's money and run off with Lola, but it didn't work out when Megan's old man cut her off. Lola lives at that trailer park north of town."

"I know it," Billy said.

"Do you know Lola, too?" I asked.

"Well, let me think a minute," Billy said, smiling.

"Do you know her address?" I asked Butch.

"No," he said. "But I can show you."

"Finish your beer," I said. "Then we'll take a little drive."

♦   ♦   ♦   ♦

As trailer parks go, this one was nice—more like a middle-class subdivision with trailers. The grounds were well kept, the streets were paved, and the trailers had adequate space between them. Darkness had descended on Mountain Center, and the trailer park's street lamps had activated.

We went through the entrance and past a sign that read, "Residents and guests only."

"Go straight," Butch Pulaski said from the front seat of my Pathfinder.

I went straight.

"Turn right at the next stop sign," he said.

I turned onto a paved road that amounted to no more than a glorified driveway. The signpost indicated that it was B Street.

"Keep going," Butch said. "It's down toward the end of this street."

Butch pointed out a white trailer with dark shutters. A red Ford F-150 pickup was in the gravel parking space at the left side of the trailer.

"I knew it," Butch said. "That's Ricky's truck."

I parked behind the F-150, reached into my center console, and removed a recent addition to my gun collection—a Ruger SP101 five-shot revolver in a sleek little black holster. Butch Pulaski's eyes widened.

"Better safe than sorry," I said, slipping the Ruger inside my belt at the small of my back.

We got out of the Pathfinder. I followed Butch to the trailer's front door. Butch seemed to be a man on a mission. He knocked loudly. A few seconds later, the door opened. A decent-looking little redhead stood there with a puzzled look.

"Hey, Butch," she said with little enthusiasm, her eyes darting from Billy to me.

"We want to see Ricky," Butch said, taking charge.

"Ricky's not around," Lola said.

"What's his truck doing here?" Butch shot back.

"He gave it to me when he left town," Lola said.

I thought I heard a noise inside the trailer. Butch must have heard it, too.

"Who's in there?" he demanded.

Then I heard a door shut. I turned to Billy.

"Back door."

Billy took off around the trailer. Butch shoved his way past Lola and went in, screaming for Ricky. I hesitated about whom to follow. Then I heard gunshots. I sprinted around the trailer after Billy just in time to see him go down at the far end. A wave of fear rushed over me. I reached him as he rolled over. Then Billy got to his feet, his back against the side of the trailer.

"You okay, Chief?" I asked, a little out of breath.

"I'm fine, Blood," Billy said. "Just getting out of the line of fire. Ricky fired a couple of shots at me and took off. I was too busy ducking for cover to see which way he went. He looked like a wild man."

I drew the Ruger and went low around the edge of the trailer, letting my gun lead the way. I saw no sign of Ricky. He must have climbed over the fence to the next road and disappeared in the darkness.

"I'm going to take a look around," Billy said.

He went over the fence as silently as a summer breeze. I holstered the Ruger and walked back around the trailer and past the pickup. A small crowd had gathered. I heard Butch inside the trailer having a heated discussion with Lola.

"Show's over," I said to the group. "Go about your business."

Nobody moved. Then I saw why. Coming down the drive toward us was a sheriff's cruiser, lights flashing. The cruiser stopped in the street in front of Lola's trailer, and a deputy got out. I recognized him from the lake. He walked over to where I stood.

"Don Youngblood, isn't it?" he said.

"Wes Lane, right?"

"Right," Wes said. "I had a report of gunfire. What's going on here?"

"You got here fast," I said.

"I was already here checking on a domestic," he said.

I walked away from the people mingling about and leaned against the back fender of the F-150. Wes Lane followed. I folded my arms and gave him the full story of the assault on Megan and our search for Ricky.

"Well, he can't get far on foot," Wes said. "Let me call it in. We'll be on the lookout for him. If we find him, we'll pick him up and call the Mountain Center police."

"Thanks," I said.

"Okay, folks," Wes Lane said loudly. "There's nothing to see here. Please disperse."

The crowd broke up and went in various directions as Butch Pulaski joined me at the pickup.

"Ricky's been here about a week," he said. "Lola said he's been high most of the time. She didn't know about Megan. She's pissed about that. He really did give her the pickup truck. So he may have a car parked somewhere, in case somebody came looking for him."

"Good work," I said.

Butch smiled. I had the feeling he didn't get many compliments.

Billy emerged from the shadows.

"No sign of him," Billy said. "He had a lot of options."

"Let's saddle up," I said.

We drove back to the Bloody Duck in silence. I slowly pulled into the parking lot and kept the motor running. Before Butch could open the door, I took the hundred-dollar bill and stuffed it in his shirt pocket. He started to protest.

"For your time," I said. "You were a big help."

Butch thought about it for a few seconds, then nodded.

"Thanks, man," he said. "I can sure use it."

I watched as he got out of the Pathfinder and headed into the bar, a guy who probably never had a break from the time he was born but was doing the best he could. I respected people like Butch. Although he was never going to have a lot of material wealth, he had found life's pleasures just the same—like a bar where people knew him, a beer with a friend, and a game of pool.

34

On Tuesday, I sat on T. Elbert's front porch for our ritual featuring coffee and bagels. The chill of the morning would soon be replaced by the warmth of an early-June day—not summer, but getting close.

"Not like you to be here on a Tuesday," T. Elbert said.

"This detective thing is interfering with my social life," I said. "Forget every Wednesday. From now on, I'll be here when I can be here."

"That's fine," T. Elbert said. "It's not like I'm going anywhere."

We ate, drank, and enjoyed the sounds of the new day.

"Heard from Roy?" T. Elbert asked.

"No," I said. "Any day now, I expect."

"Is no news good news?"

"No new is no news," I said. "Sister Sarah Agnes told me not to expect to hear anything for at least two weeks. Roy will call when he's ready."

"Any more dead girls turn up?"

"Yes," I said.

"What?" T. Elbert said. "You're just now telling me?"

"I've been busy," I snapped. "Besides, I found out only a few days ago. I have some things I don't want to put in an email."

"Tell me about it," T. Elbert said, softening a bit.

I told him what Scott had told me.

"There's going to be another one," T. Elbert said.

"That's exactly what I told Scott," I said.

◆　◆　◆　◆

On my way to the office, I called the Mountain Center Police Department. I used Big Bob's private number.

"Meet me at the office for a cup of coffee," I said to the big man.

"What's this about?" he asked.

161

"Ricky Carter," I said.

"On my way."

I flipped my cell phone closed as I reached the parking lot. I went up the back stairs and headed to the front door of my office. I had the key in the lock when I heard the *ding* of the elevator. I turned to see Big Bob Wilson emerging. The sound his boots made on the marble floor echoed in the hall. I left the door open, turned on the light, and headed to the coffee machine.

Five minutes later, we were settled in with fresh coffee.

"Two days in a row," Big Bob said after taking a long drink. "I could get spoiled. Now, tell me about Ricky Carter."

"He has a gun," I said.

"How the hell do you know that?" the big man asked in a rather loud voice.

"He took a couple of shots at Billy last night," I said.

"I assume Billy's okay," the big man said.

"He is," I said.

"Tell me the rest of it."

I did.

"Butch Pulaski told me that Ricky's parents have a farm somewhere in Byrd County," I said.

Big Bob nodded.

"I'll call the sheriff down there and get him to check it out," he said. "Why don't you stay out of it and see if law enforcement can handle it without your help?"

I was used to the big man's sarcasm. And he was right. I should stay out of it. Whether I would or not was another story.

"My pleasure," I said.

"Huh," was all he said as he finished his coffee and stood to leave.

"Let me know if they find anything down in Byrd County," I said.

"Thanks for the coffee," the big man said with a hard stare. He left without another word.

．　◆　◆　◆

Sometimes when I'm right, I wish like heck I weren't.

Scott Glass called an hour after I left T. Elbert's.

"Don, it's Scott," he said.

I knew without asking, but I asked anyway.

"Bad news, Professor?"

"Another dead girl just turned up in Great Basin National Park in Nevada, hanging naked from a tree. She's young and looks to be of Latin descent."

"Any ID?"

"No."

"How about her clothes?"

"Laid out neatly on a nearby picnic table," Scott said.

"Tattoo?"

"On the sole of her foot," he said. "A smaller version of the one on the girl at Utah Lake."

"Any leads?" I asked.

"Maybe," Scott said, surprising me.

"Maybe?" I said.

"A camper who was out stargazing before sunrise was passed by a late-model SUV or a truck with a camper. He couldn't be sure which. He thinks he remembers part of the license plate number."

"Why would he bother?" I asked.

"That's what I wanted to know," Scott said. "He said the SUV was going very fast, and he thought that was suspicious. So he tried to remember the plate number as it passed, but it was going too fast to get all of it."

"How did you find this guy?"

"We set up a roadblock and questioned campers as they came out of the park," Scott said. "We'll keep the road blocked for a few days and talk to everyone we can."

"Did he get the state the tag was from?" I asked.

"No," Scott said. "He told our agents he was concentrating so hard on the letters and numbers that he missed that. It's probably Nevada or a neighboring state—Utah, maybe. We'll develop a list and start tracking them down."

"That'll take some time," I said.

"It will," Scott said. "But at least it's something. Anything on your end?"

"No," I said. "And I'm involved in another case."

"Well, if you think of anything, let me know," Scott said. "Other than this license plate long shot, we're at a dead end."

After we hung up, I looked up Great Basin National Park. It was in the middle of nowhere in eastern Nevada near the Utah border. The closest major city was either Las Vegas or Salt Lake City. Las Vegas—now, that was scary. I had thought enough about Las Vegas in the past year to last a lifetime.

I put my feet up on my desk and leaned back in my chair and gave this whole mess some serious thought. *Think outside the box*, I told myself.

An hour later, I had a wild idea.

35

When I called and told him I wanted to come talk, he simply said, "I'll be here."

Talking to him over the phone would have been easier but I had to convince him of the urgency and get him to buy into the project. So I piled into the Pathfinder and drove for two hours.

I sat in front of his desk with my meager file on the three devils. Like the last time I saw him, his attire was meticulous—starched, open-collar white shirt, dark slacks with a crease so sharp it could slice cold turkey, and black loafers with a high-gloss shine he could see his reflection in. His black hair was well groomed and closely cropped. His dark eyes peered out through wire-rim glasses that looked new. Like last time, we drank very good coffee.

I reached into my briefcase, removed the brown paper bag, and slid it across his desk. He opened it and removed the twenty-pack of Clark's Teaberry gum. The smile on Amos Smith's face was worth the effort.

"Haven't had this in a while," Teaberry said. "Thanks for the thought."

"My pleasure," I said. I took a drink of coffee. "Did you ever do any tattoos when you were inside?" I asked casually.

Amos Smith raised his eyebrows.

"What makes you think I did?" he asked.

"You're an artist," I said. "Makes sense that you might have earned some favors doing tats."

"Very good, detective," Teaberry said. "I did do tattoos. Good ones, if I do say so myself. What of it?"

I showed him the pictures of the tattoos on Betty Lou Walker's back and Maria Cruz's foot, along with those on the other two early victims.

"Ever seen anything like these?" I asked. "Notice what happens when you overlay them."

"They match up perfectly," he said. He studied the pictures. "I can't recall ever seeing anything like these tats. And they aren't tattoos, they're transfers. The colors are too bright for tats. What's this about?"

"What I'm about to tell you has to stay between us," I said. "If it doesn't, you'll have the FBI up your ass and I'll have a couple of special agents really pissed off at me."

"Keeping secrets is part of my trade," Teaberry said. "And the farther away I can stay from the FBI, the better."

I told him about the murders and the tattoos of the three devils, omitting details he didn't need to know. He listened thoughtfully.

"So you think you're dealing with three killers," he said.

"Looks that way," I said.

"And this one with the devil behind the fire could be the leader."

"You catch on fast," I said.

"Serial killers, Three Musketeers–style," Teaberry said. "That's really screwed up. How can I help with this?"

"The FBI has had no luck tracking down these tattoos," I said.

"I don't doubt it," Amos Smith said. "Tattoo art is a worldwide sub-culture that wouldn't welcome the FBI. They would get nowhere."

"How far could you get?" I asked.

"Don't know," Teaberry said. "But a damn sight farther than the FBI."

"Will you give it a try?"

"Is this a paid gig?" he asked.

"It is," I said. "Keep track of your time and bill me when you're finished."

Amos Smith paused and rubbed his chin.

"Okay," he said. "Might be fun to see how far I can get. It'll probably take some time. I'll call you if I find anything."

◆   ◆   ◆   ◆

That night, Mary cooked a dish I had never eaten—country-style pork backbones with a secret barbecue sauce, a recipe handed down from her grandmother. Accompanying the backbones was a French-fry casserole, recipe compliments of Mountain Center Diner owner Doris Black. I made a Caesar salad.

"This is really good," I said.

"There's a secret ingredient in the sauce," Mary said.

"What is it?"

"It's a secret," Mary and Lacy said in unison, laughing as they exchanged looks.

Four of us were at the dining-room table. Lacy had asked Jonah, the boyfriend, to dinner. I guessed the womenfolk thought that would be the least awkward way for us to get to know each other. Despite my best efforts, I liked the kid. He was polite and friendly and didn't seem the least bit intimidated by the big, bad private investigator. He showed a lot of poise for a junior in high school. Maybe I should have shown him my guns.

The conversation eventually got around to basketball.

"I hear you were a pretty good player in high school," Jonah said.

And pretty good after, I thought, *just not good enough to play for the college of my choice.* But I kept that to myself and took the humble route.

"I was okay," I said.

"You averaged double figures in scoring three years in a row," Jonah said.

The kid had done his homework.

"True," I said. "But I never led the team in scoring."

"I know," Jonah said. "Big Bob Wilson did. You guys won the state title twice."

"That was a long time ago," I said.

Lacy and Mary were cleaning up but within earshot. I sensed a conspiracy.

"I hear you're a pretty good player in your own right," I said.

"I can shoot okay," Jonah said without sounding cocky. "But my dribble drive needs work."

Lacy interrupted us, putting her hand on Jonah's shoulder.

"Enough basketball," she said. "Let's go downstairs and watch TV."

"Sure," he said.

Lacy led the way as they disappeared down the stairs to the den. Mary came back to the table with a bottle of Amber Bock and a glass of white wine. She handed me the beer and sat.

"So, what do you think?" she asked.

"About what?" I replied, playing dumb.

"Jonah," Mary said, acting annoyed.

"Seems like a nice kid," I said reluctantly.

"You're so funny," Mary said. "Relax. We'll probably meet a long string of boys before it's over."

"I'm new at playing Dad," I said.

"You're doing fine."

"Let me know when I get off track," I said. "You're the one with the experience."

"You'll figure it out," she said.

I took a drink from my longneck.

"I have news," Mary said, smiling.

"Tell me," I said, though I had a good idea what the news was.

"I'm taking the detective job," she said. "I start next Monday. I'll train with John until he leaves."

"Good for you," I said. "Congratulations."

I raised my bottle to toast the good news, and Mary touched it with her wineglass. As our eyes met, I confirmed what I already knew—that I wanted to spend the rest of my life with this woman. I understood with new clarity that I had spent my whole life finding her.

"You okay?" Mary asked, sensing that something had just taken place.

"I'm way beyond okay," I said. "Way beyond."

36

When I came off the elevator the next morning, I noticed my office door was ajar. Light from the outer office spilled through a one-inch crack into the dim hallway, making a streak on the gray marble floor. My latest toy, the Ruger revolver, was resting in the small of my back, thanks to the fact that Ricky Carter was on the loose, having shot at one of the owners of Cherokee Investigations. I slipped the Ruger from its resting place and proceeded with caution. I approached the door from the left and peeked in through the crack. I saw Dunkin' Donuts coffee on the conference table and hands turning pages of the *Wall Street Journal*. I couldn't see the face or the body, but I knew who it was. I put the Ruger away and went in.

Roy gave me a wry smile.

"You're late," he said.

"Or you're early."

"Just got here," Roy said.

We shook hands.

"Welcome back," I said.

"Thanks," he said. "The coffee's still hot."

He nodded to an unopened cup sitting next to a Dunkin' Donuts bag. I sat, took the lid off, and enjoyed that magical first swallow.

"You back to stay or just visiting?" I asked.

"To stay," Roy said.

"Everything go okay?" I asked, figuring that it had or he wouldn't be here. I was trying to get information without appearing too curious.

"Everything went better than I expected it to," Roy said. "Sister Sarah Agnes is really good at what she does."

I was afraid to ask what that meant, so I let it pass.

"That's good," was all I said.

"We'll talk about it sometime," Roy said.

"No hurry," I said.

"So, tell me what's been going on since I left," he said.

"Could take awhile," I said.

"I've got the day off," Roy said. "The new guy is driving Mr. Fleet today. I think I'm going to like having him around."

I removed a poppy seed bagel with cream cheese from the bag and took a bite. I began by telling him about the interview with Missy Stone.

"If I were you," I said, "I would check her out. You could do a follow-up interview for Cherokee Investigations."

"She that hot?"

"Extremely."

"I may have to go book hunting," Roy said.

I moved on to my interview with Lawrence at Hard Bodies and then told him about the body in the Great Smoky Mountains National Park. I told him about Agent David Steele and the other dead girls. I continued with my hunt for Ricky Carter and Billy's getting shot at. I finished with my meeting with Amos Smith.

"Jesus," Roy muttered. "Sounds like a thriller movie."

"Except that it's real and people are dying," I said.

"Talking to Amos Smith was a pretty good idea," Roy said.

"We're all desperate," I said. "If you come up with anything, I'll listen."

"Sounds like you're doing all you can," Roy said.

We were quiet for a while. I knew Roy was processing everything I'd told him. He was like Billy. He did a lot of thinking before he expressed an idea.

"Seeing that dead girl hanging nude like that," Roy said. "I think that would haunt me for a long time."

"It's haunting me," I said. "A little less each day, but that image is hard to shake. If someone doesn't catch whoever is doing this, I'll never get a good night's sleep."

We talked awhile longer about sports, politics, movies—things that were not life and death. Well, except for maybe Tennessee football. Roy got up to leave. I think it was the longest time he had ever spent in my office.

"Billy asked me to come for dinner," Roy said. "I'll probably spend the night over there. Anything you want me to tell him?"

"Not that I can think of," I said. "He knows pretty much everything. I know I don't have to say it, but I'll say it anyway. Keep all of this between the three of us."

Roy nodded.

"And one more thing," I said. "When Fleet can spare him, have Oscar Morales come by and see me. I may have a little job for him."

◆   ◆   ◆   ◆

After Roy left, I called Big Bob.

"Did you ever hear back from the Byrd County Sheriff's Department about Ricky Carter?" I asked when I finally got him on the phone.

"Yes and no," he said.

"What does that mean?"

"Yes, I heard back. And no, they didn't find Ricky," Big Bob said. "A couple of deputies went by and asked if Ricky was there, and Ricky's mother said she hadn't seen him in months. Ricky's father died a few years back. They didn't have a warrant, so they couldn't search the place. They've got their hands full with a meth lab takedown and can't devote a lot of time to Ricky Carter."

"Ricky's taking shots at Billy should be enough to get a warrant," I said. "And I'll bet Ricky doesn't have a permit to carry a gun."

"You got that right," Big Bob said. "I checked. The trouble is this. If Byrd County gets a warrant and searches the farm and Ricky's not there, then we've wasted their time and the judge's time. I'd rather not do that. We need to know for sure Ricky is there before they get that warrant."

"I think I can help with that," I said.

"What do you have in mind?"

"Someone needs to sit on the place for a few days and see if Ricky is there or shows up," I said.

"You can't sit still for more that half an hour," Big Bob said. "So I assume Billy is the someone in mind."

"If he's free," I said. "If not, I'll find someone else. Can you get directions to the farm?"

"Yeah, I'll have Susie call," Big Bob said. "She'll fax you later today."

"I'll get back to you if Ricky turns up," I said.

"You do that," the big man said.

I hung up wondering why I had ever thought being a private investigator was such a good idea.

◆　　◆　　◆　　◆

I called Cherokee. Billy had recently opened our satellite office there and claimed he was doing pretty well. I wondered if I would find him in.

"Cherokee Investigations," a sultry female voice answered.

"Maggie," I said, surprised. "Is that you?"

"Hi, Don," Maggie said. "Yes, it's me."

"Aren't you supposed to be in school?"

"School got out last week," Maggie said. "I'm taking the summer off. I occasionally help Billy in the office. Believe me, he needs help."

"Is he around?" I asked.

"Yes, but he's with a client," Maggie said. "Can I have him call you back?"

"Yes, please," I said.

Billy with a client, I felt strange about that. Things were going on I didn't know about. *Well, Youngblood, you can't control everything,* I thought.

◆　　◆　　◆　　◆

Half an hour later, I was checking the market and not finding anything interesting. It was a flat day on the Street. The phone rang.

"Cherokee Investigations," I answered, hoping it was Billy.

"What's going on Blood?" Billy asked.

"How did you block caller ID?" I asked.

"Maggie did it," Billy said. "She thought there could be times a person might not answer if they saw Cherokee Investigations on their caller ID."

"She's probably right," I said. "You might have to make her a partner."

"In case you haven't heard, she already is," Billy said. "Now, why did you call?"

"If you're free, I thought we might take a drive out to the farm where Ricky Carter's mother lives."

"What time?"

"After lunch," I said. "Meet me at the office."

"Okay," Billy said.

"By the way, I heard you were with a client," I said.

"I was," Billy said.

"So, don't tell me," I said with faked annoyance.

"The shoe is on the other foot," he laughed.

"Okay," I said. "I get it."

"Runaway," Billy said. "Father wants me to find her and bring her back."

"Are you going to do it?" I asked.

"Maybe," Billy said. "First, I'm going to try what my esteemed teacher Donald Youngblood would do."

"Which is?"

"I'm going to find out why she ran away," Billy said. "The father was a little vague on that."

"Sounds like a plan," I said.

I hung up wondering if my tendency to not leave well enough alone had rubbed off on Billy. *Needing to know all the truth isn't necessarily a good thing*, I thought.

37

"Turn right," Billy said.

He was giving me directions from the fax Susie had sent. He had shown up at my office at one o'clock excited that he might be able to dish out a little payback for the shots Ricky took at him.

"This is it," Billy said a few minutes later. "Take a right on the next gravel road."

I turned right on a well-maintained gravel road and headed up a slight incline. As soon as we reached the top of the slope and started down the other side, the farmhouse was visible. I expected a run-down shack. What I saw was a well-kept two-story white house. The porch extended around two sides, flowerpots adorning the top of the wide railing. Other plants hung from the porch ceiling. The yard was landscaped and well tended. The barn looked no more than a few years old. Ricky Carter's family, or at least his mother, was not poor. Either Butch Pulaski had been drunk when he was here or the place had undergone major upgrades. I parked beside a white Ford Explorer.

Billy and I got out and walked up the steps to the front door. I pushed the doorbell and heard an old-fashioned ringing inside the house. It reminded me of my grandmother's doorbell. Whenever we visited her, I'd ring the bell just to hear the sound. She always told me I didn't have to ring it, since she could hear me coming a mile away. So, naturally, I rang it anyway.

I rang the bell again. Seconds later, the door opened. A full-figured, well-groomed woman wearing an apron smiled at us through the screen door. She was not unattractive.

"Sorry," she said. "I was in the back. Can I help you?"

"I'm Don Youngblood, and this is Billy Two-Feathers," I said. "We're looking for Ricky."

The smile evaporated.

"Why are you looking for Ricky?" she asked.

"We just want to talk to him," I said.

"Why?"

"Ricky's wife was badly beaten and is in the hospital," I said. "We're investigating the assault and want to talk to Ricky about it."

Her hand went to her mouth. Either she didn't know Megan had been assaulted or she was a fine actress.

"Megan was beaten?" she said. "Is she going to be okay?"

"She's in a coma," I said.

"Ricky wouldn't do that," she said.

The tone of her voice and the look on her face weren't very convincing. She glanced away, as if trying to decide if Ricky really could do such a thing.

"Have you seen him?" Billy asked.

"I already told that deputy Ricky isn't here," she said firmly.

The deputy had obviously not mentioned the assault.

"If Ricky shows up, it would be best for him if you called me," I said.

I removed a business card from my shirt pocket and held it up for her to see. She unlatched the screen door, and I handed her the card. She took it and then closed and re-latched the door. She studied the card.

"Nice place you have here, Mrs. Carter," I said, trying to lighten the mood. "How many acres?"

"One hundred and fifty," she said, still looking at my card.

"How long have you lived here?" I asked.

She looked up.

"Mr. Youngblood," she said tersely. "I don't want to be rude, but I don't have time for any more chit-chat. I think you should leave now. Good day, gentlemen."

The front door closed, and I heard a lock turn.

Billy and I went back down the stairs, got into the Pathfinder, and drove out to the main road.

"What do you think?" I asked Billy.

"Ricky isn't there," he said.

"Think he's been there?"

"I doubt it," Billy said.

"One hundred and fifty acres is a lot of land," I said. "Ricky could be hiding out."

"Could be," Billy said.

"Nice barn," I said.

"Looked like it could have some living quarters," Billy said.

We drove in silence as I replayed the conversation with Mrs. Carter and remembered everything I'd seen.

"Think she knew Megan is in the hospital?" I asked.

"No," Billy said.

"Did you notice how she kept one hand in her apron?"

"I did," Billy said.

"Think she would have shot us if we tried to search the place?" I asked.

"I do," Billy said. "That's a strong-willed woman."

"Think Ricky will show up?"

"God help him if he does," Billy said. "He might get more than he bargained for."

◆   ◆   ◆   ◆

I drove back to the office.

"Coming up?" I asked as we got out of the Pathfinder.

"No," Billy said. "I need to get back. A lot is going on."

"Okay," I said. "I'll see you later. Let me know how that runaway daughter thing turns out."

"I'll do that," he said. "Say hello to Mary and Lacy for me."

"Will do," I said as he got into his Grand Cherokee.

I turned and went through the back entrance and up the stairs to my office. When I came off the elevator, I saw Oscar Morales leaning against the wall next to my door.

"Oscar," I said, surprised. "Have you been waiting long?"

"Just got here," he said. "Roy said I should come by. I thought I would wait awhile and see if you showed up."

"Come on in," I said, unlocking the door.

Oscar followed me through the outer office. I went around my desk and sat. Oscar stood just inside the doorway.

"Sit," I said, motioning to the nearest chair.

Oscar sat.

"I need you to do a little job for me," I said. "You'll make a couple of hundred bucks a day, three days tops."

"On one condition," Oscar said.

"Name it," I said.

"I do this as a favor," Oscar said. "If another job comes up, then you can pay me."

"The money doesn't come out of my pocket," I said. "It's billable."

"Okay," Oscar said. "But I still owe you one."

I shrugged.

"I need you to stake out a house—actually a farm—and let me know if a certain someone shows up." I handed him a picture of Ricky and directions to the Carter property.

"Bad guy?" Oscar asked.

"Bad enough," I said. "Maybe really bad."

I gave Oscar my recently acquired Bushnell binoculars and a 35mm camera with a powerful telephoto lens.

"For your viewing pleasure," I said. "Get some pictures if you can. I want to be able to prove he's there."

Oscar put the binoculars to his eyes and looked out my window.

"Nice," he said.

"Good hunting," I said.

38

The following morning, I sat at my usual table in the back of the Mountain Center Diner. I had not been in for over a week, and Doris acted like I'd been gone for a year. I was subjected to her version of the third degree. When I finally convinced her that I wasn't patronizing any other establishment for breakfast, she finally settled down and brought me coffee. A few minutes later, she arrived with one of my Mountain Center Diner indulgences—biscuits and gravy with sausage patties. I needed a good reason to go to Moto's Gym.

Right after I finished my first biscuit, the buzz quieted and I knew the big man must have come in. I looked up. He was headed for my table.

Big Bob Wilson sat with a thud and tossed his cowboy hat on a chair close by. The hat was a gift from my recent ski trip out west. Before it had even settled on the chair, Doris placed a cup of black coffee in front of the big man.

"Want anything else, Big Bob?" she asked.

"No, thank you, Doris," he said.

Doris scurried away to tend to other customers, leaving us alone.

"Nice hat," I said. "Surprised to see you wearing it on duty."

"Sylvia said it makes me look like a real badass chief of police," he said.

"As if you weren't enough of a badass," I said.

He ignored my comment, stared at my biscuits and gravy, and shook his head.

"You're a lucky bastard to be able to eat that stuff and still not gain weight," he grumbled.

"Still trying to get back some of the pounds I lost from that Vegas deal last year," I said. "Did you come here to discuss my eating habits, or were you just passing by?"

"I was looking for you," Big Bob said. "You weren't at your office, so I figured you might be here. And if you'd carry your damn cell phone instead of leaving it in your SUV, I wouldn't have to track you down."

We had been through this before—every time he wanted to find me and couldn't, in fact. I smiled and continued eating my biscuits and gravy. I had a bite of sausage and washed it down with coffee. Big Bob sat patiently.

"Okay," I said. "You found me. What's up?"

"Megan's father called and said she woke up and told him it was Ricky who assaulted her."

"That's good," I said. "So what's the problem?"

"She supposedly slipped right back into a coma after she told him about Ricky."

"Imagine that," I said.

I took another drink of coffee. Big Bob did the same.

"Did you talk to her doctor?" I asked.

"I did," Big Bob said. "He says it's possible, but none of the staff can verify that Megan woke up."

"So what?" I said. "It's enough to drag Ricky's sorry ass off to jail, not to mention the weapons charge."

"I'd rather get him on assault, but it could be shaky in court," Big Bob said.

"I doubt it," I said. "With Ricky's history and Howard Cox as your key witness, I can hear the cell door slamming. Might even get him for attempted murder."

I finished my second biscuit and told him about visiting the Carter farm and about my stakeout.

"You really think he'll show up out there?" Big Bob asked.

"I do," I said. "The only reason for Ricky to come back here is that he's spent all his money and needs more. He had two possibilities—Megan and Mommy. Megan didn't work out too well. Sooner or later, he'll try Mommy."

Big Bob took one more drink of coffee, stood, reached down to pick up his hat, and placed it squarely on his head.

"Total badass," I said.

He smiled in spite of himself.

"If you get Ricky," Big Bob said, "bring him here and not to the Byrd County sheriff."

"My pleasure," I said.

◆　　◆　　◆　　◆

Moto's Gym is one of my local hangouts, although I hadn't hung out a lot there lately. I had gone to the condo and picked up Jake. I was working out on a rowing machine while Jake worked out in back with Moto's Siberian husky, Karate. The machine's color screen showed that I was rowing a single scull against a phantom boat at a very high level. A boat length back with plenty of time to catch up, I was sweating profusely. We passed the twenty-minute mark. Unlike me, the phantom didn't seem to be tiring. At the twenty-five-minute mark, I made my move. At the twenty-seven-minute mark, I nosed my boat in front. It was nip and tuck with one minute to go. I gave it my all and crossed the finish line a half boat ahead. Loud cheering came from the screen, and fireworks went off. I was exhausted.

Moto appeared out of nowhere.

"You win again, huh?" he said. "Probably got it set on level one."

"Level fifteen, if it's any of your business," I said.

Moto was always egging everyone on. "Be the best you can be" and all that stuff.

"Machine goes to level twenty," he said. "Win at level twenty and I give you gold medal."

"Real gold?" I asked.

"Of course not," Moto said. "You think I am crazy?"

"Where are the dogs?" I asked.

"Tired now," Moto said. "Lying in shade out back."

I toweled off and went to work on my abs. Then I worked on my chest and arms. I finished with quad work and went to the side room to hit the speed bag. An hour and a half after entering Moto's, I shuffled out like an old man with Jake in tow, feeling every bit my age and then some.

39

"Those binoculars you gave me are very good," Oscar Morales said. "The camera also."

I was in the office having my second cup of coffee when Oscar called. I had told him to call me every morning and give me a report.

"I'm glad you like them," I said.

"I could see Mr. Ricky Carter very well," he said.

"Tell me more," I said, straightening up in my chair.

"Mr. Carter showed up a little while ago," Oscar said. "He knocked on the front door of the house, and when it opened he was not invited in. The lady came out on the porch and did not seem happy to see him. They argued. Then Mr. Carter got in his car and drove around back of the barn. He took a suitcase in a side door. As far as I can tell, he is still in the barn. I took some pictures."

"Stay put," I said. "I'll be there by noon. Call me if he leaves. If he does, follow him."

"Okay," Oscar said.

I called Billy.

"Ricky's at the farm," I said.

"I'm on my way," Billy said.

◆   ◆   ◆   ◆

We picked up Oscar at the entrance to the Carter farm and drove over the ridge and down toward the farmhouse. We were passing the house when Mrs. Carter came out on the porch, hands on hips. I sensed trouble. We were, after all, trespassing. If she called the law, we could get hung up. But then again, so could Ricky. I had no intention of letting him slip away again. I stopped close to the porch and rolled down the window on the Pathfinder.

"I'm here to get Ricky," I said with as much authority as I could muster.

"Good riddance to him," she said, surprising me. "He's in the barn."

As we drove toward the barn, Ricky came out the side door and disappeared around back. I expected any second to see his car speed from behind the barn and make a run for it. I didn't want to get involved in a car chase.

"Do not worry about the car," Oscar said, smiling. "It is not going anywhere."

Seconds later, Ricky burst from behind the barn and took off across an open field.

"Stop, now!" Billy ordered as he opened the passenger door.

In seconds, he was around the front of the Pathfinder in full pursuit. Oscar and I watched in fascination as Billy closed ground on his prey. I realized what it must be like for the antelope when it senses it has no escape from the cheetah. Billy reached Ricky and grabbed him by the back of his shirt collar and jerked him to a halt. Ricky flailed, trying to break loose. Billy spun him around, slapped him hard, pointed a finger close to his face, and said something I couldn't hear. All the fight in Ricky disappeared. Billy took him by the arm and led him back to the Pathfinder.

Once Ricky was safely inside, we drove back past the farmhouse. I saw no sign of Mrs. Carter.

◆   ◆   ◆   ◆

We dropped off Oscar to get his car.

"Come see me next time you're in town," I told him.

"I will," Oscar said. "I would not mind doing these little jobs from time to time. Call me if you need me."

We drove Ricky to the Mountain Center jail. He protested most of the way that he hadn't done anything. Billy finally got tired of his yapping and told him firmly to shut up. Ricky was silent the rest of the way. I called Big Bob on the way into town. He met us in the parking lot with two uniformed officers. The uniforms relieved us of Ricky.

"Nice work," Big Bob said.

"Billy did the heavy lifting," I said.

"Good to see you, Chief," Big Bob said. "How is married life?"

"Married life is very good," Billy said, smiling.

"Wait until you have teenagers," Big Bob growled.

We drove back to the Hamilton Building parking lot to get Billy's SUV. I pulled into my parking space, and we got out of the Pathfinder.

"Want to come up for a cup of coffee?"

"I have to get back to Cherokee, Blood," Billy said.

"Okay, Chief," I said. "Anything new with your runaway?"

"I think I know where she is," Billy said. "If I'm right, she never left Cherokee."

Billy got in his Grand Cherokee and started the engine. I motioned for him to roll down his window.

"By the way," I said, "what did you say to Ricky to take all the fight out of him?"

"I told him if he didn't settle down that I would snap his neck like a dead tree limb," Billy said.

"That would do it," I said.

◆   ◆   ◆   ◆

Friday night, Mary, Lacy, Jake, and I went to the lake house. Lacy had asked Hannah to join us. I was glad to see the weekend come. I relaxed a little knowing Ricky Carter was in jail. But the gnawing feeling in the pit of my stomach reminded me that the three devils were still out there somewhere, ready to kill again. If only the FBI could run down that license tag.

Our whole group, including Jake, spent most of Saturday and Sunday on the barge puttering around the lake, occasionally fishing or swimming. Jake loved to swim. He would dive off the barge the minute one of us went in the water, giving no thought as to how he was going to get back on board. We took turns pulling him out of the water and then running to the opposite end of the barge while he shook water in all directions.

The weather could not have been better—low eighties, low humidity, lots of sunshine, and no wind. For a little while, I forgot the evil that dwells among us. In the last few years, I had seen more evil than I bargained for. And I knew I had not seen the last of it.

40

Monday morning, I felt refreshed. A perfect weekend could do that. I went online to check one of my secured accounts but had trouble getting in. I double-checked the password, and that's when it hit me.

I called Scott.

"Any luck on the tag number?" I asked.

"None," he said.

"Mind if I talk to your witness?"

"Not much of a witness," Scott said. "But sure, be my guest. I'll give you his phone number."

"In person," I said. "I'll come out."

"You know something I don't, Blood?" Scott asked.

"Maybe, Professor," I said. "Can you fax me a transcript of your interview?"

"Sure," Scott said. "You'll have it in a few minutes, but you'll have to be officially consulting on the case."

"Then I guess I'm officially consulting on the case," I said.

"Fine," Scott said. "How soon will you be here?"

"As soon as I can," I said. "I'll call and let you know."

I hung up and called Roy.

"See if one of the jets is available," I said without preamble. "I need to go to Salt Lake City."

"Hang on," Roy said.

I heard voices on the other end but couldn't make out what was being said. Roy was back in less that a minute.

"The Lear is fueled and ready," he said. "Just say the word."

"As soon as possible," I said.

"Hold on," Roy said.

I heard more indecipherable conversation.

"Jim will be at the airport in one hour," Roy said. "As soon as he can file a flight plan, you'll be off the ground."

"I'll be there," I said. "Thanks."

"You flying into trouble?" Roy asked.

"No," I said. "This trip should be rather tame."

"Let me know if you need backup."

"Thanks, Roy," I said. "I will."

◆　　◆　　◆　　◆

I fled the office and hustled home as soon as Scott's fax arrived. I packed a small suitcase for a three-day stay, gave Jake a goodbye rub, and headed to the airport. On the way, I called Mary and explained what I was doing.

"It's a pretty good thought," she said. "Try not to get shot at or beaten up."

"You can count on it," I said. "I'll expect a proper homecoming when I get back."

"You can count on it," Mary said.

◆　　◆　　◆　　◆

I was in the air almost exactly two hours after calling Roy Husky. I settled in and read the fax from Scott, which included the witness's account of the partial plate number—two letters and two numbers, 7B-5O. On my laptop, I took the numbers and letters and shuffled them around in as many ways as possible. Then I made a few notes. I looked at what I had done and got another idea. What if a Z had been mistaken for a 7 or a 2, an 8 for a B, an S for a 5, or a D for an O or a 0? I replaced and shuffled over and over until I thought I had all the combinations. It was a considerable list. And if I added surrounding states, it would become even more sizable. The flight took over three hours and gave me plenty of time to be creative. I was absorbed in the work. Before I knew it, we were on the ground.

Scott met me in the private sector of the airport. He was driving a nondescript gray Taurus—not much of a disguise with the government tags, but at least it didn't have *FBI* emblazoned on the side.

"Nice wheels, Professor," I said.

"Sorry to disappoint you, Blood," Scott said, "but the Maserati is in the shop."

As we drove out of the airport, I spotted a long-term parking lot—just the place to test my theory.

"Pull over next to that lot," I said. "I want to check something out."

Scott stopped in a no-parking zone and turned on his flashers. I got out and walked into the lot to observe license plates. I saw mostly Utah plates but also some from Idaho, Wyoming, Nevada, and Colorado. In bad light, some numbers could be mistaken for letters or vice versa—especially on fast-moving vehicles, I suspected.

As I walked back to the Taurus, an airport security car pulled in behind Scott, lights flashing. The Taurus didn't budge. The security cop walked up to the driver's window as it slid down. Scott showed his credentials as I got back into the passenger seat.

"FBI," he said. "We're finished here."

"What's going on?" the security cop said, looking at Scott's ID.

"Routine investigation," Scott said. "You have a nice day."

We pulled away, leaving the security guard scratching his head with a dumb look on his face.

"What was that all about?" Scott asked.

"Testing a theory," I said.

◆   ◆   ◆   ◆

Seated in the interview room was Dwayne Jackson, the witness who had given the FBI a partial plate of the SUV he saw speeding away from Great Basin National Park. Dwayne was a slight man with sandy hair, a ponytail, and a scraggly beard. I watched him on a monitor.

"Where's that camera?" I asked Scott.

"In the air duct," Scott said.

"And the microphone?"

"Several are built into the table," he said.

"What if he passes gas? Got something to detect that?"

Scott laughed.

"We're working on it," he said.

I walked into the interview room and immediately extended my hand.

"Donald Youngblood," I said. "I appreciate your coming in."

We shook hands.

"Dwayne Jackson," he said, standing. "I'm glad to help. It's kind of exciting, you know."

"Please," I said. "Sit down."

We sat. He seemed eager to help.

"You're an FBI agent?" Dwayne said.

"I'm an FBI consultant," I said.

I slowly pulled from my computer backpack a folder containing my notes and the long list of potential plate numbers that Scott had printed for me from a CD I had given him earlier. I was methodical in all my movements, which Dwayne followed with a look of anticipation. I placed the folder in front of me and opened it. I removed the sheet containing the list of plate numbers and slid it across the table, turning the page around as it approached him.

"Pick out the partial plate number you gave the FBI," I said.

As he looked at the list, a confused look came over him.

"I don't understand," he said.

"The partial plate number you gave the FBI is on this list," I said. "See if you can pick it out."

He looked embarrassed and shook his head.

"I've forgotten what I told them," he said, flustered. "B7 something."

"Right," I said. "B7-O5."

"That's it," he said. "B7-O5."

"Are you sure?"

"Absolutely," Dwayne said.

"Actually," I said, "you told the FBI B7-5O."

"I did?" He looked genuinely confused.

"When you were in school, did you ever turn numbers or letters around?"

Dwayne hesitated, and I knew the answer.

"Sometimes," he said. "You think I might have turned some of the numbers or letters around on the license plate?"

"Maybe," I said. "Or the plate could have been altered somehow. The FBI hasn't had any luck running it down from the partial you think you saw."

I questioned Dwayne some more about the plate color, how fast the vehicle was moving, its size, what the taillights looked like, whether it had stickers or decals, and whether or not it had a trailer hitch. I didn't get anything significant. After an hour, I gave up and sent him home.

◆　　◆　　◆　　◆

I sat with Scott in his office. He had watched on the monitor as I questioned Dwayne.

"You're pretty good at interrogation," he said.

"It's easy when your subject wants to cooperate," I said.

"Still," Scott said, "I was impressed."

"You need to expand the search on this tag," I said.

Scott pushed the button on his intercom.

"Marcie," he said. "Tell John to come in here, please."

Less than a minute later, a short, stout man came through the door.

"John Banks," Scott said, "Don Youngblood."

We shook hands.

"I want you to work with Don on an expanded search for the tag on the tattoo case," Scott said to John.

"Glad to," John said.

I picked up my folder and turned to leave Scott's office.

"Ready when you are," John said.

"Let's get started," I said.

I walked with John to his office and took a chair across from his desk. I showed him my list and notes.

"I think your witness probably turned some numbers or letters around or mistook one for another," I said. "And maybe the vehicle is not an SUV but a truck with a camper, so you better include trucks."

"I see what you mean," John said. "You could be right."

"And if the killer is smart, he could have altered the tag number."

"This list is starting to look pretty long," he said. "It could take awhile, and the first pass could produce a hundred potentials or more."

"Start with the B7s and the BZs," I said. "I noticed when I was looking at Utah plates that the Z could be mistaken for a 7 at a quick glance."

41

Early the next morning, Scott met me at the Cottonwood Residence Inn, where I was staying. We drove into Big Cottonwood Canyon to the Silver Fork Lodge to have breakfast. The Silver Fork was near the Solitude Mountain Resort, where Mary, Lacy, and I had skied earlier in the year.

We entered through the bar. A red plate hanging on the wall proclaimed the Silver Fork Restaurant the best breakfast place of 2010. I couldn't disagree.

Afterward, we drove down into Salt Lake City to the FBI offices. John Banks was already at his computer.

"How are you doing, John?" Scott asked.

"Sixteen prospects so far," John said.

"Print them out for me, please," Scott said. "Four per page."

"Yes, sir," John said.

"And stop calling me sir," Scott growled. "You're making me feel old."

"You are old," John said.

"And you're still wet behind the ears," Scott said.

John smiled. He printed the list of names and addresses on four pages and handed them to Scott. I followed Scott to the interview room, where three other agents waited. Scott made quick introductions and got right down to business, handing each agent a sheet.

"You know the drill," Scott snapped. "Interview the owners of these vehicles and find out where the vehicles were the night in question."

They took a look at their lists and nodded.

"Get moving," Scott said. "Call me immediately if anything is promising."

Then he looked at me.

"Let's go," he said, one of the lists still in his hand. "You're with me. It'll give me a chance to see your magical powers of observation."

"Don't get your hopes up," I said.

Four names were on Scott's list. He did what I would have, starting with the farthest location and working our way back toward Salt Lake City.

Our first stop was Orem, Utah. The maroon SUV in question was owned by an old couple who told us they had been in church a week ago Sunday night. Scott wrote down the name of the minister and a few people who could verify their presence. Neither of us had the feeling their alibi wouldn't check out. We saw no signs of evasiveness or deceit. They looked us straight in the eye and answered all our questions, seeming genuinely surprised we were there. The tattoo case was too big not to check every possible lead, no matter how insignificant it seemed. But we both knew this one was a dead end.

The next stop was Sandy, Utah. The dark brown SUV was owned by a University of Utah student who told us he was studying in the campus library with a group of friends on the night in question. Scott took down the names of the friends. We saw no signs that he wasn't telling the truth. We had no doubt his alibi would check.

Our day was interrupted by a call from Scott's office. He had to be back for a one o'clock conference call with the powers that be in Washington regarding a human trafficking case, and he needed some time to prepare. Scott dropped me at the Cottonwood Residence Inn and promised to call the minute he was free. I went to my suite and worked on my laptop. I checked the market. It was still going south. I emailed T. Elbert. That would make him happy. I visited some sports websites and did a little web surfing until I got the call.

◆   ◆   ◆   ◆

Scott picked me up at four o'clock, and we drove to a middle-class neighborhood in West Salt Lake. Parked in the driveway of a modest one-story home was a black pickup with a camper on the back. A middle-aged man wearing a short-sleeve khaki shirt, blue jeans, and work boots was coming out the front door carrying a lunchbox as we pulled in.

"FBI," Scott said, pulling his ID as we approached.

"FBI?" the man said. The surprise on his face was real, and I saw no sign of fear. "What's this about?"

"Just a few questions about this truck," Scott said. "Are you the owner, Randall Smart?"

"Yes, I am," the man said. "Make it quick, please. I don't want to be late for work. What about my truck?"

As with the other persons of interest, Scott told Randall we wanted to talk to occupants of a vehicle that may have seen something helpful at a crime scene. I was impressed by his professionalism, the non-threatening way he conducted the interview and his cover story.

Like Dwayne Jackson, Randall Smart seemed eager to help. It wasn't every day he got to talk to an FBI agent. It was a story an innocent man would relish telling his friends. Randall said he and a buddy had been in Idaho on a fishing trip the weekend in question. He gave us his buddy's name for verification and showed us gas receipts he still had in his wallet. I saw no reason he would be a genuine suspect.

As we pulled out of the driveway, Scott said, "Dead end. He's not our guy."

"I agree," I said.

Scott drove back toward I-15.

"It's getting toward dinnertime," I said. "Are we going to try to interview the last person on the list?"

"Why not?" Scott said. "Then I'll buy you dinner."

Unfortunately, dinner did not come to pass.

◆　　◆　　◆　　◆

Our last stop was a well-cared-for upper-middle-class house in a section of Salt Lake City known as Cottonwood Hills. A few cars were in front. We pulled in the driveway and parked the Taurus behind a black Cadillac Escalade. The Utah license plate was RBZ-508. I remembered Dwayne Jackson's recollection of the vehicle when I had pushed him on it. "It was big, and I think it was black," he said. "That's all I can remember." I had a bad feeling about this one as I followed Scott up the walk to the front door.

Scott rang the doorbell. A few seconds later, an attractive brunette I guessed to be in her mid-forties opened the door.

"Yes?" she said, a questioning look on her face.

Scott showed her his ID.

"FBI," Scott said. "Are your Darlene Asher?"

"Yes, I am," the woman said. "Is something wrong?"

"Just routine," Scott said. He repeated the spiel he had given the other persons of interest.

"Please come inside," Mrs. Asher said. "I'll be just a minute." She walked down the hall to an open doorway and stopped. "I'll be right back, girls," she said, looking into the room. "I have to talk to the FBI."

I heard mumbled conversation coming from the room as Darlene Asher headed back down the hall toward us.

"My afternoon bridge group," she said, smiling. "This will give them something to talk about for weeks."

"A week ago Sunday night," Scott said. "Where was your SUV at that time?"

"Well, let me see," Darlene Asher said. "A week ago Sunday . . ." She was silent for a few seconds, deep in thought. "Oh, yes," she said. "Jason had the car. He spent the night with a friend."

"Is Jason here?" Scott asked.

"Yes, he's upstairs," she said. "Has he done something wrong?"

I could sense that Darlene Asher was about to go on the defensive to protect her son. Evidently, Scott sensed the same thing.

"I'm sure he hasn't," Scott said casually. "Like I said before, this is routine. We just want to know if he was at a particular place where he might have seen something that would help us with our investigation."

She seemed to relax a bit.

"Jason!" she shouted.

No answer. I thought I heard the faint sound of music, a bass thump.

"Jason!" she called again.

Her voice almost hurt my ears.

"Teenagers," she said. "I can't stand some of their music."

I heard the music go silent and a door open. A tall, lanky kid appeared at the head of the stairs. Total geek—that was my first impression.

"What?" he said in an annoyed tone.

"These FBI people want to ask you a few questions," Darlene Asher said.

All the color drained from the boy's face. In a flash, he was gone. I heard the door slam. Scott started up the stairs, and I followed. Then I heard a gunshot—from a nine-millimeter, if I wasn't mistaken. Darlene Asher screamed Jason's name. Scott drew his Glock as he approached the door and tried the knob. Locked. He took a couple steps back and lunged at the door, which proved no match for a six-foot-five, 220-pound FBI agent. The frame splintered, and the door burst opened. Scott stumbled into the room, leading with his Glock.

"Shit," he said.

Over his shoulder, I saw Jason Asher on the floor, legs spread, back against the wall, eyes staring at something he would never see. Blood and brain matter clung to and dripped from the poster-covered wall behind him. My mind spun, trying to process what I was seeing. Behind me, Darlene Asher kept screaming Jason's name.

Scott turned and gave me a hard, cold look.

"Get her out of here," he said.

I knew then that the fading nightmares of my past had been replaced by a more horrific dream, one I might never purge from my memory.

42

Soon after I managed to get out of bed the next morning, I sat at the desk in my room at the Cottonwood Residence Inn with a cup of coffee wishing the previous night had been a bad dream. I had slipped away around midnight. The Asher house had turned into a three-ring circus with Scott as the ringmaster. Crime-scene techs, local police, curious neighbors, and close friends cluttered the front yard. I thanked God for the women of the bridge group, who calmed Darlene Asher enough to escort her to a neighboring house and out of the line of fire. Scott was superb bringing order to the chaos. He barked orders like a drill sergeant. He deftly handled the media, which wasted no time in finding a juicy story.

I pivoted my desk chair as I watched a replay on the morning news. An attractive young female was reporting from the scene: "Last night, in this quiet Cottonwood Hills neighborhood, Jason Asher, a high-school senior, took his own life. Why the young man did so is still a mystery. Not only are the police involved in the investigation but the local FBI as well. I talked briefly with Scott Glass, special agent in charge of the Salt Lake City FBI office."

A body under a white sheet was shown being removed from the residence. Scott appeared on the TV screen with a microphone in front of him.

"Why is the FBI involved in a suicide?" the reporter asked Scott.

"I can tell you nothing at this time," Scott said. "It is unclear why Jason Asher took his life. It may or may not be connected to a case we're working on."

The camera followed Scott as he ducked under the police tape and went back inside the Asher house. Thankfully, I heard no mention of private investigator Donald Youngblood. The segment concluded with a promise from the reporter: "We will bring you more on this tragic story as further information becomes available."

God help us, a high-school student. What had happened to the world I knew as a kid? I switched to the Weather Channel. Anything had to be better than the local news.

I called Mary on her cell phone to tell her what had happened. The sound of her voice made me rejoice and ache at the same time. I wanted desperately to be back in Mountain Center.

◆　◆　◆　◆

I was in the Salt Lake City FBI offices toting my laptop in my computer backpack by nine o'clock. The special agent in charge had not yet arrived. That did not surprise me. I was sure Scott had been up half the night.

John Banks was in his office pounding his keyboard.

"Good morning, John," I said as I stood in his office doorway.

"Good morning, Mr. Youngblood," John said.

"John, please call me Don," I said. "I feel old enough as it is."

"Sure thing," John said. "Congratulations on last night. Looks like we have one of our killers."

"How do you know for sure?" I asked.

"Scott left me a message on the office voice mail this morning about four o'clock. He said he was going to get a few hours' sleep and be in here midmorning. He said to tell you Jason Asher was definitely one of the three, whatever that means. I'm not entirely in the loop. He also said to tell you he would explain when he got in."

"If the kid is one of the three," I said, "then we got lucky. We could have been running down plates for weeks."

"Luck counts," John said. "You'd be surprised how many times we break cases on pure luck. But that expanded list you came up with, that was the key. The luck was finding the right plate so fast."

Now that one of the devils was dead, maybe the other pieces would fall into place and we could capture the other two before anyone else got killed. *Christ have mercy*, I thought, *high-school serial killers*. Were the other two high-schools kids? I hated the idea. How did I ever get in this deep?

"I'll be in the interview room working on my laptop," I said. "Tell Scott when he comes in."

"We have a visitors' office at the end of the hall," John said. "You can use that. It's a little cozier than the conference room. We have wireless. The network keys are in the middle desk drawer."

"Okay," I said. "I'll set up there."

I went down the hall to the empty office and unpacked my laptop. The room had a desk with a lamp and a comfortable chair, a few filing cabinets, two straight-back chairs for visitors, a floor lamp, and a six-foot worktable along one wall. I turned on the floor lamp and desk lamp and made myself at home.

◆   ◆   ◆   ◆

About an hour later, Scott walked in carrying a cup of coffee and took a chair in front of the desk. He looked tired.

"Long night?" I said.

"Very long," Scott said. "I got out of there around four."

"Not before you got that ugly mug of yours on television," I said. "You were superb at not answering the questions."

"I was good at that in college, too," Scott said. He took a sip of coffee. "He was one of them."

"You're sure?" I said.

Scott smiled like the Cheshire Cat.

"Absolutely," he said.

"How do you know?"

"You tell me," Scott said. "You're the hot-shot detective."

Scott loved these games. I would have been annoyed if his challenge to me didn't seem to perk him up. So I played along.

"Well," I said, "it's too soon for any forensic evidence, so I'm guessing you found some hard evidence."

"Right so far, Sherlock," Scott said.

"A piece of clothing?" I guessed.

"Nope."

"A stun gun?"

"We did not find a stun gun," Scott said. "But that's a good guess. You have one guess remaining."

Trying to sound like a game-show host was his way of relieving some of the pressure. I took some time before my final guess. When I thought it through, only one thing made sense.

"You found the transfer tattoos," I said.

"Give that man a cigar," Scott said.

"The one with the devil on the left side of the fire."

"That's the one."

"Where?" I said.

"In an envelope taped to the underside of the bottom drawer of his desk," Scott said.

"Not very original," I said.

"Good enough that a snooping mother wouldn't find it," he said.

"True," I said. "How many were left?"

"Enough for a lot more dead girls," Scott said.

"Any other leads?"

"Not yet," Scott said. "But there will be. We impounded the car and took his desktop and laptop computers. We'll find something."

"I sure hope so," I said. "I don't want to hear about any more dead girls with dancing devil tattoos."

We sat in silence for what seemed like a long time—maybe thirty seconds. Silence seems to multiply time. Scott took a drink of coffee and sighed. He looked like he might fall asleep.

"Are you going to call David Steele?" I asked.

"Unless you want to," Scott said.

"No, you do it," I said. "It'll make him feel important."

Scott nodded and took another drink.

"I owe you a lot on this one," he said. "We should have thought of the license plate thing."

"Some of my best ideas are born of desperation," I said. "I'm glad it paid off."

"You look worse than I feel," Scott said. "You can't do anything more here. I think you should pack up and get back to that good-looking woman of yours."

"Professor," I said, "that's the best idea I've heard in weeks."

◆   ◆   ◆   ◆

At nine o'clock that same evening, I sat exhausted at the kitchen bar sharing a bottle of red zinfandel with the best-looking cop on the Mountain Center police force—or any other police force, for that matter.

Much to my dismay, I had to fly commercial back to East Tennessee. I found a seat in first class on a Delta flight to Atlanta that left Salt Lake City at noon. Three hours and twenty minutes and two time zones later, I was in Atlanta with thirty-five minutes to catch my connecting flight. An hour after I boarded my connection, we touched down at Tri-Cities Airport. Mary was waiting at the gate with a much-needed hug.

"You did good work out there," she said now, taking a sip of wine. "I'm proud of you."

"I paid a dear price," I said. "I'll probably have to take those little white pills for a month to get some sleep. I may not be tough enough for this kind of thing."

"Just because you care doesn't mean you're not tough enough," Mary said. "Quit beating yourself up. You're plenty tough."

"Maybe," I said. "I've seen some bad things in the last few years, but this was the worst. Usually, I'm on the scene afterward. This time, I was there when it happened."

"Tell me about it," Mary said.

I told her, hoping it would exorcise the memory. It didn't. I told her about the first three interviews, the last house, the dead kid, and the screaming mother. She listened with a concerned look on her face but didn't interrupt. After I finished, we sat in silence.

Lacy came out of her room, down the stairs and joined us in the kitchen.

"I heard you come in," she said. "Welcome home."

"Thanks," I said. "It's really good to be here."

"You okay?" Lacy asked.

"Just tired," I said.

"I'll tell you about it later," Mary said to Lacy.

"Okay," Lacy said. "I'm going to bed."

"Sounds like a good plan for all of us," Mary said.

43

The first of the week found me back at my desk trying to concentrate on Wall Street instead of serial killers. I was halfway through my first cup of coffee when the phone rang.

"Youngblood, it's Amos Smith. I found something."

"Tell me," I said.

"The tattoos were shipped to a post office box in Knoxville."

I wrote down a box number for the city's main post office.

"Where did they come from?" I asked.

"India," Amos Smith said.

"India?"

"A lot of transfers are done there," Amos said. "After making calls and spreading some cash around, I hit pay dirt."

"You're sure about the info?" I asked.

"As sure as I can be," Amos said. "If you find out it's bogus, let me know. Heads will roll."

"What do I owe you on this?" I asked.

"A couple of good stock tips," Amos said.

"Short term or long term?"

"Long term," Amos said.

"You'll have them by the end of the week," I said, scribbling a reminder on a notepad.

"Stay in touch, Youngblood," Amos said. "Your life is a lot more interesting than mine."

"That's not always a good thing," I said. "Thanks, Amos. You did good work on this."

"Glad to help," Amos Smith said. "Don't be a stranger."

◆　◆　◆　◆

After hanging up with Amos Smith, I reheated my coffee in the microwave and called David Steele.

"Steele," he answered.

"I've got some information for you," I said.

"That you, Youngblood?"

"It is," I said. I gave him the post office box number.

"How in the hell did you come up with this?" he asked, managing to sound impressed and annoyed at the same time.

"Ouija board," I said. "I pull it out for special occasions."

"Cute, Youngblood. You should be a comedian," David Steele said. "I'll check this out and call you later. Thanks." He severed our connection.

Lost, I thought, smiling to myself, *one sense of humor. If found, return to David Steele.*

◆   ◆   ◆   ◆

For a few hours, things were quiet. Then Scott Glass called.

"What's going on, Professor?"

"We've had a busy weekend," Scott said. "I thought I'd bring you up to speed in case it hits the news."

"I'm listening."

"We found some of the dead girl's hair in the back of the Asher SUV. We also found a stun gun and a can of ether in the spare-tire wheel well," Scott said. "That pretty much seals the deal on devil number one. And we got some good stuff off the computers. Looks like the three devils met in a chat room. We tracked down one IP address to a wireless router at a residence in St. Cloud, Minnesota. Turns out it belonged to a high-school senior. When we got there, he was gone. Took the family van and disappeared. We put a bogus Amber Alert out for the van."

"Amber Alert?"

"People seem to respond when a child is missing," Scott said. "Otherwise, they don't want to get involved."

"Well, that's pretty smart, Professor," I said.

"I'm trying to catch up with you, Blood."

"I can feel this heating up," I said.

"So can I," Scott said. "You certainly got the ball rolling."

"Don't remind me," I said.

"Anything else on your end?"

I told Scott about the post office box in Knoxville and my conversation with David Steele.

"That's good work," Scott said.

"I didn't do much," I said. "I just had a good source."

"In our line of work, good sources are half the battle."

"If you get a lead on devil number three, let me know," I said.

Silence came from the other end.

"Scott?"

"One other thing," Scott said. "You're not going to like it."

"Tell me," I said.

"CNN connected the dots on the Utah suicide and the missing Minnesota person of interest, quoting sources close to the investigation," Scott said. "Since I had to send a report back to Washington, that could be anybody."

"So?"

"So private investigator Donald Youngblood from Mountain Center, Tennessee, working as an FBI consultant, was mentioned as being key in tracking down the first killer and the Minnesota person of interest," Scott said.

"How in the hell did that happen?" I asked, feeling my blood pressure going up.

"Politics," Scott said. "Somebody wants my office to look bad. They want to make it seem like we couldn't do it alone and had to have outside help. I mentioned you in my report. I had to. Besides, it will look good in your file. I was too naïve to realize someone might use it against me."

"So much for my flying under the radar," I said.

"Don't worry about it," Scott said. "Nobody watches CNN. In a few days, it'll be ancient history. It will also help me the next time you want a favor."

I sure as hell hoped devil number three didn't watch CNN.

44

Early the next morning, I went to the Mountain Center Diner for breakfast. On any given day, I knew most of the people there. Other than a nod or a hello, they usually ignored me. Not today. I walked in and was about halfway to my back table when the applause began. It turned into an embarrassing standing ovation. I stopped, made a bow, and did a two-handed motion for everyone to sit down. I made it to my seat without any further interruption. *So much for nobody watching CNN*, I thought.

I ordered breakfast as the buzz returned to normal. A couple minutes later, Roy Husky sat with me. He had a wry smile on his face.

"What?" I said.

"Can I have your autograph?" Roy said in a soft voice, leaning in.

"No."

"You celebrities are all alike," he said.

Doris appeared.

"Order something," I snapped at Roy.

◆　　◆　　◆　　◆

By lunchtime, I had talked to a dozen people who wanted to comment on my celebrity status. Some I had not heard from in a year or more. I called Billy for help. I had to escape the office.

That afternoon when he came over, we went to Moto's Gym. As I followed Billy out of the parking lot toward Moto's, I passed an old blue Ford pickup. My mind wandered to an old blue pickup from my youth. My father's best friend had a farm. One day when I was about twelve, his friend showed me how to work the column gearshift on his pickup. Then he let me practice by driving around the farm. I bounced around the fields changing gears and thinking how grown-up I was. After that, I got to drive the pickup whenever I visited. By the time I was thirteen, I was driving the family car. Of course, Dad was always in the passenger seat and was very selective about where and when I could drive. Where had my youth gone?

Billy avoided making any CNN jokes, for which I was grateful. Billy hadn't been to Moto's in quite some time. Although he tried hard not to show it, Moto was thrilled to see him. They exchanged their obligatory insults. Moto barely acknowledged me. Apparently, he didn't watch CNN.

Billy and I got down to business. We started on the elliptical machines. Twenty minutes later, I was building a pretty good sweat. Billy was barely breathing.

"You getting a lot of grief about this CNN thing?" Billy asked.

"Enough," I said.

"People like you, Blood," Billy said. "If they didn't, they wouldn't mention it."

"I'm getting more credit than I deserve," I said, breathing hard. "I didn't do that much."

"Maybe," Billy said. "Maybe not."

We worked in silence for a while.

"Whatever happened with the missing girl thing you were working on?" I asked Billy.

"Found her," Billy said.

"Where was she?"

"With a friend," Billy said.

"So what was her story?"

"Her father was getting drunk and beating up on her and her mother," Billy said. "So she ran away. She's back home now."

"Might happen again," I said, prying for more information.

"I don't think so," Billy said.

"Why's that?" I asked. I had a pretty good idea.

"I had a talk with the father," Billy said.

I could imagine how that talk went. It was more likely a demonstration of how if felt to get beaten up by someone stronger.

"So he got the message?" I said.

"He did," Billy said.

I found out later from Maggie that the girl checked in with Billy every few days to tell him how things were going. Her father was now attending AA and not drinking at all. Getting information from Billy was like trying to crack a heavily encrypted computer file.

"Maybe you should lie low for a few days," Billy said after a while. "Let this CNN thing settle down."

"Maybe I should," I said.

"And watch your back," Billy said.

◆   ◆   ◆   ◆

That night, the story made the national networks. The two Tattoo Killers were big news, and Donald Youngblood was a major character in their reality play. No network had yet mentioned that the FBI was looking for a third killer. I took that as a good sign. Lacy was excited by my fifteen minutes of fame, but Mary understood the consequences. Both of us lectured Lacy about not being alone and about watching out for strangers. That got her even more excited.

"You think I could be in danger?"

"Probably not," I said, trying to take some of the adventure out of her thought process. "We're just saying you should be aware. And under no circumstances mention the possibility of a third killer."

"Okay," she said casually.

I stared at her hard.

"Look at me," I said firmly. "I want your promise. Tell no one."

"Okay, Don," she said, getting a little color in her face. "I promise."

Lacy left us at the kitchen bar and went to her room to do computer homework that Stanley Johns had given her. I thought it was probably a euphemism for talking on her cell phone with Jonah.

"Think she can keep quiet about this?" I asked Mary.

"I think so," Mary said. "I'll talk to her again Monday morning before she goes to Stanley's."

"Think you can keep quiet about this?"

"I may need some convincing," Mary said, smiling.

"I can handle that," I said.

45

I sat underneath a large umbrella on the lower deck. On the table were my laptop and cell phone and an insulated mug filled with Dunkin' Donuts coffee I had brewed myself. It wasn't quite the same as letting Dunkin' Donuts do it, but it was still pretty darn good. My Ruger revolver, loaded with .357 hollow points, was within arm's reach. *Better paranoid and safe than careless and dead*, I thought.

Mary, Lacy, and I had spent the weekend at the lake house. Neither Mary nor Lacy had mentioned the case. I looked at the news stations a couple of times and saw nothing related to the Tattoo Killers. The story had slipped into the category of old news. I hoped it stayed there.

Before Mary had left to take Lacy to Stanley's, I overheard a conversation between the two of them at the front door. Maybe it was for my benefit. I stopped at the top of the stairs and listened as Mary reinforced my warning from Friday night.

"Remember what Don said," Mary said. "Be aware of your surroundings."

"You're serious," Lacy said.

"I am. Call me if something doesn't look right."

"Think it could be a kid in my school?" Lacy asked.

"I don't know what to think," Mary said. "I just know one more killer is out there, and young girls aren't safe until we catch him."

"I'll be careful," Lacy said as they walked out the front door.

It was midmorning, and the treetops still blocked the sun. The sky was blue, and a gentle breeze came off the lake. The stillness that surrounded me was surreal. *Not a bad place to work*, I thought. *I may have to rethink this office thing.* Jake seemed to have the same idea. He lay baking in the sun. I marveled at how a black dog could lie like that for any length of time without exploding into flames. Eventually, Jake would get hot and find some shade.

The Dow was hovering around seven thousand. I had the feeling it couldn't go much lower. I took a deep breath and bought large blocks of stock from ten different companies I felt were grossly undervalued. I was thinking long term. I emailed my recommendations to clients and asked for prompt responses.

Just before noon, I called the office to check my messages. I had three requests for interviews from major networks. I erased them all. I had just finished when my cell phone beeped to let me know another call was coming in.

"Hello," I said cautiously.

"Youngblood, it's Steele."

"What's up, Dave?"

"I'm in the area," he said. "Thought I'd spring for lunch."

"I appreciate that," I said. "But I'm not in town. I'm out at my lake house."

He paused for a few seconds.

"I could pick something up and come out," he said.

I wanted to ask why he would bother, but I didn't. I was sure he had his reasons.

"Sure," I said. "I'll be in the back on the deck. Come around the left side of the house." I gave him directions. Situated about a quarter-mile off the main road in a heavily wooded area, the lake house is hard to find unless you know where you're going. The driveway slopes gently upward to a crest, then down to the house, making it impossible to see the house from the road.

About an hour after the call, I heard the crunch of gravel under tires. A few seconds later, a door slammed. Then I heard David Steele on the stairs to the deck. Jake, now lying in a shady spot, raised his head, sniffed the air, and put his head back down. I was at the opposite end of the deck from the stairs. David Steele spotted me and walked over carrying a white paper bag from Carrie Lee's Deli and Grill.

"I see you found Carrie Lee's," I said.

"Last time I was in the area," he said. "It's pretty good."

As David Steele spread out our lunch, I adjusted the umbrella so we would both be sitting in the shade.

"Expecting trouble?" he asked, looking at the Ruger.

"These days," I said, "I'm always expecting trouble."

He nodded.

"Not a bad philosophy in this day and age."

On the table were a ham and Swiss on rye, a turkey and Swiss on whole wheat, a bag of potato chips, and a bag of Doritos. The sandwiches were cut in half.

"What do you want to drink?" I asked.

"Got a beer?"

"Beer?" I said. "You're on duty."

"So what? One beer," he said.

"Not the same tight-ass I remember," I said.

"That was then, this is now," David Steele said. "Things change."

Good for you, I thought.

I climbed the stairs to the upper deck, went into the house, and returned with two Amber Bocks and a couple of paper plates. I took half of the turkey and Swiss and the bag of Doritos. The sandwich tasted great. I was glad I didn't have a big breakfast. We ate in silence for a while.

"Nice place you have here," David Steele said, washing down a mouthful of food with a swallow of beer.

"It was my parents' house," I said. "I have a lot of great memories here."

"I don't doubt it," he said. "If I had this place free and clear, I'd retire."

I finished my turkey and Swiss and started on half of the ham and Swiss. The Doritos and the beer were disappearing fast.

"Is this a social call?" I asked.

"Half and half," David Steele said. "I needed to get away from the office to clear my head, and I have some news. Damned if I couldn't sit here the rest of the day."

"You're welcome to," I said.

"In my dreams," he said. "I've got to get going pretty soon."

"Do I dare ask what the news is?"

David Steele had just taken the last bite of his ham and Swiss. He raised one finger, washed the bite down, and set his bottle on the table.

"The post office box was a dead end," he said. "Rented eighteen months ago for six months and not renewed. The name and address on the rental form were bogus. Of course, nobody remembers anything. Too long ago."

"Too bad," I said. "It was a nice lead."

David Steele picked up the other half of the turkey and Swiss and took a bite. He swallowed and then took a drink of beer.

"And," he said, pausing for effect but not sounding very enthusiastic, "our branch in Minneapolis–St. Paul found the Minnesota high-school kid we were looking for."

"Please don't tell me he's dead," I said.

"Deader than a doornail," David Steele said. "He offed himself in a state park. Put a gun in his mouth, just like the other kid."

"Suicide pact?"

"Looks like it," he said. "Stun gun and ether in the same place as in the Asher kid's SUV. We searched the house and found his transfer tattoos, also in the same place, taped underneath the bottom drawer of his desk. We're going over the van. I'll bet we find hair or fibers that link him to the two Minnesota killings. We also have his laptop, desktop, and BlackBerry. We'll find something."

"Maybe not," I said. "He had time to clean those up."

"There's clean, and then there's clean," David Steele said. "Unless he was really good, we'll find something."

He took a large bite of sandwich, followed by a few potato chips, then drank some beer.

"Those two were followers," I said, surprising myself as I said it. "The leader may not be so kind as to kill himself. He might just recruit a couple of new players and keep going."

"Players?" David Steele asked. "You think this is a game?"

"A very deadly one," I said. "Look at the evidence. The first round of killings was almost exactly the same. The girls looked the same, the locations were similar, the cause of death was the same, the tattoos were in the same place, and the clothes were laid out the same way. I wouldn't be surprised if devil number three is keeping score."

"Son of a bitch," he said.

"We've got to find devil number three before this whole thing starts up again," I said.

David Steele drained his beer and stood up.

"We're going to catch this guy, Youngblood," he said. "I can feel it."

◆　◆　◆　◆

Jake and I went back to the Mountain Center condo just before Lacy came home from school. I drove while Jake slept. He had spent a hard three days at the lake house.

Lacy arrived a half-hour after we did.

"Mary picked me up," she said excitedly. "In her unmarked car."

"Were you under arrest?" I asked.

"I was wanted for questioning," Lacy said. "But I was released without charges being filed."

"Glad to hear it," I said.

"She'll be home soon."

"Glad to hear that, too," I said.

"How was your day?"

"Quiet," I said. "How was yours?"

"Hectic," Lacy said. "Everyone was talking about you."

"Old news," I said.

"Maybe tomorrow," Lacy said. "But not today."

◆　◆　◆　◆

I was at the bar drinking a beer and reading a just-received copy of *Rocky Top News* when Mary came in. She removed her still-holstered Glock from her belt and placed it in the small gun safe in the front closet. She was wearing black slacks with black boots and a black sleeveless top. My heart skipped a beat at the sight of her. She pulled her badge off her belt, laid it on the counter, retrieved a half-finished bottle of white wine from the refrigerator, poured herself a glass, and sat down. She raised her glass and touched my beer bottle and took a drink.

"God, that's good," Mary said.

"Long day?"

"Long enough," she said. "We're investigating some break-ins where mostly flat-screen TVs were taken. Some had tracking chips, so we made a few arrests—junkies trying to support their habits. What about you?"

"A kid in Minnesota killed himself, just like the one in Utah," I said. "They found tattoos at his place and some other evidence, so it's real likely he's the second devil."

"That's going to put this back in the spotlight," Mary said.

She was right. We watched the news and caught the story on two major networks. Donald Youngblood, Mountain Center private investigator, was once again mentioned as playing a prominent role in the case. I knew I'd be spending the next few days at the lake house.

46

Jake and I drove to the lake house the following morning. Jake sat in the front seat observing the scenery, thanks to a special dog harness the seatbelt attached to. What would they think of next? *Maybe a doggie shoulder holster*, I thought. I could put a little toy gun in it. If I put a real gun in it, Jake might end up accidentally shooting himself in the foot—or worse, shooting me. I smiled at my goofiness. The devils were driving me off the deep end.

The weather remained gorgeous. I sat on the deck as I had the day before with my laptop, my cell phone, and my Ruger. Jake found a spot in the sun and took a nap. I heard water lapping against the dock and birds singing—a top-ten day if I ever saw one.

Then my cell phone rang. So much for Shangri-La. Caller ID was blocked.

"Youngblood," I said, probably sounding a little annoyed.

"I went by your office," the big baritone voice said, equally annoyed. "Where the hell are you?"

Big Bob Wilson was never one to beat around the bush.

"At the lake house," I said.

"Chicken," Big Bob said. "Can't take the heat of being a celebrity?"

"Guilty as charged," I said. "Did you see the news?"

"I saw it," he said. "Anything I should know that wasn't on TV?"

"The girl at the lake is part of this mess," I said. "Six of them have been found so far. Three killers appear to be responsible, and the third one could be around here."

"Damn it, Blood," Big Bob said. "Just when were you going to share this information?"

"It's in the hands of the FBI," I said, soft-pedaling. "Right now, nothing is for sure. If anything solid comes up, I'll let you know."

"Does Jimmy Durham know?"

"I don't think Jimmy wants to know, but he knows some of it," I said. "The FBI has taken over the case, and I think Jimmy is happy to be rid of it."

"You stay in touch on this, Blood," Big Bob said. "You hear?"

"I will," I said.

"And be careful," he added. "You're getting way too much attention."

"Yes, Mother."

Whether he heard me or not was hard to say. The connection was broken.

I went inside, made coffee, came back down, and booted up my laptop. I had numerous emails from clients telling me to either buy or hold.

No one wanted to sell in a down market. I went about buying stock for those who wanted it. After that, I checked my personal email account. I had one from T. Elbert that made me feel immediately guilty. I had not seen him in two weeks.

It read, "Getting too big now to visit old friends? I watch the news, you know. If you're not too busy, drop me a line and let me know what's going on."

I wrote him a long email with as much information as I cared to share and promised I would drop by soon.

Then I went to the University of Tennessee website to see what the latest football news was. Two starters had just quit the team. But before I could get the particulars, my cell phone rang again. I was about ready to chuck it into the lake. Again, caller ID was blocked. *What the hell good is caller ID if everyone can block it?* I thought.

"I called the office, Blood," Scott Glass said. "Where are you?"

"At the lake house, Professor," I said. "Hiding out."

"Damn," Scott said. "I wish I could do that."

"More bad news?" I asked.

"Not really," Scott said. "We found hairs from both Minnesota victims in the van. No big surprise. And we found some stuff we didn't understand until I talked to David Steele and he told me your theory about a game. You could have run that by me first."

If I didn't know better, I might have detected hurt in his voice.

"You had to be there," I said. "It just popped out of nowhere, an epiphany of sorts. I said it and then it started to make sense."

"It makes more sense now," Scott said. "We found one email that said, 'Game tied,' and another that said, 'Game still tied.'"

"Could you track them?" I asked.

"Yeah," Scott said. "They came from the kid in Utah."

I felt something cold move past me, and then it was gone.

"Scott," I said, "somewhere on one of those computers is a connection to East Tennessee. You've got to find it."

47

I laid low for a few days and then on Friday returned to the office. I left
Jake at the condo. He was tired of traveling. The Tattoo Killers had
faded into the background, as far as the news was concerned. I had heard
nothing from Scott Glass or David Steele, and I was thankful for that. But
I couldn't shake a feeling of impending doom.

My office door opened and closed, and I heard footsteps approaching
my inner office.

"I was in the area," a newly familiar voice said. "Got a minute?"

"Sure," I said. "Sit down."

Troy Walker looked like he had aged since I last saw him. Losing a
daughter can do that. I had watched Joseph Fleet age the same way. Fleet
finally came to grips with what had happened and made a comeback.
I hoped Troy Walker could do the same. The sooner the FBI wrapped up
the Tattoo Killers Case, the better for him. For a while, I had sent Troy
weekly updates. In the last couple of weeks, things had been so hectic that
I forgot.

"I've been watching the news," he said. "I heard your name mentioned
a few times."

"A few too many times to suit me," I said.

"Do these killers have anything to do with Betty Lou?" Troy asked.

"Not directly," I said. "But we have reason to believe they knew who
killed Betty Lou or were at least connected in some way. We have one
more to catch. And believe me, we're going to catch him."

He nodded but didn't respond. He seemed distracted. We sat in
silence. He looked on the verge of tears.

"Why?" Troy Walker said sadly. "Why would anyone want to kill my
daughter?"

"No reason," I said. "A random act of violence. Wrong place at the wrong time. She may have been killed just because she was young, dark haired, and dark eyed."

"What?" He looked incredulous.

I gave it to him straight. He deserved to know.

"We think they were playing a game," I said. "Someone established the parameters for the kills, and then each player had to follow the parameters to score points."

"Score points?" Troy Walker said, choking on the words. "Oh, God." He turned white as a sheet. I thought he might pass out. "Bathroom?" he said, getting to his feet.

I pointed to my private bathroom.

He moved quickly, slamming the door behind him. When I heard the retching, I moved to my outer office and sat at the conference table. Moving didn't help much. The sound traveled. After a few minutes, I heard water running. The bathroom door opened, and Troy walked slowly into the outer office and sat at the table across from me.

"Sorry," he said.

"Don't be," I said.

"A game," he said, more to himself that to me. "Goddamn them to hell."

I couldn't agree more, I thought.

◆   ◆   ◆   ◆

That afternoon, I went to the Mountain Center Medical Center to check on Megan Carter, soon to be Megan Cox again. I went through the main entrance and straight to the elevators and punched the button for the fourth floor.

Brenda Knox was at the nurses' station. She smiled as I approached.

"She's awake," Nurse Brenda said. "About an hour ago. The doctor just left. Her father is with her now. We moved her a couple of days ago. She's at the end of the hall. Go ahead down."

"Thanks," I said, trying not to notice how good she looked.

Megan was sitting up in bed and talking to her father. They noticed me at the same time.

"Mr. Youngblood," Megan said, looking confused. "What are you doing here?"

"I came to check on you," I said, smiling. "It's nice to see you awake. How do you feel?"

"A little groggy," Megan said. "My father told me I've been in a coma."

"I need to talk with Mr. Youngblood for a few minutes, Megan," Howard Cox said. He made a head motion toward the door. "A waiting room is down the hall," he said to me. "Let's take a walk there."

I followed him. A Bunn coffeemaker was set up, and someone had just brewed a fresh pot. Howard Cox poured himself a Styrofoam cup full. No half-and-half was in sight, so I passed.

We sat side by side in chairs with a table in between. Howard Cox set his coffee on the table.

"She doesn't remember a damn thing," he said.

"She doesn't remember waking up and telling you it was Ricky who assaulted her?" I asked, straight-faced.

"No," Howard Cox said, smiling. "She doesn't remember that either."

"Not surprising," I said. "She'll remember sooner or later."

"That's what the doctor said. She needs to remember soon or Ricky will get away with this."

"Ricky is still facing a gun charge," I said.

"I've talked to a few people," Howard Cox said. "Ricky doesn't have any record, so it's likely he'll get a fine and probation."

"Even though he tried to shoot Billy?" I asked.

"I was told his lawyer will claim he was protecting himself," Howard Cox said. "That you and your partner didn't have any legal right to be in pursuit of him. You know, lawyer hocus-pocus."

"When is his court date?" I asked.

"Next week," he said.

"Well, let's hope Megan remembers something by then," I said.

"And if she doesn't?"

"Ricky is not going to skate on this," I said. "One way or another, he'll pay."

❖   ❖   ❖   ❖

"You don't know for sure he did it," Mary said.

"I do know," I said. "I'm ninety-nine percent sure."

"That's not one hundred percent," Mary said.

"But it's close enough," I said.

We were at the lake house. It was Friday evening, and Lacy was spending the night with Hannah. We had driven both SUVs, since Mary had to stay late to finish some paperwork. On Saturday night, Hannah would spend the night with us. Mary and Hannah's mother, Suzanne, had worked something out so we could be alone. Tomorrow night, Suzanne and her husband would have the benefit of being teenager-free. I didn't ask questions, since I was perfectly happy with the arrangement.

"You cannot take the law into your own hands," Mary said, sipping a glass of white wine.

"I know," I said. "But Ricky is not getting away with it."

"Is he still in jail or out on bail?" Mary asked.

"You're a poet and don't know it," I said.

"Good Lord, I haven't heard that one since I was in grade school," Mary laughed.

"That just kind of popped out of my head. Sorry." I took a drink of beer, thinking how silly I felt. "Rollie told me Ricky's mother wouldn't put up bail, but later someone else bailed him out," I said.

"Is Rollie his lawyer?" Mary asked.

"No way," I said. "I talked to Rollie this afternoon as I was leaving the office. Ricky has a public defender. He told the court he couldn't afford a lawyer."

"Does Rollie think he'll walk?"

"He feels he might," I said. "Rollie says that unless Megan identifies Ricky as her attacker, he could get off."

"Think she'd lie about it for Ricky?" Mary asked.

"I don't think so," I said. "She seems intent on getting rid of Ricky once and for all. But you never know."

Mary took another sip of wine and gave me that seductive smile I knew so well.

"Want to get in the hot tub?" she said. "In our birthday suits?"

Silly question!

◆　　◆　　◆　　◆

I was down to my boxer shorts and Mary had on only her black bikini panties when the phone rang. I groaned. I recognized the number—Big Bob Wilson's personal cell phone.

"What's up?" I asked.

I couldn't believe my ears.

"On my way," I said, and hung up.

I also couldn't believe the next words that came out of my mouth.

"Get dressed," I said to Mary.

Then I called David Steele.

48

Mary drove. The red flasher Big Bob had given her for the top of her SUV warned those in our path that a speed demon approached. When we arrived, a county deputy blocked the street, but Mary flashed her badge, and he let us through. The scene was another three-ring circus. Lights pulsated from various cruisers, and uniformed officers were scattered around. The Mountain Center police and the county sheriff's department were both at the scene.

We were far on the other end of the same trailer park where Ricky Carter had taken shots at Billy. I spotted Big Bob and Jimmy Durham in front of a trailer with a white extended-cab late-model pickup in the driveway. All the lights were on inside the trailer. A crowd was forming behind the police tape. I walked through the crowd and went under the tape to Jimmy and Big Bob. Mary stayed behind to help Sean Wilson with crowd control. She looked spectacular in her jeans and T-shirt. But with her badge and Glock on display, she was all business.

"Anybody inside?" I asked.

"Billy," Big Bob said.

"How'd he get here so fast?" I said.

"I phoned him the minute the call came in reporting a gunshot and a dead body," Big Bob said. "I didn't call you until I had a look for myself."

"The FBI is on the way," I said to Big Bob.

"I figured as much," he said. "They can have this one."

"Can I get a look?" I said, not really wanting to.

"Be my guest," he said, nodding toward the trailer door.

He walked away from me and went to talk with Mary. I saw her nod and leave Sean. She pulled a notebook and pen from her back pocket and headed toward a trailer across the street.

I turned and went up two steps and inside the trailer. To my left was the living room. Billy was moving around taking pictures of everything. He looked at me and shook his head but remained silent. The body of a young man was on the couch, his head at an odd angle, rolled over on his right shoulder. Most of the back of his skull was missing. Blood, bone, and brain matter were on the couch and the wall behind it. A .45 caliber Colt lay beside him on the couch at his right hand. On the other side of him was a sheet of paper with two words in big, bold letters: **"GAME OVER."**

Except for the note, it was eerily similar to the scene I had witnessed in Salt Lake City. I was surprised at how detached I was, viewing the gore. *A bad sign*, I thought. When I'd seen enough, I went back outside and rejoined Big Bob. Jimmy was thirty feet away talking to a couple of his deputies. He walked toward us. Over his shoulder and down the street, I noticed a van from a local TV station.

"You got this one?" Jimmy asked Big Bob as he approached. "We got other things to do, and this part of the trailer park is inside the city."

"Yeah, we got it for now," Big Bob said. "The feds will be here soon, and then they can have it."

"Call me when you get a chance, Blood," Jimmy said. "We'll get caught up."

"I'll do that," I said. I felt a little guilty I hadn't kept him more in the loop.

Jimmy gathered his men and moved on.

A few minutes later, Billy came out of the trailer.

"I'm done," he said.

"Thanks," Big Bob said.

"I'll email you a file later tonight," Billy said.

"No hurry," Big Bob said. "The feds will take over soon."

"See you later, Blood," Billy said.

"Okay, Chief," I said. "Be careful going over the mountain."

Billy grinned widely.

"Yes, Mother," he said.

I laughed. He'd been waiting a long time to say that. I had said it to him for years when I thought he was being too protective.

•　　•　　•　　•

David Steele arrived with his entourage fifteen minutes after Billy left. He and three other agents climbed out of a black Crown Victoria, doors slamming one after another. I introduced him to Big Bob Wilson.

"We'll take over from here, Chief Wilson," David Steele said. "This certainly appears to tie into our case. If it doesn't, we'll turn it back to you."

"It's all yours," Big Bob said. "I have enough on my plate with break-ins, meth labs, and the other usual bullshit."

He rounded up his on-duty officers.

A few minutes later, Mary walked over, and I introduced her to David Steele.

"Nice to meet you," he said, smiling.

I had never before seen him that gracious. Beauty calmed the savage beast.

Mary turned her attention to me and looked at her notes.

"The kid, Russell Goode, was a senior at Byrd County High School," she said. "His father, Paul, is a long-haul trucker. He left for the West Coast yesterday. I got his cell-phone number, but one of the neighbors volunteered to call him."

"That's not a call I'd want to make," I said.

"Neither would I," Mary said. "Some of the neighbors watch out for the kid. One of them was outside and thought he heard a gunshot from inside the kid's trailer. He came over to check it out. Knocked on the door and got no answer, so he tried the knob. It was open, and he went in and found the kid and called the police."

"Good work," I said.

"I'm going to talk to a few more people to see what else I can find out."

She turned and walked back toward the crowd as David Steele and I observed her movements.

"That's a fine-looking woman," he said. "Nice that you get that kind of cooperation from the local police."

"Probably because we're living together," I said.

David Steele did a double take and then said, "You're kidding."

"No kidding," I said. "That's my lady."

"You know, a guy who can attract that kind of woman must be okay," he said with admiration.

"Or just plain lucky," I said.

"Agent Steele," a voice called from the doorway of the trailer.

David Steele and I walked over and stood looking up at the young agent, who leaned down toward us.

"We found the tattoos," he said softly. "Hidden in a book in the bedroom."

"Good work," David Steele said.

The agent smiled and disappeared back inside the trailer.

"Guess that about wraps this one up, Youngblood," David Steele said.

"Not soon enough for me," I said.

I caught Mary's eye and gave a little head motion toward her SUV. We met at the edge of the front yard about ten feet from the police tape and the press, who were now out in force.

"Let's get out of here," I said so only she could hear. "It's the FBI's problem now. There's nothing more we can do."

"Give Peggy Ann Romeo a couple of minutes," Mary said quietly. "I've gotten to know her a little. She has a daughter in Lacy's class. Peggy Ann's nice, and she won't put you on the spot. It would mean a lot to her."

Peggy Ann Romeo was a local TV on-the-scene reporter. I had seen her on the news once or twice but had never met her.

"You talk to her already?"

Mary nodded.

"Damn it, Mary," I said, more than a little annoyed. As if I didn't have enough press coverage already.

"Please," she said.

Might as well, I thought. *The three devils are no longer a threat.*

"Okay," I said. "A couple of questions."

We went under the police tape. Peggy Ann was waiting with her cameraman a few feet away.

"A minute please, Mr. Youngblood," she said.

"Turn off the camera and mic for a second," I said.

She made a slashing sign toward the cameraman, and the light went out. I led her a few feet away from the fray.

"I do this and you owe me one," I said. I didn't want to make it too easy. Being owed a favor by a local TV reporter could come in handy someday.

"Deal," she said.

She nodded toward the cameraman. The light went back on: Showtime.

"I'm here with Mountain Center private investigator Donald Youngblood, who has been working closely with the FBI on the Tattoo Killers Case," Peggy Ann began. "Word from the neighbors indicates that Russell Goode committed suicide. Is his suicide connected to the Tattoo Killers Case?"

She moved the microphone a few inches from my chin. I took a deep breath and tried to act professional.

"The FBI will have to completely process the scene," I said as calmly as I could. "But some indications suggest this suicide may be connected."

"Are there any indications that Russell Goode was the third killer the FBI was looking for?" Peggy Ann asked.

I wondered how she knew about the third killer. I gave Mary a quick look. She shrugged.

"You'll have to ask the FBI about that," I said. "Right now, I wouldn't want to speculate."

"Will you continue to work with the FBI on this case?" Peggy Ann asked.

I raised an eyebrow at her as if to say, *Last question.*

"I was actually conducting a parallel investigation for a private party and consulted with the FBI when it looked like my case intersected with theirs," I said. "I have no plans to work with the FBI any further on this case."

"Thank you, Mr. Youngblood," Peggy Ann said, turning back toward the camera.

"Very impressive, big boy," Mary said as we walked to her SUV. "Thanks for doing that."

"How'd she know about a third killer?" I asked.

"Not from me," Mary said. "Maybe she just made an assumption, since this was the third suicide and you and the FBI were both here."

"Maybe," I said.

We slipped quietly into the darkness and left.

◆　　◆　　◆　　◆

Mary came out of the bathroom wearing a nightshirt that read, "Chick with Brains." I had given it to her as a Christmas present. She was beautiful and smart, and I wanted her to know I knew it. As she usually did at night, she had taken out her contacts and was wearing round black-framed glasses that made her look even smarter. The room was cool, and her erect nipples showed through the nightshirt, raising my powers of observation to level red.

"What?" she said.

"I like your nightshirt," I said, leering.

"I know you do," she said, looking down. "Want me to take it off?"

"How about in the morning?" I said. "It's been a long night."

"In the morning works for me," Mary said. "You better get a good night's sleep."

She turned off her bedside lamp and slipped underneath the quilt beside me. She rolled on her side, back to me, and I scooted close, spooning her, and kissed her neck. We would sleep that way until one of us got hot.

"I'm glad this case is over and you can relax," she said.

"Well, I still have Ricky Carter to deal with," I said.

"Forget Ricky Carter," Mary said. "And forget the three devils."

Something still nagged me. *Let it go*, a little voice inside my head said. *Easier said than done*, I said back.

49

The following Tuesday, I was on T. Elbert's front porch. After getting some grief for staying away so long, I settled in for coffee and bagels. T. Elbert told me I was all over the weekend news. I had refused to watch. I had gone to the office on Monday to lie low.

David Steele had faxed me a copy of the forensics and a copy of the on-the-scene report from Friday night. Payback for the fast phone call, I guessed. The report said that hairs from both victims were found inside the truck. The father, who had now been questioned, confirmed that he was on the road on the dates of both murders. An IP address from one of Jason Asher's computers was traced to Byrd County High School, where Russell Goode was a student. Jason had referred to whomever he was emailing as Lucifer. Lucifer was the supposed leader of the three devils— the head devil, so to speak. The Tattoo Killers Case, the FBI concluded, was open and shut. At the bottom, the report was stamped, "Case closed." I had filed it with my other paperwork from the Walker case and vowed to forget about it.

"You did some good work on that tattoo case," T. Elbert said.

"I got lucky," I said. "I pulled on the right thread, and the whole thing unraveled before our eyes. It's not very common that serial killers oblige you by committing suicide."

"Luck counts," T. Elbert said.

"It does indeed," I said.

"How was it working with Agent Steele?" T. Elbert asked.

"Agent Steele turned out to be a pretty good guy," I said. "I think he's tired of being an FBI agent."

"I can understand that," T. Elbert said.

We both sat in rocking chairs. I rocked back and forth. My coffee sat on a table beside me. It's not easy to rock and drink coffee. I stopped, took a drink, set the cup back down, and continued my rocking. It had a mesmerizing effect.

"Something's bothering you," T. Elbert said.

"I'm afraid to talk about it," I said.

"Probably best to get it out."

"I keep thinking we didn't finish this," I said.

"Go on," T. Elbert said.

"All these kids seemed to be followers," I said. "What if someone else was orchestrating the whole thing? I believe the first two kids were part of this. We ran both of them down, and they committed suicide. But we were nowhere close to catching Russell Goode. That was way too convenient. The report I read said they tracked an IP address to Russell's high school. I'm sure the high school uses a wireless router. I'll bet the router isn't secure. If it's not secure, then anyone could go online through that router."

"You're way over my head now, but keep going," T. Elbert said.

"Let's say the third devil thought we were closer than we really were," I said. "So he picked out this kid for a fall guy. He must have known Russell. Knew his father traveled. So he killed the girls when he knew the father was going to be away."

"Like a backup plan," T. Elbert said.

"An escape tunnel, so to speak," I said. "So Friday night, he subdued Russell somehow—spiked a drink, used ether, I don't know. Then he killed the kid and made it look like a suicide, left the note, and went out the back door, had a vehicle parked somewhere."

"Maybe he used a stun gun," T. Elbert said.

"I doubt it," I said. "That would leave marks and point to a set-up. If this guy is as smart as I think, it would be something hard to detect. Something the FBI would have no reason to look for."

"What about the hairs in the truck?" T. Elbert asked.

"He could have planted them that night, after the kid was out cold, or sometime earlier," I said.

"Sounds like you have more work to do," T. Elbert said.

❖　❖　❖　❖

Later that morning, I sat in my office watching a steady rain falling on Main Street. The more I thought about it, the more I was convinced that the third devil was still out there.

I called Scott Glass.

"Hey, Blood," he answered. "Thanks for all your help on the tattoo case. It's nice to wrap that one up."

"Maybe not, Professor," I said. "I have a theory."

I heard silence from the other end of the phone.

"I know I don't want to hear this," Scott groaned. "Go ahead, tell me."

I told him.

He was silent for a while.

"Damn," he said. "My gut tells me you could be right."

"I was hoping you'd tell me I'm crazy," I said. "Now what?"

"I'll call Steely Dave and tell him to come see you," Scott said. "Lay it out for him and see what he thinks. Maybe we're both crazy."

❖　❖　❖　❖

A couple of hours later, David Steele walked into the office and sat.

"Where's the pooch?" he asked.

"At my condo," I said. "He's got the day off."

"Lucky him," he said. "Why am I here, Youngblood?"

"I don't think we're finished," I said.

"I was afraid we weren't," David Steele said. "Scott said you have a theory. He hopes I think you're both crazy."

I laid it out for him. After I finished, he sat and stared out my window at the pouring rain.

"Son of a bitch," he said finally.

"Does that mean you don't think I'm crazy?" I asked.

"That's what it means," David Steele said. "If I'm going to put any more manpower on this, I need something solid."

"Where's the body?" I asked.

"With the Knox County Coroner's Office," he said.

"Have them do a blood screen and see what pops up," I said. "Our killer had to incapacitate Russell Goode in some way. I'm betting drugs or ether. And I'm betting he knew Russell."

"I guess I need to work the high school," David Steele said, standing to leave.

"No," I said. "Let me poke around. I've got a few ideas. We need our killer to think he's in the clear."

David Steele stopped in my doorway and turned to face me.

"I've enjoyed working with you, Youngblood," he said. "And for what it's worth, you made the right decision not to pursue a career in the FBI."

"Thanks, Dave," I said.

"I'll be in touch," he said.

Without another word, he turned and walked through the outer office and out the door, a tired man worn down by years of working for a government that would never notice.

50

Wednesday morning, I went to Mountain Center High School to visit the new principal. Summer school was in session, and I knew Dick Traber would be there because I had called ahead. The last time I saw Dick he was a middle-school principal. He was a dark, slender man about six feet tall with wire-rim glasses. He wore dark slacks and a white shirt with a dark tie that had some nice color in it. Dick welcomed me with a handshake, and we went into his office.

"You're pretty dressed up for summer school," I said.

"I'm new on the job," he said. "Have to make a good impression."

"I understand," I said. "Congratulations on your promotion. I'm sure it was well deserved."

"Thank you, Mr. Youngblood," Dick Traber said. "I appreciate that. Please, sit down."

I sat in a not-so-comfortable chair in front of his desk. I guessed that most people who found themselves there were not supposed to be comfortable.

"You've been busy since we last talked," he said. "I've read about you in the paper and seen you mentioned on the TV news."

"It appears that's sometimes unavoidable in my line of work," I said.

"At least you're on the side of the good guys," Dick Traber said. "How are things working out with Lacy?"

"So far, so good," I said. "Lacy is a good kid."

"An exceptional kid, I hear," he said. "And you rescued her. You did a good thing."

"I think I'm blushing," I said.

"Sorry," Dick Traber said. "I didn't mean to embarrass you. How can I help?"

"I'm looking into Russell Goode, the Byrd County High School student who apparently took his own life on Friday night," I said. "I need to interview some of his teachers, but I don't want to go in there cold. I thought maybe you knew the principal."

"I know her well," Dick Traber said. "She was also just promoted. Want me to give her a call and see if I can set something up?"

"I'd appreciate it," I said, standing and offering him my card.

"I'll get back to you as soon as I talk to her," Dick Traber said, scribbling something on a notepad in front of him. He took my card and laid it on the notepad.

"For whatever it's worth," I said, "Lacy tells me the kids really like the new principal."

"Now I'm going to blush," he said.

◆   ◆   ◆   ◆

That afternoon, thanks to Dick Traber, I packed up my laptop and visited Byrd County High School. I met with the principal, Grace Parker. She set me up in the school's conference room to interview a few teachers who had taught or known Russell Goode. A few others were not working the summer session, but she promised to ask them if I could speak with them over the phone.

I spent the afternoon talking to some of Russell's teachers one by one. I heard a consensus among them. Russell was quiet, respectful, and an average student who was probably underachieving. None of them would ever have thought Russell could kill someone or take his own life.

The last teacher I spoke with taught computer science.

"How many PCs do you have in your computer room?" I asked.

"Twenty computers," he said. "Half are Macs."

"Are they wireless?" I asked.

"Yes," he said. "We have a basic Linksys router."

"Does is require a network key to use it, or is it open access?"

"It's open," he said. "We weren't too concerned about security, since it has limited range."

"I'd like to see your computer room," I said.

"It's part of the library," he said, standing. "Come with me and I'll show you."

We went to the second floor, using the elevator. The library was to the left and down the hall. It was surprisingly large. The computer room was all the way in the back. Each computer sat on a small desk in a cubicle, offering some degree of privacy. I looked out the window. A parking lot was located below.

"Was Russell particularly adept with computers?" I asked.

"He knew the basics but never really showed a lot of interest," the teacher said.

I thanked him for his time and went back to the principal's office to thank Grace Parker. She gave me a list of three more teachers and the phone numbers for each.

I got in the Pathfinder, drove around back, and parked underneath the windows of the computer room. I took my laptop out of my computer backpack and powered it up. It took less than a minute for it to acquire the school's wireless network. I launched Internet Explorer and was online in seconds. That was not good news. The router had enough range to reach the parking lot. That meant that anytime, day or night, someone could drive in and go online. The IP address the feds tracked had led to Byrd County High School's router. It could not be pinpointed to a specific computer. I logged off and shut down my laptop.

◆   ◆   ◆   ◆

That night after dinner, I spoke to a few more teachers on the phone. They all had the same opinion of Russell. Not one teacher thought he could kill anyone or himself. None mentioned the words *strange* or *weird*. Russell seemed pretty normal.

When I finished, I went downstairs and into the kitchen. Mary and Lacy were finishing the dishes from dinner. Lacy was unusually quiet.

"You okay?" I asked her.

"That kid killing those girls and then himself creeps me out," she said, turning to face me.

Mary continued to dry dishes, facing the sink. She was going to let me handle this. I sat on a barstool.

"Sit a minute," I said.

Lacy sat beside me.

"I'm going to tell you something because I know you can keep a secret," I said.

Mary turned around, interested now.

"I don't think Russell Goode killed those girls or himself," I said. "I'm going to try and prove it. So you still need to be aware of what's going on around you. I think we still have a killer out there."

"Really?" Lacy said.

"Really," I said.

"Okay," Mary said. "I think it's time to do that homework that Stanley gave you. I want to talk to the famous Mountain Center private detective."

"I'm going," Lacy said. "Thanks for telling me that, Don. I'll be careful."

Mary poured a glass of Bailey's Irish Cream on the rocks and a glass of white wine and sat at the bar across from me. She slid the Bailey's in front of me.

"Thanks," I said, taking a sip.

"When did you come to this conclusion?" Mary asked.

"This morning on T. Elbert's front porch," I said.

I told her my theory. I told her about my conversations with Russell's teachers. I told her about the high school's wireless setup.

"What do you think?" I asked when I was finished.

"I think I want this to be over," Mary said, taking a long drink of white wine. "And I think you may be onto something."

51

Thursday morning, I picked up Oscar Morales at his new house and went back to the trailer park. I told him most of what I knew about the three devils and shared my theory about the apparent suicide. I wanted to canvass the neighborhood to see if anyone on Friday night had seen a vehicle they didn't recognize. Many of the residents were Spanish speaking, and I knew they would tend to be reticent toward an investigating gringo. That's where Oscar came in.

We went to the trailer-park office. I asked the middle-aged overweight woman behind the front counter if I could see the manager.

"What's this about?" she asked defensively.

"I'm working with the FBI on a very sensitive case," I said, flashing my ID and trying to sound important.

Invoking the Federal Bureau of Investigation worked. She hurried off through a rear door. I heard muted conversation.

Beside me, Oscar stood looking amused.

"Name-dropper," he said softly.

I shrugged.

A minute later, the manager appeared. He was short, stocky, and bald and did not have a warm and fuzzy demeanor. He reminded me of a bulldog, slack jowls and all. He would have made a good mascot for that rival university to the south.

"Whadda you want?" Bulldog asked in an accent from somewhere north of the Mason-Dixon line. "And what's this bullshit about the FBI?"

"I *am* working with the FBI," I said, showing him my ID.

"A private investigator's license don't mean shit to me," he said.

"I'm hurt," I said.

"Who's this guy?" he asked, nodding toward Oscar.

"The Cisco Kid," I said.

"Take a hike, wise guy," Bulldog said.

Charming fellow. I ignored the invitation to leave.

"Do you have a layout of the trailer park showing the names of all the residents?" I asked.

"What if I do?" Bulldog growled. He looked like he might actually jump over the counter and bite me on the leg.

"I'd like very much to see it, please," I said, verbally patting him on the head.

"No," he said sharply. "That's confidential, and you got no real authority."

I looked at Oscar. He shrugged. I turned and gave Bulldog my best glare.

"Look," I said, no longer Mr. Nice Guy. "If you don't want the Mountain Center police up your ass, you'd better stop being a hard case and cooperate."

"You're bluffing," he said. "Police don't like private dicks."

"Wait here," I said to Oscar.

I walked outside and called Big Bob on his private cell phone.

"Hey, Blood," he said when he picked up.

"I need your help," I said. "I'm doing some follow-up on the Friday-night thing, and the manager out at the trailer park is being an asshole."

"I know him," Big Bob said. "He is an asshole. Put him on the phone."

I walked back inside and laid my cell phone on the counter.

"For you," I said.

Bulldog looked at the phone as if it were a coiled cobra.

"I'd answer that if I were you," I said.

Bulldog reluctantly lifted my phone to his ear.

"Yeah?" he said. His eyes grew wide. "Chief Wilson?" Bulldog looked as if he'd eaten some bad puppy chow. Loud, indistinguishable sounds came from the phone. "Yeah, okay. Sure. If I'd known he was a friend of yours . . ." Bulldog showed the early signs of a full meltdown. "Yeah, sure, chief, right away."

He flipped the phone closed and handed it to me.

"You should have told me you was a friend of the chief's," Bulldog said, his eyes as big and friendly as a puppy's. "I'll be right back."

Within minutes, a schematic of the trailer park was spread across the front counter. The map showed the entire complex, including the streets and the lots. Each trailer had a name written in pencil inside a trailer icon. I judged about one-third of the names to be Spanish.

"You guys want coffee?" asked the manager, a completely changed man.

"No thanks," I said.

I looked at Oscar. Oscar looked at the manager.

"Black," he said.

Bulldog hurried away to get Oscar's coffee.

"Coffee?" I asked.

"It's free," Oscar said, smiling.

I helped him make a list of all the Spanish surnames on the schematic. I listed the other names. We agreed to meet back by the trailer-park office at noon.

For the next two hours, I knocked on doors. Some didn't open because the occupants weren't home. Some didn't open because the occupants chose to ignore me. Of the ones that did open, I was recognized a half-dozen times from the news and was offered a dozen cups of coffee, three lunches, and one roll in the sack with a not-so-bad-looking waitress. I declined the lunches and the roll in the sack. None of the open doors had any useful information.

At noon, Oscar and I leaned against the Pathfinder for a few minutes as I told him about my morning.

"How good looking was the waitress?" Oscar asked.

"Not bad," I said.

"And you turned her down?"

"I'm committed to someone else," I said.

"Remember the trailer number?"

"You're a married man," I said.

"That is true," Oscar said. "But wives in my culture are a little more forgiving than in your culture."

"Lucky for you," I said. "Let's go get some lunch."

"You understand that I was only kidding about the trailer number," Oscar said as we drove off. "I would never cheat on my wife. She would cut my balls off."

"Nice motivation," I said.

◆　◆　◆　◆

We were at a back table in Carrie Lee's Deli and Grill sharing a huge turkey sandwich with Swiss cheese on grilled marble rye. A large order of French fries sat between us. We drank sweet iced tea.

"So I take it you drew a blank," I said to Oscar.

"Nobody saw anything," Oscar said. "Which does not surprise me. I am sure some of them are here illegally. The rest don't trust law enforcement."

"Our local guys are pretty decent," I said. "You need to get the word out."

"I will do the best I can," Oscar said. "But it has been my experience that when people are on foreign soil, they tend to be very cautious."

"Like you," I said.

"Well," Oscar said, grinning widely, "maybe not quite like me."

◆　　◆　　◆　　◆

We spent the afternoon knocking on doors. At four o'clock, Oscar met me in front of the trailer-park office.

"Anything?" I asked.

"*Nada,*" Oscar said.

We got in the Pathfinder, drove to Paul Goode's trailer, and pulled in the driveway. His pickup truck was not there. Oscar and I got out and went to the front door and knocked. No answer.

Oscar followed me around the back of the trailer. Beyond the small backyard was a field of wildflowers, weeds, and enough scattered trees to give reasonable cover. Past the field lay an old county road maybe a half-mile away. A barbed-wire fence separated the yard from the field. I could tell by the posts that the fence was old. I walked the fence line in both directions, looking for any signs of someone coming to or going from the trailer. Near the corner of the lot, I saw weeds that had been mashed down and a sort-of path leading into the field.

"You thinking what I'm thinking?" Oscar asked.

"Someone came or went through this field recently," I said.

"Could be someone taking a shortcut," Oscar said.

"Could be," I said. "Or it could be the killer."

I looked for signs of torn clothing or blood on the barbs but found none. Whoever had come this way was careful. I handed Oscar the keys to my SUV.

"Take the Pathfinder and meet me on that road over there," I said. "Go left out of the trailer park and then take another left about a half-mile down. Follow that road until you see the back of the trailer park, then pull over and wait for me. I'm going through the field."

"See you in a few minutes," Oscar said.

I climbed the fence and began a trek through weeds, high grass, wild-flowers, and briar bushes, following a vague impression of a path. Fifteen minutes later, I climbed another barbed-wire fence and walked up a slight bank to the old county road. My Pathfinder was parked approximately fifty yards up the road on the other side. Oscar leaned against the front fender, arms folded, watching me come toward him. I noticed three widely spaced houses on the road opposite the field.

"Wait here," I said when I reached him. "I'm going to knock on a few more doors."

At the first house, no one answered. At the second, I showed my ID and explained I was looking into the trailer-park suicide. The lady of the house told me she and her husband had been out Friday night for dinner and a movie and returned home late.

At the third house, I got lucky. A blue-haired woman answered the door. I introduced myself and explained what I was doing.

"Ma'am, were you home Friday night?" I asked.

"Yes, I was," she said in a Southern drawl.

"Did you happen to notice any cars or trucks parked on the road that night?"

"Well, yes, I did," she said slowly, as if dredging up a memory. "When I let the kitty out right before eight o'clock, I saw a pickup truck parked up the road on the other side."

"Do you remember the color?" I asked.

"Well, no, it was gettin' dark," she said. "I could tell it was medium colored, not real dark and not real light."

"Could you tell if it was new or old?"

"It was old, kinda square lookin'," she said. "Not one of those fancy new models."

"How old, do you think?"

"Pretty old," she said. "And a little beat-up."

"Did you see anyone?"

"No, I didn't," she said.

"Anything else you can tell me?"

"Well, the truck was gone by nine o'clock," she said. "I let the kitty back in right after my TV show was over, and the truck was gone."

I thanked her and rejoined Oscar. We got in and drove back toward Mountain Center.

"Anything?" Oscar asked.

"Maybe," I said. "She saw an old pickup parked up the road on Friday night between eight and nine o'clock."

"A pickup," Oscar said. "Well, that sure narrows it down."

◆   ◆   ◆   ◆

I dropped Oscar at his house.

"Want to come in and meet the wife and kids?" he asked, smiling. Oscar seemed to be in a perpetually good mood.

"Some other time," I said. "Thanks for your help."

"*No hay problema*," Oscar said. "And thanks for the lunch. Call me if you need anything."

On the way back to the office, I called David Steele and told him what I had learned in the past two days. If he was impressed, he contained it well. Then he told me some news that reinforced my theory.

"The M.E. found alcohol and traces of chloral hydrate in Russell Goode's blood," he said.

"Someone slipped him a Mickey and then staged the suicide," I said.

"Certainly looks that way," he said. "Now what?"

"You could have your computer geek make a list of old pickup trucks that are registered within a fifty-mile radius of the crime scene," I said.

"I'm guessing that'd probably be more than a couple," David Steele said.

"Probably," I said. "Give you something to do."

"Washington was pretty happy with us when we told them this case was closed," he said. "They won't be happy if they hear I'm spending more time and manpower on it."

"They'll be even less happy if dead girls start turning up again," I said.

"You got a point," David Steele said.

"So reopen it," I said.

"Right," he said. "The big dogs are really going to love me for this."

52

The following afternoon, I had a visitor. He stood in my inner-office doorway holding a baseball cap in both hands. He was a lanky man about six feet tall with medium brown hair and a mustache. He wore a brown work shirt with the sleeves rolled up a couple of turns, jeans, and cowboy boots that had a nice shine on them. His belt had a big Harley-Davidson buckle. I guessed he was between forty and forty-five years old.

"Mr. Youngblood?" he asked tentatively.

"Yes," I said, standing.

He took a step into my office.

"I'm Paul Goode," he said. "Russell's father."

"Would you like to sit down, Mr. Goode?" I said, motioning to the nearest chair.

He sat and looked around, as if wondering what to say. He seemed distracted.

"I'm sorry for your loss," I said, breaking the awkward silence. I was getting damn tired of telling parents I was sorry they had lost their kids. I prayed this would be the last time.

"Thank you," he said.

Staring out my window, he looked so fragile I thought he might break apart. I noticed the redness in his eyes.

"Why don't you tell me why you're here?" I said, trying to get him focused.

"Sorry," he said. "I haven't been able to concentrate on anything since I got the news about Russell."

"I understand," I said.

"Some of my neighbors told me you were at the trailer park asking questions about Friday night," he said.

"Yes, I was," I said. "Myself and an associate."

"Mr. Youngblood," he said earnestly, "I know my son didn't commit suicide. Somebody killed him. And I know my son didn't kill anybody. I know it just as sure as I know any truth."

I looked at him for a long moment. Joseph Fleet, Troy Walker, and Jason Asher's mother flashed through my mind, all enduring a grief I could only guess at.

"I think you're right," I said finally.

Paul Goode glanced down and let out a long breath. Then he looked up at me.

"I figured so," he said. "Couldn't figure any other reason you'd be out there. Did you learn anything?"

"I did," I said. "And I'll tell you what I learned, and I'll tell you my theory about Russell's death, but it has to stay between us for now."

"I swear I won't tell a soul," he said.

I believed him. I told him what I promised.

"You going to catch this guy, Mr. Youngblood?" Paul Goode asked.

"I'm sure going to try," I said.

Paul Goode was silent as he stared out my window. Watching him, I felt my anger rising. I wanted very much to find justice for Paul Goode and his dead son, not to mention all the dead girls.

"The newspapers and the TV are saying my son did this thing," Paul Goode said finally. "That's not right."

He was certainly correct about that. Knowing his son didn't do it and having everyone think he did must have been almost as bad as Russell's death.

"I may know how to change that," I said.

"That would really help me get my head straight," he said. "It's bad enough to lose your only child, and even worse when people think he's a killer."

After Paul Goode left, I sat and pondered my dilemma. I would rather the killer think he was in the clear and the case was closed. But the agony Paul Goode was going through was unbearable. Being so close to his grief had changed my perspective.

I called David Steele.

"I want to give my theory to a local TV reporter who was at the scene Friday night," I said. "You can blame me if somebody higher up gets on your ass. The father was just in my office, and I swear, Dave, he's breaking apart. We can't let people keep thinking his son was a killer."

I heard silence on the other end. I really didn't know what to expect.

"Go ahead and do it," David Steele said. "I can take care of myself with the higher-ups. Have your TV person give me a call, and I'll offer some vague confirmation."

"Thanks, Dave," I said. "It's the right thing to do."

"The case is officially reopened," he said. "I got the approval from Scott, since he was in charge of the original case. He'll take the heat if there's any. I'm working on that truck list. We'll start running them down tomorrow."

I hung up with Dave and made the call.

"Mr. Youngblood," Peggy Ann Romeo said. "This is a surprise."

"Get over here with that cameraman of yours," I said. "Have I got a scoop for you."

◆   ◆   ◆   ◆

Mary and I sat with our drinks on the couch in the den and watched the six o'clock news on my wide-screen TV. The Tattoo Killers Case was the lead story. A close-up of Peggy Ann Romeo with my office bookshelves in the background flashed on the screen.

"New developments in the apparent suicide of Russell Goode have now been brought to light by Mountain Center private investigator Donald Youngblood, who is assisting the FBI with this case," Peggy Ann reported. "The new evidence uncovered by Mr. Youngblood suggests that Russell Goode was murdered in an attempt to divert the authorities from the real killer."

The camera swung in my direction.

"What can you tell us about the new evidence?" Peggy Ann asked.

"Apparently, someone entering the trailer through the back door drugged Russell Goode and staged the suicide," I said. "We have reason to believe he might have known his killer. I have some very credible leads."

Another close-up of Peggy Ann appeared on the screen. She was in the television station's studio.

"I later spoke to an anonymous source at the FBI, who confirmed the Tattoo Killers Case has been reopened and that they are vigorously pursuing leads," she said.

"You're getting to be a regular TV star," Mary said, nuzzling close to me on the couch.

"Maybe I should get an agent," I said.

Mary laughed.

"Maybe you should just stick to what you do best," she said.

"And what's that?" I asked innocently.

Mary rolled toward me and kissed me.

"Take a guess, big boy," she said, smiling seductively.

53

Saturday mornings usually found us at the lake house, especially in the summer. But Mary had paperwork to do at the station and Lacy had plans with Hannah, so I went to the office. I thought about taking Jake, but he was in a deep sleep, so I left the old man alone. That turned out to be a mistake.

The parking lot was almost empty at eight o'clock. I punched in my security code and went up the back stairs to the second floor. As I came out the side door and headed to my office, I sensed something behind me, and then I had the sensation of being stung by a thousand bees. My muscles quit working, and I went down hard, banging my head on the marble floor. I barely felt the blow. I was more interested in the hooded stranger about to place a rag over my face. I tried to resist but couldn't. I had no control anywhere—arms, legs, neck, or vocal cords. I tried without success to move my head away from the rag. Everything faded away. I thought I heard a distant sound, like a ping from sonar in those old submarine war movies.

◆　　◆　　◆　　◆

I heard distant, unrecognizable voices. Then I smelled an awful odor, like someone had shoved chlorine up my nose. I moved my head to get away from the smell and heard a voice say, "He's coming around."

As I floated toward consciousness, I recognized how much my head hurt. I still felt distant as I scanned the room, like a drunk waking up with a bad hangover. I was in one of the oversized chairs in the inner office. I saw Big Bob, Mary, Rollie Ogle, and someone I didn't know with a uniform on. As my head cleared, I recognized him as an EMT. He was standing over me and holding an ice pack to the back of my head.

"Don, are you with us?" Mary asked, kneeling so she was looking up at me.

"Yeah, I think so," I said. "What happened?"

"You were Tasered and drugged, probably with ether," the EMT said. "You also have a nasty bump on the back of your head."

"Guess you were in the news one time too many," Big Bob said. "This psycho son of a bitch came after you. If it hadn't been for Rollie here, you might be hanging naked in the woods somewhere."

"Thanks for the visual," I said, wondering why the big man couldn't just once keep his thoughts to himself. "And don't talk so loud. My head hurts. Now, what's this about Rollie?" I rolled my head toward Rollie, who was sitting on the edge of the other chair. The movement made it throb.

"Well, as I came off the elevator, I saw this guy bending over you with a rag in his hand, placing it over your face," Rollie said in his sophisticated drawl. "So I hollered, 'What's going on?' and pulled my gun, and he took one look and bolted down the back stairs."

"You carry a gun?" I asked, incredulous.

"I'm a divorce lawyer, Don," Rollie said, as if I were an idiot. "A lot of pissed-off husbands out there would like to kill me."

"Well, why didn't you shoot the son of a bitch?" Big Bob said, way too loudly.

"Well, it happened so fast," Rollie said. "I've never shot anyone before. I'm not a cowboy like Don here."

"Thanks for that, Rollie," I said.

"No offense, Don," Rollie said. "I meant that I have no experience in those kinds of things. Let me get him in court and I'll tear him to shreds."

"I hate to interrupt," the EMT said, "but this man needs to get to the hospital to check out his head injury."

"How did he get in?" I asked, ignoring the EMT.

"Who the hell knows?" Big Bob said, still agitated. "The guard says he didn't see anybody, but he could have been away from his desk taking a leak. Now, get your ass to the hospital."

I knew that didn't happen. I had discussed it with the guard. If he had to be away from his post, he locked the door and put up a sign that said, "Back soon." My attacker got into the building some other way.

"I'm okay," I said, sitting up a little straighter. "I've seen enough of hospitals."

Mary, still kneeling and watching me intently, said, "You're going to the hospital, cowboy, and that's the end of it."

◆   ◆   ◆   ◆

And that was the end of it. Not only did I go to the Mountain Center Medical Center, I checked into a private room. Who checks in overnight for a bump on the head? Did it have something to do with my excellent medical insurance?

"You do not have a skull fracture," Dr. Evan Smith said. "But you do have a subdural hematoma, and you probably have a mild concussion."

Subdural hematoma, I thought. *Medical-speak for a puffed-up bump on the head.* I remembered this was the same Dr. Evan Smith who had treated Mary last year. He had paid a lot of attention to her, as I recalled.

"I see from the x-rays that you had a skull fracture recently," Dr. Smith said, looking more at Mary than me.

"Last year in Las Vegas," Mary said.

"Bad luck in the casinos?" Dr. Smith asked.

"Bad luck in a parking garage," I said.

Dr. Smith looked at Mary.

"Long story," she said.

"Well, we'll keep you for observation," Dr. Smith said. "If everything looks okay in the morning, I'll release you."

"Thank you, doctor," Mary said.

"I'll check back with you later," Dr. Smith said.

I wasn't sure if he was talking to Mary or me.

•   •   •   •

Mary stayed a few hours and then went home to check on Jake. Lacy was at Hannah's. I convinced Mary there was no need for her to come back. She reluctantly agreed and said she would see me bright and early in the morning.

Dinner was grilled chicken, steamed vegetables, mashed potatoes with gravy, and a biscuit—not bad for a hospital. I couldn't convince the nurse to bring me a couple of beers, so I drank sweet iced tea.

About an hour after dinner, I had a visitor.

"I heard they brought you in," Howard Cox said. "How are you feeling?"

"I've got a sizable headache," I said. "Other than that, I seem to be okay."

"What happened?" he asked.

"I got too close to solving a case I'm working on," I said. "I really can't say any more."

"Did you know a cop is guarding your door?" Howard Cox asked.

"What does he look like?" I asked.

"Tall, dark hair. Nametag says he's Sean Wilson," Howard Cox said.

"Chief Wilson's younger brother," I said. "I think the chief is being a little overprotective. Ask Sean to come in here for a minute, please."

Howard Cox left my room. I heard mumbled voices. Sean Wilson came in looking like a kid caught with his hand in the cookie jar.

"You're not supposed to know I'm here," he said. "I'm supposed to keep a low profile."

"Hard to do when you're in uniform," I said. "I assume this was Big Bob's idea."

"Among others," Sean said.

"Mary," I said.

Sean smiled.

"One hell of a woman," he said. "I wish she was looking out for me. Now, relax and get some rest and let me do my job."

I wanted to protest, but my head hurt and I was tired. Having Big Bob Wilson's younger brother guarding my back wasn't such a bad thing.

"Thanks, Sean," I said. "Try not to shoot anyone."

"Well, if I do, they'll get treatment right away," Sean said as he turned to leave.

"Send Mr. Cox back in if he's still out there," I said.

A few seconds later, Howard Cox returned.

"How's Megan?" I asked.

"Improving quickly," Howard Cox said. "She's being released tomorrow."

"Good for her," I said. "I'm glad to hear that."

"And her memory is coming back," he said. "She said it was definitely Ricky who assaulted her."

"She already said that once, right?"

Howard Cox smiled sheepishly.

"I may have embellished that a little," he said.

"Well, no matter," I said. "Megan's testimony should be enough to put Ricky away for quite a while."

"It should," Howard Cox said, "if they can find him."

"He's missing?"

"Didn't show up for his court date," Howard Cox said. "No one has heard from him."

"He'll turn up sooner or later," I said.

"I certainly hope so," he said, turning to leave. "I want to see Ricky get what he deserves."

So did I, but at this point Ricky Carter was the least of my worries. I was trying to figure out how my attacker had gotten onto the second floor of the Hamilton Building on a Saturday. The guard had told Big Bob he didn't see anyone. My attacker hadn't slipped by the guard, so he must have had the security code to the back entrance. I wondered how he got it.

My train of thought was interrupted when David Steele walked into my room. He looked concerned.

"You okay?" he asked.

"I'm fine," I said. "Bump on the head. They're keeping me overnight for observation. How'd you know I was here?"

"Your lady cop called me," he said. "Said she thought I should know. Didn't sound too happy about your doing the FBI's job."

"She can get a little hot sometimes," I said.

"I don't blame her. I saw the news last night," David Steele said. "It didn't take our boy long to come after you."

"He's spooked," I said. "He thinks we're closer than we are."

"Did you get a good look at him?"

"No. He had on a black hooded sweatshirt and something covering his face," I said. "Maybe a ski mask."

"We're running down old pickup trucks," he said. "Maybe we'll get lucky."

The nurse came in with my evening meds.

"He needs to rest," she said, looking at Agent Steele.

"I'm leaving," he said. Then he looked at me. "I'll be in touch."

"Dave," I said before he got out the door. "Are you checking antique plates? This truck may be older than twenty-five years."

"I don't know," David Steele said. "Could be a separate database. I'll check. That's a hell of a good thought, Youngblood. Maybe you should get hit on the head more often."

The nurse handed me a paper cup containing one little white pill and one big white pill. My head hurt, and I didn't have the energy to think about the case anymore. I gulped the pills and within minutes floated off into a peaceful, dreamless sleep.

54

Sunday morning, Mary and Lacy were sitting in my room when I woke up. Whatever the nurse had given me the night before had knocked me out for eight hours.

"Good morning, sleepyhead," Mary said.

I felt groggy.

"Bathroom," I said, struggling to get out of bed.

I moved at the fastest pace I could muster and slammed the bathroom door. A couple minutes later, I came back out feeling much relieved.

"When you gotta go, you gotta go," I said in my best Tony Soprano imitation.

Lacy laughed.

"I brought you some fresh clothes," Mary said. "Shave, shower, and get dressed and we'll break you out of here."

"Local law enforcement is outside my door," I said. "I may not be able to leave."

"I sent Sean home," Mary said. "Now, get moving."

I got moving. The warm water from the shower felt great, even on my bump—my subdural hematoma, I mean—which had dissipated considerably overnight.

I wrapped a towel around myself and poked my head out the door.

"Clothes," I said.

Mary handed me a shopping bag, and I closed the door and got dressed. When I came out, Mary was gone and Lacy was sitting in a chair watching the Weather Channel.

"Mary said wait here while she checks you out," Lacy said.

I sat in the other chair and stared at the TV. No rain and highs in the mid-eighties—not a bad forecast for midsummer in East Tennessee.

Mary returned a few minutes later.

"You're sprung," she said.

"I want to go back to the office," I said.

"What you want doesn't matter," she said sternly. "We're going to the lake house and relax, and I don't want any argument from you."

Something in her voice let me know I wasn't going to win the argument, so I let it go. The idea I had could wait one more day.

"Yes, dear," I said.

Mary and Lacy both laughed.

◆   ◆   ◆   ◆

By nine o'clock that morning, we were eating on the lower deck. Cereal, fresh blueberries, and cheese Danish were the breakfast fare. We kept our coffee hot in an insulated thermos. A pleasant breeze came off the lake. My head hurt less and less, and I was actually starting to relax a little.

"I'll get the barge ready, and we'll take her out," Lacy said.

I looked at Mary. She gave me an almost imperceptible nod.

"Sounds good," I said to Lacy.

"I'll get my bathing suit on first," she said, bouncing up the stairs to the upper deck and into the house.

"She's crazy about you, you know," Mary said.

"The feeling's mutual," I said.

"She was really upset when she found out what happened."

"Goes with the territory," I said.

"Still," Mary said, "you make a big deal about Lacy being careful, and then you're careless and almost get yourself killed."

I heard fear in her voice, and I felt responsible for that. She was right. I had been damn careless, and fate had been kind to me.

"I'm sorry," I said. "It won't happen again. I thought he might move on me, but not that soon. I could have had the son of a bitch, and I blew it."

"This private investigator thing is not a game, Don," Mary said. "It's serious business. You are way too cavalier about it sometimes."

I could have argued, but what was the point? She was mostly right. I deserved a lecture, so I sat silently and took it.

"You're right," I said. "I'm sorry I scared you and Lacy."

"I don't want to be a nag," she said. "I've said my piece, and that's the end of it. I love you, but your carelessness scares me sometimes."

"I'll be more careful," I said. "I promise."

55

Monday morning, I felt fine. It took me awhile to convince the females, but they finally relented and cut me loose. I drove straight to the office from the lake house. I had to find some things out. Sometimes, I believed I knew something, but the more I thought about it the more I wasn't sure. I was almost positive security cameras were located at the back of the bank, but as I drove toward Mountain Center I began to have the feeling that I imagined it because it should have been so. I pulled into my reserved spot in the parking lot, got out, looked up, and breathed a sign of relief—they were there, two of them. One was mounted above a second-floor window and the other just below the rooftop.

I punched in my security code and went up the back stairs to the elevator. I looked around the hall to see where my attacker had come from. A tiny alcove with a vending machine had just enough room for someone to hide out of sight. It was well lit. I found a light switch and turned it off and stepped back into the hall. It was dark enough for someone to hide unnoticed, especially if I hadn't been paying attention.

I took the elevator down to the first floor and went into the bank to see Ted Booth. Ted was a few years ahead of me in high school. An all-American success story, he had started at the bank as a teller after graduating from the University of Tennessee and worked his way up to president. He had prematurely gray hair and wore wire-rim glasses and looked every part of his title. He was alone in his office when I walked in. He looked up and smiled.

"I know why you're here," he said.

"You do?"

"You want the security tapes," he said.

"How'd you know?"

He laughed.

"Chief Wilson told me when he took them that you'd probably be by looking for them," he said. "He told me you'd figure it out sooner or later. He told me to tell you to go on over to the station when you got here."

"Yeah, that sounds like him," I said. "Thanks, Ted."

"You okay, Don?" he asked.

"I'm fine, Ted," I said as I turned to leave. "You might think about changing the security code. I'm almost positive that's how my attacker got in."

"I'll do that," Ted said, scribbling on a notepad as I left.

◆   ◆   ◆   ◆

"You watch the tapes yet?" I asked as I walked into Big Bob's office.

"No," he said. "I was waiting on you. I figured you wouldn't be long. How you feeling?"

"I'm fine," I said. "Let's play those tapes."

Big Bob put one of the tapes in his VCR and pressed the play button on his remote. This particular tape was from the lower camera and started at 6 A.M. He fast-forwarded to 7 A.M., when we saw a hooded figure walking toward the back entrance. He disappeared beneath the camera.

"He had the security code," I said.

"Seems that way," Big Bob said. "How'd he know you'd be in on a Saturday?"

"I don't know," I said. "Maybe he just took a chance."

"Or maybe he's been watching you and knew you came in on Saturday sometimes," Big Bob said.

"Maybe. I'll ask him when I catch the SOB."

We fast-forwarded past 8 A.M. and saw the hooded figure leave in a hurry around 8:07. He disappeared from the camera into the parking lot.

"Let's look at that other tape," I said. "I'll bet it has a view of the entire parking lot."

Big Bob inserted the other tape and fast-forwarded it to 8:07. We saw the hooded figure running across the parking lot and disappearing around the corner of another building.

"Well, that's it," Big Bob said, stopping the tape.

"Play a little more," I said.

Big Bob pressed the play button, and we watched cars go by on the street beyond the parking lot. A minute later, I saw it.

"Stop," I said. "Back it up."

Big Bob stopped the tape.

"What'd you see?"

"Give me the remote," I said.

He handed it to me. I pressed the rewind button. When I saw it, I pressed the pause button.

"There," I said. "I think I've seen that truck."

On the TV screen was an older-model pickup truck. Since the tape was in black-and-white and the truck was at a distance, I couldn't tell the color or the make. But I knew it was blue, and I knew I'd seen it before.

"That doesn't make sense," Big Bob said. "Why would he drive back that way in front of the camera?"

Indeed, why would he? It took me a few seconds.

"You should get out more often," I said. "Franklin is a one-way street. If he parked around the corner of that building, he had to go back that way."

"I knew that," Big Bob said, grinning.

◆   ◆   ◆   ◆

I felt the pace quickening. I sensed we were being propelled toward a conclusion, and that it was coming soon. I went back to the office and called David Steele.

"I have a video of the truck," I said when he answered his cell.

"How?"

"Security tapes," I said. "The bank has two cameras set up in the back. We got video of the guy and the truck—two cassettes."

"I'll send one of my guys to pick them up," David Steele said. "Will you be in your office?"

"I'll be here," I said.

After hanging up, I went online to check my email. I had over forty. The ones I needed to answer, I kept as new emails. The others, I deleted. When I finished, I clicked on my spam folder. It had an additional twenty emails. Sometimes, something important went into my spam folder, so I always checked it. I had deleted the first couple of emails when I heard the door. I opened the desk drawer that held my Beretta—better safe than sorry.

"Mr. Youngblood," a voice said. "FBI."

"In here," I said, closing the drawer.

I recognized the young agent when he entered my office. I handed him the package.

"Agent Steele said he'll call you later," the agent said.

He turned and left without another word.

I went back to my spam folder. As I worked my way down the list, I came to one that gave me pause. "Sorry I had to run," it said. That was just too coincidental. I opened it. It read, "So sorry we were interrupted. You were being so cooperative. I am about to take the game to the next level. It's time for another funeral. I hope you are around to play."

I stared at the email address. It was garbage—a series of meaningless letters and numbers. Untraceable, I was sure.

I called David Steele.

"I just got an email from our killer," I said.

"Read it to me," he said.

I did.

"He's escalating," David Steele said. "He's pulled you into the game to see if you can catch him."

"Well, let's not disappoint him," I said.

"Has my guy been there yet?"

"He left a few minutes ago," I said.

"Forward that email to me," David Steele said. "I'll see if our guys have any luck tracing it."

"I doubt it," I said. "But it's worth a try. Give me your email address."

He did. I forwarded the email while we were still on the phone.

"Got it," he said. "Stay in touch, Youngblood, and watch your back."

56

That afternoon, I paced the office like an expectant father. I could not sit still. Finally, I closed up and went to the condo. I changed into my workout clothes, loaded up Jake, and headed to the gym.

I couldn't tell if Moto was happy to see me, but he was happy to see Jake.

"Karate needs exercise," he said. "He is getting fat."

After we turned the dogs loose out back, I went to the rowing machine. I set it on level sixteen and rowed like a man possessed. I went through my weight routine, then moved to the back room and worked on the speed bag and the heavy bag.

Two hours after arriving, I sat in a corner of the side room with a bottle of water. Although I felt like a whipped puppy, I'd been able to exorcise my frustration. I loaded Jake, who was as whipped as I was, and went back to the condo. Jake headed straight to his bed. I headed straight to the shower.

♦　　♦　　♦　　♦

By the time I dressed, Lacy was home in her room talking on her cell phone. A few minutes later, Mary arrived.

"Want a glass of wine?" I asked.

"I'd love one," she said.

I poured her a glass of wine and myself a beer and told her about my day.

"First, he Tasers you, and then he sends you an email," Mary said. "This guy is nuts."

"It's all part of his sick little game," I said. "I don't think he intended to kill me. If he wanted to, he could have."

"Then what was he going to do with you after he had you unconscious?"

"Good question," I said. "I'm glad I didn't find out."

Lacy came bounding down the stairs.

"Hi," she said. "What's for dinner?"

"I hadn't thought about dinner," Mary said. "What sounds good?"

"Well," Lacy said, "we haven't had Chinese in a while. Let's go pick up Chinese."

Mary looked at me.

"Sounds good," I said.

As soon as they left, my cell phone rang.

"I need your help," David Steele said. "And I need it now."

"Tell me," I said.

"An hour ago, the Knoxville police reported a possible abduction of a teenage girl in the East Town Mall. The details were a little sketchy. One thing the witness was sure of was the vehicle—an old blue pickup truck."

"Christ, have mercy," I said softly. "How can I help?"

"Our computer guy did his thing with some fancy software, and we've got four good possibilities on the truck," David Steele said. "You're closest to one of them. The address is at the far end of Byrd County."

Dave gave me the address.

"I'm on my way," I said.

"Don, prepare for the worst," Dave said. "This truck has an antique tag."

•   ◆   ◆   ◆

As I pulled out of the parking lot, I dialed Mary's cell phone. No answer. Then I dialed Lacy's. No answer.

Twenty minutes out of Mountain Center, my cell rang—Mary calling back.

"I tried to call," I said. I was using Bluetooth so I could be hands-free.

"Sorry, we both left our phones in the condo," Mary said. "Stupid of us. Where are you?"

I told her.

"Give me the address," Mary said, "and don't argue. You need backup, and the backup is going to be me."

I gave her the address. On some level, I found the thought of her backing me up thrilling.

"Watch yourself," she said. "I'm on my way."

I guessed I was fifteen minutes away. I activated the built-in GPS that I hardly ever used and keyed in the address. I could feel the adrenaline rush.

57

Fourteen minutes later, I turned off the main road and headed up a dirt road toward an old two-story farmhouse surrounded by trees. I reduced my speed so as to make as little noise as possible. When I saw the truck, I slowed even more and pulled behind some trees that would hide the Pathfinder and give me some cover.

I got out, careful not to slam the door. I weaved through the trees, trying to keep at least one between me and my line of sight to the front windows of the farmhouse. The old blue pickup was parked facing me. I walked to it and felt the hood. It was warm. I looked through the open window on the driver's side and saw a cell phone. I picked it up for a closer look. It was a stun gun disguised as a phone. I didn't know such a thing existed. It explained a lot. On the floor was a rag and next to it a bottle of ether. I drew my Beretta. I knew I had found the master devil, the one called Lucifer.

I approached the house and slowly climbed the stairs to the porch. A few steps from the front door, I noticed that it was slightly open. I sensed trouble but felt somewhat secure with the Beretta in my hand. I had loaded it with hollow-point shells. It held ten—enough firepower to bring down a grizzly bear.

Hearing a scream, I pushed the door open wider, slipped inside, and scanned the room, my Beretta at arm's length. I heard another scream. It came from the basement. Moving as quietly as I could, I located the basement door. It was open. I started slowly down the stairs, letting the Beretta lead the way.

I heard a girl's voice pleading.

"Please don't hurt me," she said between sobs.

"We're going to have some fun," I heard a voice say.

"No, please," the girl said.

I was halfway down the stairs when I saw them. His back was to me. The girl, a slender redhead, was tied to a support beam in the middle of the basement, which smelled of mold and mildew. The man held a hunting knife. The blade looked very sharp. I needed to get off the stairs so I could have a clear shot at him.

I was negotiating the final few steps when the girl caught sight of me. Her eyes went wide. I shook my head as if to say, *Don't let him know I'm here*, but fear had control of her.

"Help me!" she cried, looking over his shoulder.

The man spun around behind the support beam, keeping the girl between him and me. He was dark, slender, and less than six feet tall. I guessed he was around my age. His eyes were wild, his hair disheveled. He held the knife to her throat.

"Donald Youngblood," he said. "I didn't expect to see you so soon. Did you get my email?"

"I got it," I said, pointing the Beretta at his forehead. I couldn't take the shot. It was too risky. But I had to make him think I would. "Let her go and I'll let you live."

He laughed the laugh of the insane.

"What makes you think I want to live?" he said. "I'll just be moving from one hell to another."

I saw a trickle of blood where he pressed the knife at the girl's throat.

"Tell you what," he said. "I'll trade her life for that gun of yours."

I paused as if thinking it over. I didn't want to agree too soon.

"Okay," I said. "Take the knife away."

He shifted it slightly so the blade was no longer touching her. She sobbed softly, probably going into shock, her brain shutting down.

"Slide the gun over here or I'll slit her throat," he said.

"Please don't hurt me," the girl repeated, choking back tears.

I knelt and slid the Beretta toward him, but far enough away from the girl so he couldn't reach it and keep the knife at her throat. The sound of the Beretta skidding and bouncing across the concrete floor made me grimace.

He looked at the gun. It was about eight feet away.

"Don't move," he said.

"I don't intend to," I said.

Then he made a fatal mistake. He left the girl and went quickly for the Beretta. In one fast, fluid motion, I pulled up my right pant leg with my left hand and with my right hand drew my newly acquired Ruger .32 caliber six-shot revolver from my ankle holster. He reached my Beretta, picked it up, and swung it toward me. I put two rounds in the center of his chest before he could get off a shot. The sound of the Ruger reverberated around the basement. He stumbled backward, hit the wall behind him, and slid down it, dropping the Beretta.

The girl shrieked. I went toward him with the Ruger still pointed at his chest. I picked up the Beretta and placed it back in my carry holster.

He looked past me and blinked.

"Sammy," he said. "Is that you?" Then his eyes went blank, and he was gone.

I turned to the girl. She was sobbing uncontrollably. I gently took her head in both of mine and looked straight at her.

"You're okay," I said.

No response.

"Look at me," I said. "You're okay."

She blinked through the tears.

"Focus," I said. "Say, 'I'm okay.' "

She stared into my eyes.

"I'm okay," she said faintly.

"Louder," I said.

"I'm okay," she said, stronger this time. The crying slowed.

"I'm going to cut you loose," I said.

I retrieved the knife and cut the duct tape he had used to tie her. When she was free, she fell into my arms and started sobbing again. I held her as she let it all out.

When she calmed, she pushed away from me.

"Thank you," she said. "You saved my life. Who are you?"

"Donald Youngblood," I said. "I'm a private investigator from Mountain Center. What's your name?"

"Toni," she said. "Toni Correll."

"You're welcome, Toni," I said. "Now, let's get out of here."

We walked up the basement stairs, through the house, and out on the front porch. Fresh air had never felt so good. In the distance, I saw a cloud of dust moving fast up the dirt road to the house. The SUV skidded to a halt, and the blond Wonder Woman got out and came toward the house, Glock drawn. Lacy emerged from the passenger side and followed her.

Mary reached us with a questioning look on her face.

"You can put your gun away," I said. "The game is over."

58

I was sitting on the steps to the farmhouse, a little dazed by what had happened.

"You okay?" Mary asked.

She was beside me. Lacy had taken Toni to sit in the Pathfinder.

"I guess so," I said. "It's occurred to me that I've just taken another life."

"You just saved another life," Mary said. She had a way of not letting me forget the obvious. "Call Billy," she said.

"What?" I said, my mind still in the basement replaying the events there.

"Call Billy. He'll want to know about this right away. And it might be a good idea if he photographs the crime scene."

I flipped open my cell and dialed Billy. In the distance, the sun was low in the sky, filtered by a heavy haze. I guessed we had maybe an hour of daylight left.

"Hey, Blood, what's happening?" Billy asked.

"It's over, Chief," I said. "I killed him."

I gave Billy a quick recap of the last two hours and directions to the farmhouse.

"I'm on my way," he said.

Then I called David Steele. My mind was settling down and starting to refocus.

"Please give me good news," David Steele said as he answered. "We struck out here."

"I've got the girl, and our killer is dead," I said.

"God Almighty, Youngblood!" he exclaimed. "That is great news. Damn good work."

"You and your crew need to get out here right away," I said.

"We're on our way."

"And call Scott," I added. "Tell him it's over."

"My pleasure," David Steele said.

◆   ◆   ◆   ◆

The occasional chirping bird and the gentle breeze rustling the leaves in the maples belied the fact of the dead body in the basement. I had helped chase this guy for over two months, and the chase was finally over.

We continued sitting on the stairs, listening to the sounds of an East Tennessee summer evening. I could see Lacy and Toni talking in the Pathfinder. Billy was in the basement photographing the scene. He had arrived faster than I thought possible and in typical Billy fashion walked past us with only a nod, camera in hand. Billy had unerring judgment about when to speak and when to keep quiet. Mary and I enjoyed the peace and quiet. I knew in a few minutes it would be chaotic again.

"I'm surprised you brought Lacy," I said.

"I couldn't get Hannah's mom on the phone, and I was in a damn big hurry," Mary said. "I gave her a lecture on the way about staying in the car if things didn't look right. It's not a bad thing for her to be here. She needs to know what we do and how serious it is. I don't think she's likely to forget what almost happened to that girl."

◆   ◆   ◆   ◆

The peacefulness of the evening ended when a black Taurus tore up the dirt road, leaving dust in its wake. Minutes later, another arrived. David Steele had the same crew with him that had been at Paul Goode's trailer Friday night. It seemed so long ago.

As David Steele approached the porch, Mary got up and headed back toward my Pathfinder. They nodded but didn't speak as they passed. David sat on the steps beside me. His other agents went past us into the farmhouse.

"Tell me about it," he said.

I recounted the events step by step.

"That second gun in the ankle holster," David Steele said, "that was real smart."

"You said to prepare for the worst," I said. "So I did."

We sat there in silence as darkness fell, each with our own thoughts. Finally, David Steele rose and started into the farmhouse.

"Go home, Youngblood," he said. "You've done enough. We'll take it from here."

"Did you call the girl's parents, Dave?" I asked.

"I did," he said. "They're on the way."

◆　　◆　　◆　　◆

We stayed until Toni's parents arrived. They were so effusive with their thanks that I thought they'd never leave. Mary rescued me by telling them their daughter needed to get away from the farmhouse and back to her secure environment.

"Thanks for that," I said as the three of us watched them drive away into the darkness.

"I could tell you were starting to get embarrassed," Mary said.

"Let's get out of here," I said. "I'll follow you two."

"Can I ride with Don?" Lacy asked Mary.

Mary looked at me and smiled.

"Sure," I said.

Mary pulled out, and I followed. We drove awhile in silence, my mind going over every move I made and everything I said in that farmhouse basement. Could I have done anything differently? I didn't think so.

"Don," Lacy said softly.

"Yes?"

"You did really good back there," she said, choking a little on her words. "I'm sorry for you that you had to kill somebody, but you did really good."

I glanced over and saw tears on her face, made visible by the headlights of oncoming cars.

"Thanks, Lacy," I said.

"That girl was so scared," she said. "She was shaking. I didn't know what to say. I just kept telling her that she was okay now, that it was over."

"That's about all you could say," I said. "I think you handled it well."

She didn't say anything else right away. I kept Mary's taillights a few car lengths ahead of me. To my surprise, she was going the speed limit.

"That could have been me," Lacy said finally.

"No, it couldn't have," I said, trying to get that thought out of her head. "You're a blonde. Toni was a redhead. Our killer was looking for a redhead. It was part of his game." Whether or not that was true, I hoped she would buy it.

Lacy didn't respond. She took some tissues from a box on the backseat and wiped her eyes.

"You can bet the next time you tell me to be careful, I'll listen," she said softly.

59

My life started returning to normal—no one tried to kill me, at least. For a few days, the news went wild with the story of the Tattoo Killers. Then a junior senator from one of the northeastern states was caught in bed with twin girls just past the age of consent, and the three devils were soon forgotten. The parents of the girl I saved visited me to again offer their thanks. It was an awkward few minutes.

Two days after the showdown at the farmhouse, I received an early-morning phone call from David Steele to update me on the case. The man we now referred to as Lucifer, the master devil, had been identified as Trevor Smith. The FBI had found a driver's license, registration, credit cards, and even a Social Security card to prove it.

When they tried to track down a family for Trevor Smith, they reached a dead end. Digging deeper, they stumbled onto an old case file of a Trevor Smith who had gone missing about twenty years ago. The Social Security numbers matched. Trevor Smith had run afoul of the law on several occasions, so his fingerprints were on file. The problem was that they didn't match those of the man I killed in the basement. The FBI's best guess was that our killer had murdered the real Trevor Smith and assumed his identity—the ultimate identity theft. The fingerprints of the man we knew as Lucifer were not on file.

When the FBI tracked the Social Security number to employment records, they found that Trevor Smith had been a part-time janitor last year at Byrd County High School. For her sake, I hoped Grace Parker hadn't hired him.

"Well, that might explain how he knew Russell Goode," I said. "Have you tried military records?"

"Yes," he said. "But not everything that far back has been put on computer. We've got people digging, but a dead killer in a closed case file isn't top priority."

"I understand," I said. "Still, it would be nice to know who he was."

"I don't care who he was," David Steele said. "He's dead and soon to be buried. You need to let go of this, Youngblood."

"Right," I said, realizing I was getting nowhere.

"I wanted to tell you I'm retiring," David Steele said. "I put in my papers for the end of the year. I'm fifty-two, and I've been on the job thirty years. It's time for a change."

"Good for you," I said. "What are you going to do?"

"My daughter's in college at New Mexico State, so we're moving to Santa Fe," he said. "My wife is an artist and wants to open a shop and see if she can sell some of her work. I'll run the shop. We have money put away, and I'll get a pension, so we'll be okay."

"I'm happy for you," I said. "You've served your country well. I know a lot about moving and doing things differently."

"Well, I'm not gone yet," he said. "I'm sure we'll talk a few times before I leave. If I find out anything else on Lucifer, I'll let you know."

"Hey, Dave, before you hang up, did your agents do a thorough search of the farmhouse?"

"Not after we found the tattoos," he said.

"Where were they?"

"In an envelope in his desk," David Steele said. "I guess he wasn't too worried about our finding him. Either that or he didn't care."

"Do you mind if I go back out to the farmhouse and snoop around?" I asked. "I might turn up something."

"Be my guest," he said. "I'll have one of my guys bring you a key."

◆   ◆   ◆   ◆

I arrived at the farmhouse around noon. I searched the living room first, then the kitchen, methodically checking every nook and cranny. I moved on to the bedroom. I had no idea what I was looking for, but I knew I'd know when I found it. I went through the drawers and looked under the bed and the mattress but found nothing.

In the closet on the top shelf in the far right-hand corner, I found a small replica of a pirate's chest. I pulled it off the shelf and sat on the bed with it. The chest was not locked. I flipped the latch and opened it. The chest was a jewelry box. In it were an old wristwatch, two very old pocket watches, a few rings, a few old coins, and some cuff links. The box had a false bottom. I lifted the top tray and set it aside. The bottom was littered with old baseball cards. I sifted through them. They were from the mid-1900s. Some had to be worth a small fortune.

Mixed in with the baseball cards was a professional snapshot of a young boy on high-quality card stock. On the back was a one-word mystery I had been trying to figure out since the farmhouse shooting.

Sammy.

◆ ◆ ◆ ◆

"You're going to Lexington, Kentucky?" Mary said, disbelieving. "Because you found an old photo?"

We had just finished dinner and were still at the dining-room table. Lacy had been excused to go to her room, which was code for getting on the telephone with her boyfriend, Jonah.

"Correct," I said.

Mary was getting annoyed with me, I could tell. I knew the tone of voice.

"You know, Don, most of the time, you're one of least curious people I know," she said. "You're not nosy, you don't participate in gossip, you don't volunteer information, and you can keep a secret. So what's this obsession all about?"

"Right or wrong," I said, "in my mind, this case isn't over until I exhaust all avenues to find out who this guy was and what compelled him to do what he did. His last word is haunting me. I know this picture is the key. I need some closure on this."

"You know, it's over thirty years since that photo was made," Mary said. "It'll be a miracle if the studio is still in business."

"I believe in miracles," I said, smiling. "And in Yahoo. I did a search, and the studio is still in the same location that's printed on the back of that photo."

"Then by all means go and get this out of your system," Mary said, seeming to approve but annoyed nonetheless.

60

I decided to drive to Lexington. I would have felt guilty asking for the Fleet jet for such a short trip.

I got up early Thursday morning, packed an overnight bag, and took the fastest route to I-40 West. From there, I drove to I-75 and went north. I was in Lexington by noon. I located the Lewis Art and Photography Studio in the downtown area, exactly where it had been for forty years. I found a parking spot on the street and walked inside. A bell jingled over my head.

A man a few years younger than me glanced up from behind the counter.

"Can I help you?" he asked.

"I hope so," I said. "I'm trying to track down the kid in this picture." I slid the photo across the counter.

He examined it like it was a rare artifact.

"You don't see paper like this anymore," he said, turning it over. "It's one of ours, all right. This was made a long time ago. Way before I started working here."

"Who was here at the time?" I asked.

"My father, Peter Lewis," he said. "I took over day-to-day operations about twenty years ago. I'm Peter Jr., but most people call me Bud."

"Please tell me your father is still alive, Bud," I said.

"I can do better than that," he said. "He's in the back doing some framing, and he has a memory like a computer. He'll know who this is, I guarantee it. Let me get him."

He laid the photo down and disappeared through a door behind the counter.

"Dad!" I heard him call.

A minute later, a short, white-haired man maybe seventy-five years old came out, followed by his son.

"Bud tells me you have an old photograph you'd like me to identify," he said.

"This one," I said, sliding it back across the counter in front of the elder Lewis.

He took reading glasses from his shirt pocket, perched them on his nose, and studied the photo.

"This looks like the pictures we used to take for a private school not far from here. Freemont Academy, I think it was. Public schools wouldn't pay for this kind of paper. This looks like a kindergarten or first-grade picture. I recognize the face now, if I can just remember the name." He tapped the picture on the counter and stared off into space, trying to dredge up the memory. He turned it over. "Sammy." He read the name on the back out loud. "Yes, I remember now, Sammy Sherman. What a cute little boy he was."

"Do you know if he's still around here?" I asked.

"Oh, no," the elder Lewis said. "Sammy died soon after this photograph was taken. Leukemia, I think it was. He wasn't more than six years old."

"I'm sorry to hear that," I said. "Do you remember the family?"

"Yes," Peter Lewis said, rubbing his chin as he revisited the past. "Mother and father, of course, and one older brother. I can't remember his name."

"Do they still live here?" I asked.

"The mother died about ten years after Sammy," Peter Lewis said. "Cancer, I think. Such a tragedy for that family. I don't know where the brother and the father are now. Bret Sherman was the father's name. Nice fellow, much older than his wife."

"Do you know anyone who might remember what happened to Bret Sherman?" I asked.

Peter Lewis scratched the side of his head.

"You might try the Mallory Memorial Methodist Church," he said, handing the photo back to me. "I know the Shermans were longtime members there. I remember that Sammy's funeral was at Mallory."

"Can I ask what this is about?" Bud Lewis said.

I had anticipated the question and decided in advance that a short version of the truth would best serve my purpose.

"I'm a private detective working on a case that requires identifying a recently deceased person," I said. "I have reason to believe Bret Sherman might be able to help. The person I'm trying to identify had this picture among his possessions. It might be something, or it might be nothing. I'm just tracking it down."

"Well, good luck," the elder Lewis said.

◆   ◆   ◆   ◆

A half-hour later, I was in the church office at Mallory Memorial Methodist waiting to see the minister. The church secretary was new to the job and had never heard of Bret Sherman. She told me the Reverend Jesse Taylor had been at Mallory for eight years.

"I'm sure Reverend Jesse will know," she assured me with a pleasant smile.

Reverend Jesse was in a meeting with the head of the finance committee. I waited, then waited some more. I wondered if I might be able to see him sooner if I made a large donation.

"So sorry to keep you waiting," he said to me twenty-five minutes later.

I sat in a large, comfortable chair in front of his desk.

"I'll be brief," I said. "I'm trying to track down a former member of this church, Bret Sherman. I'm a private investigator. It's about some insurance."

Lying to a Methodist minister. Well, it was for his own good. I didn't want to alarm Reverend Jesse with tales of suicide and murder.

"Bret Sherman," he said. "I haven't heard that name in a while. Someone told me last year, or maybe it was two years ago, that he was in a nursing home in Louisville. Bret must be past eighty by now."

"Do you know which nursing home?" I asked.

"I don't," he said. "But I might be able to find out."

He brought up a file on his computer. After studying it a minute, he dialed a number.

"John," he said. "This is Jesse. How are things? Good. I need to ask you a question. Are you the one who told me some time back that Bret Sherman was in a nursing home in Louisville?" He waited a moment. "Yes, I thought that was you. Do you remember the name of the home?" He waited again. "Maple Oaks, right. I remember now. Someone was asking about him recently, and I couldn't remember where he was."

Well, even ministers bend the truth sometimes, I thought.

"How is Nora? Great, say hello for me. Thanks, John. I have to run. See you on Sunday. God bless." He hung up the phone. "Maple Oaks."

"Maple Oaks," I said, standing to leave. "Thank you very much, reverend."

♦   ♦   ♦   ♦

I knew I wasn't going to make it back to Mountain Center by dark, so I called the Marriott reservations number and arranged to stay at the Louisville Residence Inn East at Exit 15 off I-64. An hour and a half later, I checked into a Studio King suite. I was grateful for having the good sense to pack an overnight bag. I looked up Maple Oaks in the phone book and got the address. Then I set up my laptop and went online to MapQuest for the driving directions. Maple Oaks turned out to be only fifteen minutes from the Residence Inn.

♦   ♦   ♦   ♦

The heat and humidity of the summer afternoon were kept at bay by a nice breeze that had a hint of rain in it. Dark clouds were forming to the west. *A thunderstorm may be in my future*, I thought.

A tasteful sign informed me that I was entering the Maple Oaks Retirement Community. The place reminded me of a small college campus. It contained at least seven buildings. The grounds were immaculate.

Not a cheap place to retire to, I thought. A sign pointed me to the office. "All visitors must check in at the main desk," it read.

At the desk, I encountered a pleasant-looking woman in her mid-thirties with short, dark hair and black-framed glasses similar to the ones Mary wore at night.

"May I help you, sir?" she asked.

"I'm here to visit Bret Sherman," I said.

"One minute, please." She looked at her computer screen. Her hands went flying over the keyboard. "Mr. Sherman is in the nursing-home section. That's building five. Let me call," she said. "I have a male visitor for Bret Sherman," she said into her phone. "Is he able to receive visitors today?" She waited maybe ten seconds. "Fine, I'll send him around." She gave me directions. "Ask for Jane," she said.

◆　◆　◆　◆

Jane was a tall, athletic-looking woman maybe fifty years old who had a kind face and dark hair with streaks of gray.

"How long has it been since you've seen Mr. Sherman?" Jane asked.

"A long time," I said. "He may not remember me." Distorting the truth went with the territory, but it bothered me that I did it so easily.

"Well, then, let me explain," she said. "Mr. Sherman is in the early stages of Alzheimer's disease. He has good days and bad days. I checked with the nurse, and she told me that today he's pretty lucid. Let me take you around."

I followed Jane to a room where the residents were participating in various activities from playing cards to using crayons on coloring books. A nurse came over to meet us. She was a young, short, cute redhead with a freckled face and a big smile.

"He's down in the common area," she said. "Follow me." She led the way through double doors to a patio. "That's him down there on the bench next to the fountain," she said, pointing. "Whether he remembers you or not, he loves to have visitors. His short-term memory isn't so good, but his long-term memory seems to be okay."

I left the nurse, descended the stairs, and walked toward the man next to the fountain. He had chosen a shady area. Considering the breeze, I imagined he was quite comfortable there.

He looked up and smiled as I approached.

"May I join you?" I asked.

"Sure," he said. "It certainly is a nice day, isn't it?"

"Very pleasant," I said. "Looks like you have the premier spot."

He laughed.

"I do, indeed."

Bret Sherman was a tall, lean man. His long legs were stretched out and crossed at the ankles. His hair was snow white, his face clean-shaven, and his eyes a watery blue. He looked tan and healthy. I wouldn't have guessed him to be the other side of eighty.

"My memory isn't so good," he said. "Do I know you?"

"No, you don't," I said. "My name is Don."

He stared off for a while, then looked back at me.

"Are you here to see me or someone else?" he asked.

"I came here to see you and to give you something," I said. I handed him the picture of his younger son.

"My God," he said. "That's Sammy. Where on earth did you get this?"

"I found it in an old farmhouse in Tennessee," I said. "I was curious, so I tracked it back to the photography studio and eventually to you. You can have it if you want."

"Yes," Bret Sherman said. "Thank you so much."

I wanted to push him for information about Sammy's brother. I wanted to ask about the significance of the neatly folded clothes and the dancing devil tattoos. But this man had suffered so much in his life that I didn't have the heart to probe. He seemed content in his surroundings, and I didn't want to disrupt that. So I sat there and enjoyed the day and kept silent and waited to see what came up.

Bret Sherman looked at the picture, then stared off in the distance, then looked at the picture once more.

"Sammy's dead, you know," he said sadly.

"Yes," I said. "I heard that. I'm sorry for your loss."

"It was a long time ago," he said, sounding tired now. "Leukemia. He was only five years old."

He was silent for a while, almost trancelike.

"I had another son, you know," he said.

"No, I didn't."

"Matthew," he said. "I don't know where he is now."

"Tell me about Matthew," I said casually.

He was silent. I waited.

"Matthew was seven when Sammy died," he said finally. "He worshipped Sammy like Sammy was the older brother. Sammy's death killed something in Matthew, brought out the dark side of him. He was never the same. Then my wife died of cancer, and Matthew went to an even darker place, one with no hope or joy. I didn't know him anymore. He got into some trouble and was institutionalized. He wouldn't see me or talk to me. He got out when he was twenty-one, and I've never heard from him since."

"I'm sorry." I didn't know what else to say. I felt a little unnerved talking to a man who had lost one son to leukemia and another to a bullet from my Ruger.

"Did you get this picture from Matthew?" Bret Sherman asked, looking confused.

"No," I said. "Remember, I told you I found it."

"It's a kindergarten picture," Bret Sherman said as if he hadn't heard me. "It was taken a few weeks before Sammy went back into the hospital. Funny how things turn up in the oddest places."

Maybe he had heard me. He took another long look at the picture of Sammy.

"I want to thank you for bringing this to me," he said. "I had others, but I don't know whatever happened to them. This means so much to me."

"You're welcome," I said. "I'm glad I was able to find you."

"Time for you to go up, Mr. Sherman," I heard a voice say. "They'll be serving dinner soon. You don't want to miss that."

I turned and saw the cute little red-headed nurse who had shown me the way down.

"No, I surely do not, Nancy," he said, smiling and getting to his feet. "Nice talking with you," he said, looking at me. "What did you say your name was?"

"Don," I said.

"Come see me again sometime, Don," he said. "I don't get many visitors."

"I will, sir," I said, promising myself that I would.

Bret Sherman turned and walked away, Nurse Nancy steadying him with her hand under his elbow. At that moment, for the first time in my life, I thought about getting old.

61

I was back in Mountain Center on Friday afternoon. As soon as Mary got home, we headed to the lake house. Lacy was at Hannah's. Hannah would be with us on Saturday night. I was really beginning to like that arrangement.

"Maggie and Billy are coming over on Sunday," Mary said.

"That's good," I said. "I haven't seen Maggie in a while."

We were on the lower deck. The sun was setting, and the day was beginning to cool.

"Have you gotten that whole mess out of your system?" Mary asked.

"Just about," I said.

"What does that mean?"

"I want to have a conversation with Sister Sarah Agnes about the psychology of the whole thing," I said. "After that, it's ancient history."

"So you decided not to tell Bret Sherman his son is dead," Mary said.

"Yes," I said. "He's already lost a wife and one son. That's more grief than anyone should have to bear. If he can live out his remaining days not knowing his other son is gone, he's better off."

"A compassionate decision," Mary said.

"And if you were there, you would have seen for yourself that it wasn't a hard decision to make."

"Having second thoughts about being a private investigator?" Mary asked.

I hated it when she did that mind-reading thing.

"Maybe," I said. "For a small-time PI, I sure do seem to attract some big-time messes."

"What you need is some TLC," Mary said.

She was reading my mind again.

◆   ◆   ◆   ◆

"How does it feel to have this one over?" Billy asked.

We were on the lower deck on a gorgeous Sunday afternoon that same weekend. The bikini brigade—Mary, Maggie, Lacy, and Hannah—had taken the barge out on the lake to swim and sunbathe. Billy and I were told politely to stay behind because we'd be bored by all the girl talk. What that really meant was that they wanted a chicks' day on the lake. That was fine with us. We sat and enjoyed the breeze off the lake and drank iced tea.

"Strange," I said. "I was so emotionally involved. I feel relieved, depressed, guilty, confused, and maybe a few more things I can't identify."

"You'll settle down as you get farther away from it," Billy said.

"I hope so," I said. "I never thought I'd encounter such evil as I have in the last three years."

"There's always been evil in the world, Blood, and there always will be. Most people don't encounter it like we have."

"I just don't know if I should keep doing this, Chief."

"You can't deny your destiny," Billy said cryptically. "You're very good at what you do."

"Maybe, but I've killed three people," I said.

"All bad men," Billy said. "And you saved good people doing it."

We sat for a long time and didn't say anything. I knew Billy was right. I had to move on. As far as he was concerned, saving lives absolved me for the killings. I wasn't so sure. Only one thing was I certain of—the more time I put between the three devils and me, the better off I'd be.

"I have some good news," Billy said.

"I can use it," I said.

"Maggie's pregnant," Billy said nonchalantly.

I was stunned.

"Damn, Chief," I said. "When you have good news, you really have good news. Congratulations."

Billy smiled from ear to ear. I felt a weight lift from me. I was so happy for Billy I forgot all about the last two months. But I was also a little jealous. My chances at real fatherhood were fading fast. I was sure Mary didn't want to give birth again. I could be a father to Lacy, but according to Big Bob taking on a teenager was doing it the hard way.

"That's great," I said. "Just great."

"You'll be an uncle," Billy said.

"Uncle Don," I said. "I can live with that."

62

I went to the office on Monday. Billy's news had really lifted my spirits. Roy was waiting with coffee and bagels. I'd given him a key so he wouldn't have to show off by picking the lock.

"I didn't see the limo," I said. "Where did you park?"

"Oscar has the limo," Roy said. "Hiring that guy was the best thing Mr. Fleet has done in years. We're both wondering why it took so long."

"I'm glad he's working out," I said. "So, what are you driving?"

"The silver Mercedes parked across the street," Roy said. "Mr. Fleet's personal car. He almost never drives it."

"Nice," I said, sneaking a peek out my window.

We were close to finishing the coffee and bagels, but Roy seemed in no hurry to leave. I knew he wanted to say something about my farmhouse showdown. I didn't have to wait long.

"I see you iced another bad guy," Roy said.

"Had to," I said. "It was either him or me."

"How are you dealing with that?" Roy asked.

"About the same as last time," I said. "I'm feeling guilty about not feeling guilty. I'm very confused about the person I'm turning into."

"You're still the same person," Roy said. "You've been through the ringer lately. Your problem is that, on the surface, you're pragmatic. So you know you did what you had to do. But beneath that, you're a hopeless romantic. That gets you in trouble. Sometimes, it's better to listen to your head and not your heart."

Roy, like Billy, was a man of few words. I was surprised by his eloquence and insight.

"You spent too much time with Sister Sarah Agnes," I said.

Roy laughed. He ate the last bite of his bagel and finished his coffee. I did the same.

"You've had a lot of gunplay in the last two years," Roy said.

"All in self-defense," I said.

"Good thing you can shoot, gumshoe."

"A real good thing," I said.

◆　　◆　　◆　　◆

After Roy left, I immersed myself in Wall Street and forgot about murder, suicide, and the most recent life I'd taken. I had killed a bad guy to save a good girl—not the first time I'd done that. But I quickly found that a morning of analyzing, buying, and selling what the Street had to peddle no longer held the appeal it once had.

That afternoon, I had a visitor. He stood silently in my doorway. I pointed to a chair.

"I want to thank you for what you did for Russell," Paul Goode said.

"For the others, too," I said.

"Of course," he said. "But you put yourself in danger so as to let everyone know my boy wasn't a killer."

"No sense in not letting the truth be told," I said. "It drew the killer out and gave us a chance to catch him."

"Still, it was a brave thing to do," he said. "If I can ever help you, let me know."

I thought about that for a few seconds. I didn't want Paul Goode thinking he owed me anything.

"How often do you get to California?" I asked.

"About once a month," Paul said.

"If you think of it, pick up a couple six-packs of Lagunistas Censored Copper Ale. Lagunistas is a microbrewery in Petaluma, California."

"I'll do it," he said, smiling widely.

◆　　◆　　◆　　◆

Tuesday morning, I had a visit from Oscar Morales. He stood in my doorway snappily dressed in a dark suit.

"I was in the neighborhood and had a few minutes," he said. "Roy filled me in on all your adventures in the last week. Was the guy you killed responsible for Maria Cruz's death?"

"Yes," I said.

"I'll let Miguel know the death of Maria Cruz has been avenged," Oscar said. "It will mean a lot to that community."

"Okay," I said, feeling a little uncomfortable about being an avenger.

"Did Ricky Carter turn up?" Oscar asked.

"Not yet," I said. "I may want you for a day's surveillance on the farm again."

"I can do that," Oscar said. "Let me know when."

♦   ♦   ♦   ♦

Nothing much happened the rest of the day. I went to the diner for a late breakfast and ate in relative peace and quiet. I read the *Wall Street Journal* front to back and got a few ideas for purchases, though none of them were very exciting. Nobody walked through my office door looking to get me involved in something sinister. I left early and went to the gym and had a light workout. I took Lacy and Mary to The Brewery for a burger.

That night, I slept like a baby.

♦   ♦   ♦   ♦

Wednesday, I got bored and went looking for Ricky Carter, who was still lying low.

Roy and I had a drink at the Bloody Duck. No one paid attention to us when we came in. Maybe they considered me a regular by now. As expected, Rocky was behind the bar and Butch Pulaski was shooting pool. Neither had seen Ricky since the last time I was there.

I went out to the trailer park and talked to his ex-girlfriend. She hadn't seen him and didn't care if she ever did again.

I had Oscar sit on the Carter farm that afternoon and evening. When he called me late that night, he said he saw no signs of Ricky.

◆　　◆　　◆　　◆

On Thursday, I called Sister Sarah Agnes and asked her to help me make sense of the Tattoo Killers Case. I explained in detail how the case had unfolded over a period of more than two months. I told her about the neatly folded clothes, the tattoos, and the game they were playing. As usual, she listened without interruption.

When I finished, we were both silent for a while.

"That's quite a tale you spun, Galahad," she said. "I don't know how you can get yourself into such predicaments."

"It's an art form," I said.

"With you, it certainly is," she said. "You have questions, I assume. So ask them."

"Was this all about his brother dying?"

"Yes and no," she said.

"Typical shrink answer."

"Let me finish," Sarah Agnes said. "The deaths of the younger brother and the mother triggered something in the killer. Without the brother dying, this whole thing probably would never have happened. Most brothers wouldn't react to the death of a younger sibling or even their mother by becoming a serial killer. So, for lack of a better term, Matthew Sherman had some loose connections in his brain, and the deaths of two people he loved very dearly triggered some kind of revenge mechanism."

"What about the folded clothes? Why were all the victims young girls? Why were they naked? Why did he involve high-school kids? Why did he think it was a game?"

"Mercy," Sarah Agnes said, exasperated. "Slow down. If I could interview your killer over a long period of time, I might be able to answer some of those questions. But since I can't, they will have to remain a mystery.

The mind is a universe within itself, Don. It's like the ocean. We know the surface but very little about the depths. That's all I can tell you. You need to move on."

I sat for a long while after we hung up. Somehow, my conversation with Sister Sarah Agnes gave me closure. When she said to move on, I knew it was time. I understood there were some things I'd never know. I would have to live with that. I put the case file away in my closed-file drawer and told myself it was over.

Gradually, I would begin to believe it.

63

Friday, I had visitors—a stampede, compared with what I was used to. Troy Walker came first. He didn't stay long.

"Thanks for killing that animal," he said, standing in my doorway.

I wanted to explain how Matthew Sherman had become the way he was, but I didn't think Troy Walker would much care. His pain was too deep.

"He would have killed me and another girl," I said. "I didn't have many choices."

"Obviously, you made the right one," he said. "I'm glad you're okay, and I'm glad you saved that girl."

And I wish I could have saved your girl, too, I thought.

"Send me a bill," he said on his way out.

"I'll do that," I said.

♦   ♦   ♦   ♦

Two hours later, Rasheed Reed appeared. He was dressed to the nines in a beautiful brown pinstriped suit, a brown-striped tie, and a cream shirt.

"Nice suit," I said. "You should be on the cover of *GQ*."

"They'd be lucky to have me," Rasheed said, smiling.

"Want to sit down?" I asked.

"Can't stay," Rasheed said.

"Is this a social call?"

"I was in the neighborhood and thought I'd drop by," Rasheed said.

"Nice of you to think of me," I said.

"Heard you were looking for Ricky Carter," he said.

"From time to time," I said.

"I wouldn't waste time on that if I was you," Rasheed said.

"You know something I don't?" I asked.

"I know a lot of things you don't," Rasheed said. "Take care of yourself, Youngblood. You're all right for a rich white dude."

He turned and left as quickly as he had come in.

◆　◆　◆　◆

When Rollie Ogle visited after lunch, I made a fresh pot of coffee for the occasion. Rollie was famous for drinking coffee all day.

"I love smelling your coffee when I get off the elevator in the morning," Rollie said, taking a drink.

"My first cup in the morning is usually Dunkin' Donuts," I said. "But I always brew a short pot for another cup later on. Feel free to help yourself anytime."

"I just might take you up on that," Rollie said.

"What's the occasion?" I asked. "You never just drop in."

"I need to serve divorce papers on Ricky Carter," Rollie drawled, "but no one seems to know where he is."

"Oh, boy," I said.

"What?"

"I have a feeling Ricky Carter is gone for good, if you know what I mean."

"As in never coming back?" Rollie asked.

"As in that," I said.

"Well," Rollie said, finishing his coffee, "that's a minor problem. I can work around that."

◆   ◆   ◆   ◆

I had one more thing to do to put the finishing touch on the Ricky Carter file. Late that afternoon, I phoned Howard Cox.

"I have it on good authority that Ricky Carter isn't going to be coming back to face charges," I told him.

"As in never?" Howard Cox asked.

"And ever, amen," I said.

"Thank you, Mr. Youngblood," he said. "You made my day."

Epilogue

We sat on the balcony of my Singer Island condo eating a light lunch and drinking sweet tea. Somewhere below us, Lacy and Hannah were showing off their tans in their new bikinis and drawing the attention of some teenage boys. It was early August, and we had been here a week. One more week and we had to go back to Mountain Center. Lacy would be starting her sophomore year in high school, and the Mountain Center Police Department needed Mary back on the job. Criminals, it seemed, didn't take vacations.

"I love it here," Mary said.

She was tan, healthy, and altogether gorgeous. I felt that electrical surge I always experienced when I stopped to take a good look at her.

"Me, too," I said. "We probably love it more because our time here is short."

I took a bite of tarragon chicken salad and one of rosemary sea-salt flatbread. Mary had a drink of sweet tea.

"Jimmy's starting the next preseason game," she said. "I talked to him yesterday."

Mary's son was the backup quarterback for the Tennessee Titans, in his second year in the NFL. I was sure he was destined to be a starter someday. He had all the tools.

"Good for him," I said. "Maybe we can watch it on TV."

"I hope so," Mary said.

"What do you hear from Susan?" Mary's daughter would be a senior at Wake Forest, where she was a starting guard on the basketball team.

"She just finished her summer classes," Mary said. "Straight A's."

"Of course," I said. "Smart, like her mother."

Mary smiled as if to say, *You better believe it.*

We finished our lunch. Mary gathered our plates and took them inside and came back out and refilled our glasses. She put the pitcher of tea on the table between our chairs and sat.

"We've been together about two years now," she said.

"I know." I started to say that was a record for me, but I stopped myself. I sensed this conversation was more than idle chitchat.

"I love you," Mary said.

"I know that," I said. "And you know I love you."

"Yes, I do," she said.

She took a long drink of sweet tea. I waited. I knew more was to come.

"I never thought I'd want to get married again," Mary said. "But you're rich and good looking and you love me."

"All of that," I said, smiling.

"And I want this to be permanent."

"It's already permanent," I said.

"But not binding," she said.

"Are you proposing?" I asked, surprised.

She drank more tea and made me wait for her answer.

"Yes," she said finally. "I am."

"Well," I said, trying hard to keep a straight face, "I'll have to think about it." I drank some tea and stared at the ocean. I might have even wrinkled my forehead.

Mary turned toward me and gave me a dazzling smile.

"You've got ten seconds, cowboy," she said.

I took about five.

"In that case," I said, "I accept."

"To us," Mary said, raising her glass of tea.

I touched my glass to hers.

"I'd want us to adopt Lacy," Mary said.

"I'd want that, too," I said. "Think Lacy will be okay with that?"

"She will," Mary said.

"You two have already talked?"

"We have."

"So I'm the last to know," I said.

"You are," Mary said.

"And when do we do this deed?"

"Soon," Mary said, laughing. "Very soon."

Acknowledgments

My thanks to:

Bob Miller, Management Assistant, National Park Service, United States Department of the Interior, for valuable information about the Great Smoky Mountains National Park

James Robert "Bobby" Donnelly for his computer expertise

Meri Saffelder, the webmaster for my website:
www.donaldyoungbloodmysteries.com

Buie Hancock, master potter and owner of Buie Pottery, who has given Donald Youngblood a spotlight in the Gatlinburg community

Steve Kirk, my editor at John F. Blair, Publisher, for a great job as always

And especially those members of the Science Hill High School class of '62 who have stayed in touch through the years and have supported me in my writing endeavors—and who are too numerous to list but know who they are

Author's Note

Although this is a work of fiction, most of the places in the story are real. Mountain Center, however, is not one of them. I chose a wide-open space on a map of East Tennessee and decided that's where Mountain Center should be. You might recognize places from Gatlinburg, where I reside, and Johnson City, my hometown. I have transplanted them to Don's fictional town. Don's lake house is very much like my mountain home in Gatlinburg, except that below my bottom deck is not a lake but rather a tennis court and hundreds of acres of undeveloped land beyond.

Of course, the Great Smoky Mountains National Park is a very real place. The cover photo was taken on the Sugarlands Valley Nature Trail on the Tennessee side of the park, where the body of a fictional young woman was discovered in *Three Devils Dancing*. The author photo was taken near the trailhead. The concrete half-mile loop trail is nearly flat and wheelchair friendly. It was the one place in the park I could think of that T. Elbert Brown could negotiate in his wheelchair.

GSMNP is only minutes from my house, and I go there often to walk, hike, and enjoy nature. On more than one occasion have thoughts or conversations or plot lines hatched as I took in the peaceful sounds of the Great Smoky Mountains. God's country, many of us call it.

An interesting side note: My house was built in the early seventies by a former park superintendent.

A few facts worth knowing: The Great Smoky Mountains National Park spans over half a million acres in North Carolina and Tennessee. It is the most-visited national park in the United States, with an estimated 10 million guests expected in 2010. The higher elevations receive so much rain annually that they qualify the park as a temperate rain forest. The park is home to a wide variety of wildlife including red wolves, coyotes, wild hogs, elk, and approximately fifteen hundred black bears, including a few that from time to time stop by my house to say hello.

As of this writing, entrance to the park is still free. For more information on this national treasure, visit the Great Smoky Mountains National Park website at www.nps.gov/grsm.

Visit the Donald Youngblood Mysteries website at:
www.donaldyoungbloodmysteries.com

You may write the author at:
DYBloodMysteries@aol.com

Praise for Keith Donnelly's *Three Deuces Down*

"*Three Deuces Down* was such fun to read!"

—P. Buckley Moss, Artist

"Big surprises in debut whodunit, Donnelly finds
right blend of actions, characters."

—Edward Clarkin, *BostonNOW*

"A high-stakes conflict ensues, where cunning is just
as crucial to staying alive as dexterity and sweat!
The forthcoming second Donald Youngblood mystery,
Three Days Dead, can't arrive soon enough."

—Midwest Book Review

"[Donnelly's] words are breezy with lots of dialogue.
His characters are funny and romantic."

—Joe Tennis, *Bristol* (VA) *Herald Courier*

"*Three Deuces Down* is a fast-paced, page-turning book
that readers might compare with John Grisham's novels.
No heavy lifting, but a book you won't want to put down."

—Joe Biddle, *The Tennessean*